JAMES A. ROSS

Coldwater Revenge

A Coldwater Mystery

LEVEL
BEST BOOKS

First edition

ISBN: 978-1-953789-54-9

Cover art by Rebecacovers & Ryan Mahan

This book was professionally typeset on Reedsy.
Find out more at reedsy.com

For my sons, Guy and Drew, may they never fall for the same person.

"And a man's foes shall be those of his own household."

Praise for Coldwater Revenge

"From the first page, I was drawn into Jim Ross' captivating novel, Coldwater Revenge. More than a crime novel over the death of a local boy who ran with the wrong crowd, this story has layers in the depths of its characters. The warmth between Tom Morgan and his brother as they work to investigate the murder adds a touching humanity to the story, and the care with which Tom nurtures his neurodiverse nephew brings the dynamics of this family alive on the page. It doesn't stop there. Ross imbues the many characters in his setting with rich backstory that comes out in the present. In the hands of a lesser writer, the intensity of the different sub-plots might overwhelm the main story, but Ross deftly brings all the story threads together in a gripping read. This is a book not to miss!" — Vanitha Sankaran, author of Watermark: A Novel of the Middle Ages

"Author James A. Ross grabs you and keeps you spellbound as this fast-paced thriller plunges into the icy depths of a dangerous lake on the Canadian border, and two brothers reconnect to solve a crisis which grows from a murder investigation into potential international terrorism." — Lenore Mitchel, author of DYING TO RIDE

"Coldwater Revenge by Jim Ross is a testament to how great mystery stories should be written; with grit and style, and with unnerving characters that blossom into palpable genre-representations that foil each other marvelously with each new page. Detailed and vividly conceived, there's little doubt the story takes its readers to a place of intrigue where it's near impossible to gage an outcome, and instead we must let it come, sometimes suddenly, while praying that there will continue to be more left to read.

To call it a page-turner would be an understatement." — Josh Michael, Associate Fiction Editor, Mud Season Review

CHAPTER 1

Billy Pearce was still alive, though neither he nor his killer knew it. The plunge into the icy darkness of Coldwater Lake brought Billy back to consciousness, but not awareness. His body filled the narrow sleeping bag. Cement blocks at his feet ensured that it found bottom and stayed there. Where his face filled the opening at the top of the bag, strobes of sparkling moonlight made prisms of the bubbles that could well be his last mortal breath. But Billy didn't think about that. His mind was somewhere else. This had happened to him before, a long time ago, and his mind went back there now.

When Billy was thirteen, he'd decided to break into a golf course clubhouse on the far side of Wilson Cove to steal liquor that he'd heard had been left in the basement storeroom over the winter. Temperatures had been unseasonably warm for most of the month. But Billy had decided to chance the walk across the late winter ice, rather than risk being spotted along the lake road at an hour when boys his age were presumed to be in school.

The frozen ice crackled and popped beneath his feet like a bowl of breakfast cereal. Billy imagined the party he would have with the liquor he was going to steal. And while he busied himself with a short mental list of who he could invite that would not rat him out, the *snap, crackle pop* went *WHOOSH!* and he plunged like a clown through a trap door into the freezing lake. In an instant, his heavy winter jacket sponged its weight in brain-numbing ice water, boots filled like pails and the whole soggy weight of it dragged him rapidly toward bottom.

But Billy didn't panic. His egghead family may have thought him deficient because of his constant troubles in school and his indifference to books, but Billy was brighter than they knew, and a childhood of disapproval had made him stoic and unflappable.

As his body drifted toward bottom, Billy methodically removed everything that was weighing him down: jacket, boots, shirt and trousers—everything but underwear. That done, he looked for the halo of light that would mark the spot where his fall had punched a temporary hole in the rotting ice. When he found it, and before his breath could give out or his mind succumb to the numbing cold, Billy had kicked and clawed his slim, nearly naked body through the hole and onto the ice.

Now, on a starless October night a dozen years later, his mind went back to that time where his body knew what to do and his brain was confident that everything would be all right if he just didn't panic. Inside the sleeping bag, his hands methodically removed a coat that was not really there, kicked off a pair of heavy boots that were not there either and lastly slipped-off the trousers that were. Then, as his face turned to find the wall of white where memory told him a patch of brighter white would guide him to a hole he must find and climb through if he were to survive, he abruptly ceased to remember, or to think at all. Because this time, Billy Pearce was dead.

CHAPTER 2

"Sir, you'll have to turn that off until we land."

"Sorry," said Tom, dropping the Blackberry into his jacket pocket, "force of habit." From habit as well, he shut his eyes while the turbo prop made its descent to the Coldwater County Airport, keeping them shut until wheel touched tarmac and held straight. Fifteen years of first class business travel hadn't diluted the formative memories of white knuckle landings on this pocked strip of macadam. Laid crossways to the wind that swept east from Coldwater Lake and surrounded by acres of succulent field corn, the seasonal challenges of fog and ice were minor compared to the obstacle course of white tail deer that guarded the sweet grass along the cracked tarmac as though it were a field of Bambi heroin.

He grabbed the vibrating Blackberry as soon as the plane came to a stop. "Tom Morgan."

"Stu Bailey," said the voice on the other end. "Do you know your phone's been off for the last hour?"

"It's called vacation, Stu. What can I do for you?"

"I'm sorry, Tom, but I need to follow-up on your response to the conflict of interest questionnaire you filled out before you left."

What could be ambiguous about a one word answer? "Too verbose?" he asked.

The voice on the other end forced a chuckle. "That depends. Are you sure you haven't handled anything for Eurocon in the last ten years?"

"Yep."

"Or any of its subs or affiliates?"

Tom cradled the phone, opened the overhead compartment and retrieved a laptop and garment bag while the plane taxied toward the single room terminal. "A company the size of Eurocon can have hundreds of those, Stu. You know that, and that not all of them use the parent company name. If you've got a list, email it to me. But like I said, I'm on vacation. And I'm about to get off a plane and start it."

"Okay, Tom. But call me when you get the list. It's important."

Tom held the phone away from his ear and made a face, slinging the laptop strap over his shoulder and dragging the wheeled suitcase up the aisle.

"One more thing, Tom. Have you done any political fund-raising?"

"What?"

"Campaign fund-raising, that sort of thing."

"I know what fundraising is. What's that got to do with a conflicts check?" The phone remained silent.

"Stu?"

"It's not a conflicts check, Tom. The Compliance Committee needs to know if you've done any political fund-raising."

"What? Hold on." He lifted the suitcase and descended the half dozen steps to the tarmac. Fifty yards away, a Paul Bunyan-sized figure leaned against the door of a police car parked and idling in the No Parking Zone in front of the terminal.

"Of course I have," he growled into the phone, dragging his suitcase toward the car. "And charitable fund raising and Greenpeace fundraising and practically every other kind. The firm knows that. They encourage it. Now what's this about, Stu? Because you're starting to put a damper on my hard-earned vacation."

"Sorry, Tom. I guess that's enough for now. I'll get back to you if we need more."

"Take your time."

4

* * *

The outsized man beneath the Smokey the Bear hat detached himself from the Crown Victoria, revealing the words "Coldwater County Sheriff" painted in red across the door panels. "That better be a girl you're talking to, or I'm supposed to take that Crackberry away from you."

Tom slipped the phone into his pocket and hugged his younger brother, trying not to wince at the bone-crushing return. "Good to see you, too."

"Don't stay away so long, you won't miss me so much."

Tom felt his heels return to earth.

"Throw that stuff in the back. Bonnie and the girls are at school. Luke's at daycare. Mom's home and everyone's excited to see you."

"How is our favorite girl?"

"A pistol, as usual. Broken leg hasn't slowed her down much. The cast comes off next week. Some geezer from the Senior Center's been calling every day. But don't mention that unless you want a crack to the shins with a metal walker."

Tom had been about to start a long overdue, lie-on-a-beach–brushing -sand-off-your-stomach-and-deciding-what-to-do-next-with-your-life vacation when his brother called with the news that their mother had fallen and broken her leg. Changing plans was a simple matter of adjusting flights, discarding his Italian phrase book and postponing any life-altering decisions. It was simple enough that it should have come with a warning label. He threw his bags into the back of the patrol car and climbed into the passenger seat while his brother took a call on the hands-free mounted on the dashboard. "When did you get rid of the two way?" he asked when Joe had finished the call.

"Ten days ago, when Paulie Grogan and all three deputies jumped ship to join some new BCI Terrorist Task Force. The mayor says that the sheriff's department doesn't need a dispatcher for just one cop, so the town let Helen go, too. But they gave me this flip phone thing so I can take citizen calls directly."

Tom felt his jaw hang open. "You're out three cops and a dispatcher? It's down to just you?"

"It's temporary. Just until the town council can meet to authorize replacements. In the meantime, I patch over to DuBois at night and pick up again in the morning."

Tom gave a weak whistle. "Is Bonnie okay with you out there herding the bad boys all by yourself?"

Joe stared straight ahead. "She's pissed, which you'll no doubt hear about later. In the meantime, that was a call from a concerned citizen who thinks I should rescue some idiots who got their boat stuck on the rocks in Wilson Cove before they freeze or drown or something."

"Flip on the bubble lights, brother. It'll be like making rounds with Mad Dog again."

Joe turned the cruiser onto the highway and headed downhill toward the lake. "Could be kids; but there was a boat out there last night running without lights. It went dark when I started after it in the patrol boat. Nearly peeled off the bottom on a rock. If I find out it's the same punks, I'll let them swim home."

Tom gestured at the fresh cuts on the back of his brother's muscled forearms and across the top of his dirty blond buzz cut. "You fall out and land on the propeller?"

Joe smirked. "Different bunch of assholes. Dopers planting on Watermelon Hill. I go up there sometimes to have a look and pull up plants. But they plant thorn bushes around them now, to keep the deer away. Spray, too. The stuff itches like hell."

"You get a kick out of Dad's old job, don't you?"

"More than you get out of yours."

Bull's eye. Flagging interest in a legal practice that had brought Tom white collar wealth in his early forties might come as a surprise to his partners. But it had never been possible to keep a secret in the Morgan house. Too many natural detectives. Joe's comment was a gentle probe. Their mother would bring out the backhoe and start digging before he had time to put down his suitcase.

Even so, it felt good to be home. He missed the hills above town that clung now to the last of their fall plumage, and the salmon-filled lake that gave its name to the community and shared its shoreline with French Quebec. The only thing he didn't miss were the "Call Of The Wild" winters which would come at any time now, and the lack of meaningful work for anyone with more than a high school education.

"Be funny if it were the Dooley twins out there," said Tom, dragging out old names and shared memories. "Remember when Dad caught them red handed with a haul of salmon, took their boat and left them stranded on Sunken Island up to their nuts in forty-five degree water?"

Joe's carrot-sized fingers squeezed the steering wheel. "Not everyone appreciated the old man's idea of instant justice, Tommy. That's part of what got him killed, don't you think?"

The cruiser accelerated.

Let's not go there.

The patrol car turned onto the lake road, past gabled houses with wraparound porches and vistas of blue water that stuttered by like subliminal advertising for turn of the century splendor. The elms that had lined the road when Tom and Joe were boys had long since succumbed to disease, their crippled skeletons lending the lakeshore road an air of permanent Halloween.

Where the road turned east to follow the knuckle of Wilson Cove, Joe pulled the car to the gravel shoulder. A hundred yards offshore, visible through patchy but rapidly lifting fog, a battered twenty-foot Boston Whaler churned circles in the cove's muddy shallows. Joe took a pair of binoculars and a battery-operated bullhorn from the trunk, slapped on his Smokey the Bear hat, tossed the binoculars to Tom and swaggered toward the shoreline.

Through the binoculars, Tom watched a short, wiry figure leap from the stern of the Whaler into knee-deep water. A graying ponytail swung from the back of his sun-faded tractor cap. Oblivious to Joe's approach, the man waded beside a taut down-rigger cable, pulled a long-handled filleting knife from a sheath on his hip and started to saw away on whatever was there.

Joe's amplified voice boomed across the water. "You guys need help?"

Tom swung the glasses toward the man who'd remained in the boat. He was pony-tailed too, slightly built, and as oblivious as his companion to the arrival of local law enforcement. Tom steadied the glasses against the dashboard and moved them to the man in the water and then back to the man in the boat. *The Dooley Twins?*

Some things never change. The poacher brothers padding the winter larder with fat fillets weeks after the season ended. Rods springing from downriggers, trolling reels screaming like toy tops, Kevin Dooley whooping like a kid, and brother Mickey angrily shushing him. Though as soon as they realized it was a snag, not a fish, the bickering must have started. Other than fishing and hunting out of season, that's what the Dooley twins were known for: world-class bickering.

Turning the glasses to the back of the boat, Tom watched the ponytailed man lift the lid on the fish box and dump its contents into the lake on the side of the boat opposite the shore. His partner in the water continued to do whatever he was doing with the knife. Then, as a gentle wind began to ripple the cove, pushing the fog away from the shoreline, a line of floating fish carcasses spread across the water in a slow, incriminating drift from boat to shore.

Joe bellowed through the bullhorn, "Gotcha, Mickey!"

The man in the water turned toward the amplified boast. As he did, a large cloth-covered something floated to the surface and began to drift behind the fish carcasses. Tom focused the binoculars to get a closer view of the thing bobbing in the water. Disbelieving seconds ticked by before he recognized what and then who it was.

"What" was a lean, pock marked face peering out of a water-logged sleeping bag. "Who" was Billy Pearce.

CHAPTER 3

When the ambulance left with Billy's body, Tom and Joe walked the shoreline looking for what might have floated out of the bag Billy had been stuffed into. Bickering voices wafted from the back of the patrol car. *Morgan has no right to take our boat!*

"Billy must have really pissed somebody off this time," said Joe.

"What do you mean?" asked Tom. "Billy was harmless. His sister even let him tag along on our dates. How many big sisters do that?"

"Ones whose boyfriend won't behave?"

"I'm serious, Joe. Who would want to harm a nice kid like Billy Pearce?"

"Kill," said Joe quietly. He picked up a stick and used the crooked end to snag a soggy sneaker that had drifted beside a floating fish carcass. "He may have been a nice little kid, Tommy. But he hung with a different crowd after his cute little brother days."

"Like who?"

"The Cashins, Frankie Heller, that bunch."

Tom couldn't picture Billy Pearce having anything in common with local bad boys, and he said so.

"Pickings get slim around here after the school crowd leaves for college," Joe reminded him. "What's left is all there is, unless you want to stay home and drink."

That Billy Pearce was a disappointment to his over-achieving family was something the family never hid. But Tom couldn't imagine the aristocratic Dr. Pearce sitting idle while his offspring dragged the family name to the trailer park. He kicked a spray of stones toward the water and, as if in response, the Blackberry in his pocket began to bleat. A swift, smothering hug pinned Tom's arm to his side, preventing him from answering it.

"Fair warning, Tommy. You had that thing glued to your ear the whole time you were here last year. Mom says that if she sees it there again, she's going to shove it in with her cane."

Tom tried to free his arm, but it was pancaked to his ribcage.

"Unless it's a girl calling."

The phone continued to vibrate. "Look, I got a cryptic phone call as I was getting off the plane. I may have to go back to New York."

"Sweet Jesus, brother!" The squeeze tightened. "Mom will kill you. Bonnie will help her. The girls will truss you up with their jump ropes, and Luke will gnaw off your feet at the ankle."

"Norman Rockwell meets the Far Side," The words escaped with the last of Tom's breath.

"We love you too, brother. But if you don't stay off that god damned phone... or if you try to leave early because some fat cat snaps his fingers... be afraid for what your loving family will do to you."

Tom struggled to free his arm. "Let me answer the phone, Joe."

"Not a chance. If you need an action fix while you're here, put that Ivy League brain of yours to work on something important for a change. Help me find out who killed Billy Pearce."

* * *

Joe drove the patrol car into the hills east of town, where the pavement gave way to gravel and then dirt. Minutes later, he turned onto a one-lane track that came to an end in front of a three thousand square foot log cabin on ten acres of cleared land overlooking Coldwater Lake.

Tom whistled. "You win the lotto or something? This is your new place?"

"It's private," Joe growled. "And secure." He punched a code into the keypad next to the front door. "I'll leave you here to visit with Mom, if she isn't napping. I need to get over to the morgue. But if she's up, try not to push each other's buttons, okay? It'd be nice to have a quiet, peaceful visit for a change."

Easier said... Tom loved his mother, and knew that all of his best qualities came from her. But a wall had risen between them that had not been there when he was growing up, bricked and layered by his choice of career and lifestyle, and mortared by her displeasure with both.

He set his bags in the hall, catching his jet-lagged reflection in the polished copper pans that dangled above the island kitchen. A timbered room filled the greater part of the ground floor, bordered by a ceiling-high stone fireplace on one side and bedrooms on the other. Sliding glass doors led to a wraparound porch that overlooked the lake.

A thin, raspy voice rose from a couch at the center of the room. "You're letting your hair grow."

Tom crossed the room and gave his mother a kiss. A policeman's widow for a dozen years, Mary Morgan had long since decided that life doesn't get much better than a quiet afternoon on the magic carpet of a moderate alcohol buzz. She was thinner than when he had visited a year ago, and the thigh-high cast made her seem frail.

"I'm on vacation, Beautiful."

"You didn't grow that in a week."

He laughed. "A client talked me into it."

"Does she have a name?" Mary didn't hide the hope in her voice. She exaggerated it.

"Ed," he said firmly, moving a pile of magazines from the end of the couch to clear a spot beside her.

"Pshaw!"

Suppressing a smile, he watched his mother's graceful fingers comb a crop of silver curls that had been black and straight when he and Joe were growing up, with an off-center streak of white as if her habit of running her

11

hand through her hair had worn away its colors.

"You know I worry about you flitting around all those foreign cities. So does your brother—though he'd never say so to your face. It isn't safe. Americans aren't as popular as they used to be."

Tom reminded himself to be patient and let her work her beads. Afterwards they could relax and enjoy each other's company. But as his brother had cautioned, if Tom tried to stop or shorten what had become an annual ritual, there would be no peace for any of them. "I'm in London more than any place other than New York," he said. "It's pretty safe these days... as long as our people don't start blowing up pubs again."

Don't bait her, Tommy.

Mary's face puckered, and she gave him *the look*. Her maiden name had been Flynn, but she refused to admit the Irish were her people. "Ne'er-do-well cousins" was as close as she'd come. "And you stayed, I suppose." It was a statement, not a question, and an unveiled reference to the congenital recklessness she believed infected the Morgan lineage.

"We were working on a three billion pound tender offer. You leave the room with chips like that on the table, and they don't ever ask you to come back." *Can't you be home more than one minute without showing off?*

She dismissed the preening. "Your father risked his life for strangers. I never understood that. I was always after him to stop."

"He should have listened to you."

"Your brother, too. There's too much testosterone in this family."

She'd skipped a few questions. 'You look tired. You should rest. Maybe you should stay another week. The last usually signaled the end.

"You worried about someone blowing me up?"

"Killing yourself with work is more like it. You look exhausted."

A carousel of images triggered by finding Billy's body, and the phone call from New York that might mean he would have to cut this visit short, clamored for Tom's attention. He hadn't wanted to mention any of it right away. But the dead body of a childhood acquaintance is not something that can go unmentioned for long. "Look, mom. On the way in from the airport..."

"Is that why your hand's hovering over your pocket like there's a pack of cigs in there and you just quit this morning?"

He sighed, reminding himself to be patient. "Joe delivered your warning about the phone."

She placed her fingers on his forearm. "Leave it, Tommy. Just for a week. You need your family time."

"And happy to have it."

The opening was small, but she plunged. "And about time you started your own, don't you think?"

He laughed. "No." *And not fair asking questions out of order.*

"You're wearing yourself out."

He shrugged.

"You're obsessed."

That wasn't part of the usual litany. He smiled, hoping it didn't encourage.

"With money," she pressed.

Ouch! Then the words slipped out. "I wonder why?"

Her chin jerked up and back as if he'd slapped her from below. But before he could sweep question and subject back under the rug where they belonged, one of the wireless gizmos on the table beside the couch began to trill. Lost among the bottled water, snack packs and piles of paperbacks, it was a moment before either of them could find the source. Mary grabbed the phone first. "No, I'm afraid he's not," she said. "I would try him at the station house... No, I really don't... As I told you before, Miss Pearce, this is his home not his office." Click.

Tom lowered his chin and peered at his mother from beneath compressed eyebrows. "Susan Pearce?" The name of his high-school girlfriend came out a rasp.

"Three times in the last half hour."

"She's here? Already?"

"She's been back a year."

"What? The Dooley brothers just fished her brother's body out of Coldwater Lake less than an hour ago. Joe got the call on our way here. That's what I was trying to tell you."

Mary's hand moved to the top of her forehead where her long white fingers combed a meticulous hairdo. "Oh, dear. No wonder you're so testy. I wish you'd told me. And the poor girl's just after losing her parents, too."

"What? Dr. Pearce is dead?" It came out nearly a shout. "*And* Mrs. Pearce?"

Mary closed her eyes, sighed and then opened them again. "Didn't you know? That's what brought Miss Pearce back to Coldwater. The parents drowned in a boating accident in Wilson Cove last year. She and her brother inherited that beautiful estate."

* * *

Susan's back in Coldwater?

Tom felt like a kid who's just heard the jingle of an ice cream truck rolling down the street—alert, excited, ready to blast off. But the sound of an SUV coming to a stop, a door flying open and cries of, 'Uncle Tom! Uncle Tom!' forced him to tuck the feeling away for later.

Two pairs of sticky hands wrapped around his neck. Four gangly legs slid into his arms. He staggered upright like an out-of-shape circus strong man. "Girls!" he groaned. "You make your daddy do this?"

"He can lift us over his head!"

"Well, I can drop you!" Tom flexed his knees and a staccato of pink flip flops slapped the hardwood. Squeals of laughter blasted his ears.

"And who's this? Somebody's new boyfriend?" A dark haired boy of about six ducked behind his sister's legs and peered shyly around them. Tom bent at the waist and held out his hand.

"That's Luke, Uncle Tom!"

"No way! Luke's about yeah high." Tom turned his palm upside down over his knee. "Are you Luke?"

The boy nodded.

"Let me feel your muscle." Tom reached toward the boy, who lifted his arm slowly while holding tight to his sister's leg. Tom wrapped his fingers gently around the boy's bicep. "Wow! You've grown, buddy." The boy smiled. "Where's your mom?" He pointed toward the door. "She got packages?" He nodded and stepped cautiously from behind his sister. "Okay, let's put those muscles to work."

Tom and the kids helped their mother carry groceries to the kitchen, then she sent them off to play and do homework. Rising on her toes, Joe's pretty wife gave Tom a quick peck on the cheek, and whispered, "Good to have you back." A petite girl-next-door type with a slim figure and short brown hair, Bonnie Morgan was even-tempered, competent and forgiving of her husband's many shortcomings, including his family. Tom didn't often see that combination in his colleagues' marriages. If his brother's wife had been a tall redhead, there might have been some fraternal competition.

Joe came home an hour later and pulled Tom aside. "I got a call from somebody who saw Billy's picture in this afternoon's Coldwater Gazette and claims it looks like the guy who broke into his business a few weeks ago. I told him we'd meet him in an hour."

Bonnie came out of the kitchen and gave her husband a hug and a kiss, saying that dinner would be ready in five minutes.

Joe took her hand. "Did Tommy tell you about Billy Pearce?"

"We've been whispering about it all afternoon. It's terrible. But don't say anything in front of the kids. Please. We don't want nightmares."

Joe squeezed her hand. "Look, I hate to do this, but Tommy and I need to run."

"Joe!"

"I'm sorry. It's a lead on this Billy Pearce business. I need to jump on it."

"At least eat, babe."

"Maybe I should stay," said Tom. He had altered his vacation plans to help Joe's wife, who had her hands more than full taking care of three kids and a self-medicating mother-in-law with a broken leg. If he said yes to Joe, they could be doing the Holmes/Watson thing all week, and then so much for helping Bonnie.

"I need you, Tommy. The guy who called is the owner of that new bio-research company that moved into Coldwater Park last year. He's a corporate wheeler dealer, like you. I need someone to translate the bullshit."

"Joe!" said Bonnie.

"Sorry, sweetie. I need Tommy's help, that's all. We've got to run."

She put a hand on his arm. "Eat, then run. Don't disappoint your mother. She's been waiting all day to have the two of you together."

Used to be she couldn't wait to get rid of us.

The brothers carried their mother outside to the picnic table, while Bonnie and the girls brought out plates of hamburger and sweet corn. It was too late in the year to dine comfortably outside, so they ate hurriedly while the sun sank toward the horizon. When they finished, Tom produced a bag of exotic presents from foreign locales: geisha kimonos for Kate and Meghan, a scrimshaw pocket knife for Luke. The girls put on the kimonos and performed an energetic hip hop while the sun dropped over the trees beyond the lake. Luke toyed with the knife under the watchful eye of his mother.

"Do you know how to play Mumbly peg?" Tom asked.

The boy moved his head from side to side.

"Your dad used to be pretty good at it, until grandma took away his Barlow. Get him to tell you the story sometime."

"Careful, brother. I've got stories, too."

"But not the right audience." Tom turned to Luke. "Anything you want to know about your dad, you ask me. He was a wild man before he met your mom."

Bonnie laughed. "I might like to hear those stories."

"Tommy!" Mary's voice was a warning.

"He gets it from Grandma," said Tom. "Do you take after your mom?"

The boy shook his head.

"*adic-*I s-*adic-*ee," Tom said, in a soft, conspiratorial whisper.

The boy cocked his head.

"I used to do the same thing to Grandma. Drove her n-*adic-*uts."

"Tommy!" Mary's voice rose again. Bonnie's head swung back and forth between mother and sons. Joe raised his eyes to the sky.

"It's a secret language," Tom explained. Only eldest male Morgans are allowed to speak it. I spoke it with my Dad. He spoke it with his. Luke and I are allowed to speak it, too—but no one else." He put his arm around his nephew. "I thought I saw some rushes down there by the pond. Why don't you cut a big one and I'll show you how to carve a whistle they can hear all the way to town."

The boy nodded vigorously and took off down the hill toward the pond at the bottom of the property. As soon as he was out of earshot, Mary cautioned, "Be careful, Tommy. Don't embarrass the boy."

Bonnie spoke quietly. "We took him to Upstate Medical last month. They said the same thing as the doctors here. There's nothing wrong with his hearing or his vocal cords. He understands everything. He just won't speak."

CHAPTER 4

Neurogene occupied the first floor of a prefabricated metal building on the outskirts of town where the Coldwater drive-in movie theater used to be when Tom and Joe were growing up. Tom felt himself smile as they drove past the oak tree that had been the unofficial line of demarcation between the families who were there to see the movie, and the teenage couples who were there to make out. Joe stared straight ahead. He was in his hunter mode. Nothing extraneous was going to register until the bio research company owner was bagged, or released.

Joe parked the patrol car in front of a steel frame building skinned in faux stone and tinted glass. Holes in the stone showed where the lengthy logo of a previous tenant had been replaced by the single word NeuroGene. Tom expected a blast of over-air conditioned air. But the air inside the glass-fronted reception area felt tepid and stuffy. New Age Muzak filtered through stands of spindly bamboo on either side of a metal reception desk. Joe leaned a hand on the desk, and it slid toward the wall.

"Hey careful!" The girl behind the desk braced it with her forearm, keeping a phone wedged tightly between shoulder and ear.

Joe flashed his badge. "We're here to see Mr. Willow."

She sighed into the phone, "Back in a sec," then pressed numbers on a keypad. "They're here." Then she pressed some more buttons and showed the Morgan brothers the back of her head.

Tom noted the absence of visitors' chairs in the reception area or any

18

magazines, company literature, corporate art or other visual distraction beyond the single word *NEUROGENE* painted on the wall above the receptionist's head in a fashion-y script that looked like something you might see on the window of a hair salon.

When the door next to the reception desk finally opened, a lanky, middle-aged man in need of a haircut and sunlight stepped forward to greet them. The outstretched hand and simian show of outsized teeth were perfunctory. "Dave Willow," he said, "Follow me."

The NeuroGene owner led them down a hall lined with inspirational posters and empty offices to a tiny unpainted room containing a single metal desk, two unmatched chairs and stacks of files and loose paper that looked less like they were passing through in any commercial sense and more like permanent residents. To Tom's well-traveled eye, the venue was more academic than entrepreneurial and not too successful at either.

Willow motioned his guests to sit, and then settled into a faux leather chair behind the cluttered desk. Joe produced a blown-up copy of a New York State driver's license, and Willow leaned forward to look at it. "That's him," he said. "No question."

"The guy you found rummaging in your mail room?"

"I don't know that he was rummaging. He was just there where he shouldn't be."

"When was that?"

"About three weeks ago. I'd just come back from a speaking engagement in Chicago and I stopped here on my way home to pick up some mail."

"What time?"

"About midnight."

"Do you come here often at that hour?"

"No, thank God. When I'm traveling, I usually have my mail sent to my condo so I can read it when I get back. But our part-time mail room person was out sick that week, so I stopped on my way in from the airport to pick up my mail."

Joe tapped the blown-up photo. "What did this guy say when you walked in on him?"

"Nothing at first. I asked him who he was and what he was doing, of course. He told me to ask my partner."

"And who is that?"

"Was. A man named Michael Sharp. He's no longer with the company."

Joe made a note in his pad. "And this intruder was looking for him?"

"I don't know that for sure," said Willow. "He just said to talk to my partner, as if that's all the explanation I needed. So I told him just what I told you, that I no longer have a partner."

"Then what?"

"Then he left."

"And you didn't report the break-in?"

"I wasn't sure there'd been one. He didn't seem to be doing anything. He was just there. And he did mention my partner."

"How can I get hold of this partner of yours?"

"Former partner." Willow took an embossed business card from his wallet and slid it across the top of the desk. "I wrote his new address and phone number on the back."

"You call him yet?"

"I called him the day after I found that man here." Willow pointed to the photocopied license.

"And what did he say?"

"That he didn't know anything about it and had no idea who he was or what he might have been doing."

"Anything else?"

Willow paused. "Some business loose ends. Nothing about the man in that photo."

"Have you spoken to your former partner since you saw the picture in today's Gazette?"

"I assumed you wouldn't want me to."

Tom interrupted. "He said check with your partner. Did he use his name?"

Joe frowned at the interruption.

"No, he didn't," said Willow.

Joe opened the leather-covered notebook, looked at some notes and made a few. Willow watched and waited for him to resume, which Tom understood was the point. *I'm in charge here. My brother's along to keep his ears open, not his mouth.*

Joe closed the notebook. "It might be helpful if you give me some background on this company of yours. What it does for example. No offense, but I thought Neutrogena was a women's face cream."

Willow forced a chuckle. "NeuroGene, Sheriff. We do gene research, primarily as it relates to brain chemistry."

"Anything I might have heard of?"

Willow smiled. So did Tom. Asking an entrepreneur about his company was like asking a mother about her children. This wasn't going to be short.

"We're not a household name yet," said Willow. "But I believe our research will get us there, eventually. What we do is attempt to unlock the genetic determinants of human behavior: why people smoke tobacco for example, or drink alcohol even though they know it to be harmful. We try to identify the specific brain chemistry at work in making the body want what the brain knows to be toxic or reject what it knows to be beneficial. Then we try to come up with things that enhance or block those impulses." He went on to give several examples.

"So you're a drug company?" Joe asked.

"No. We're a research company with a focus on brain chemistry. Drugs, or ideas for drugs, come from that research."

Tom interrupted again. "So where does the money come from?"

Joe folded his Popeye forearms and stared at the ceiling.

"Ah, money." Willow templed his fingers as if in prayer, and rested his chin on the tips. "Basically NeuroGene survives by patenting the ideas that come out of our research and by licensing the patents to the major drug companies. There's considerable interest among the large pharmaceutical manufacturers in what we do. But they can be tight with their cash until there's a demonstrated commercial demand."

"So you're broke?" Tom pushed.

Willow stiffened. "We've been through a few dry patches now and then. Nothing atypical for this line of business. We're fine at the moment."

Tom had heard that wishful line before. "Are you the sole owner?" Willow's answer would tell him if NeuroGene was still limping along on founder money, or if the corporate vultures had already started to tear off the digestible pieces in exchange for short-term cash. Willow's slow, drawn-out 'yes' seemed to pass through several filters of weighed consequences before he let it out.

Joe took back the lead. "So where do you keep the brainiacs that do all this research? This place looks kind of sleepy to me."

"It's late, Sheriff. I'm sure most of the staff have gone home."

"And that would be how many?" asked Tom, wondering why the receptionist would be there if everyone else had gone.

Willow paused again before answering. "At the moment, I employ three researchers. In addition to myself. We should be staffing up again soon."

Joe tapped the photo on the desk. "So this guy didn't steal anything?"

"Not that I know of."

"Or threaten to?"

"No."

"And aside from mentioning your partner, there's no connection between him and your company? He wasn't a customer? Or here to pick up or deliver something for one?

Tom watched Willow's eyes move up and to the left, as if the answer might be somewhere at the top of a flimsy shelf jammed with photos and corporate trinkets.

"He didn't say anything like that when I asked," Willow answered.

Joe closed his notebook. "Now that you've had a few weeks to think about it, what do you think he was doing here? Or what do you think he might have intended to do before you busted in on him? Any guess?"

"Guess?" Willow's neck arched like a fastidious egret's. "I'd rather not. The potential for serious mischief in a bio-research lab should give nightmares to any thoughtful person. It's a field that attracts its share of brilliant misfits, I'm afraid."

Joe gestured toward the open door. "Did he leave anything behind?"

"Not that I noticed. But then, I'm afraid I didn't think to look."Willow clasped his hands behind his neck and looked again toward the shelf of photos and corporate memorabilia above his desk. "My sense now is that I came in before he could get started on whatever it was he intended to do."

Joe pursued. "And what's usually in your mail room? Anything out of the ordinary?"

"Mail, of course. Overnight packages. Dry chemicals. Wet chemicals. Refrigerated culture dishes. Scientific journals. Junk mail."

"Could he have been looking to steal something?"

"He didn't act like it. Like I said, he was pretty bold."

While Joe worked his questions, Tom sat with the sense that there was something familiar about the NeuroGene owner. But the answer didn't come right away.

When Joe had finished taking careful notes of Willow's unremarkable answers, he gave the NeuroGene owner a copy of the driver's license photo and asked him to show it around the office in case the intruder had been there more than once and someone else had run into him.

As Willow took it, Tom noted the demeanor of a witness who has not been asked the question he'd over-prepared to answer. At the risk of pushing his brother over the edge, he prompted. "I think Mr. Willow has something to add."

Willow's head swung toward Tom and then slowly back to Joe, who was busy staring holes into Tom's skull.

"I'm sorry, Sheriff," said Willow. "I know you blacked out the name and address on that license. But the Gazette printed the name and address of the man whose body was found in the lake this morning."

Joe's face hardened.

Willow's voice was almost apologetic. "I'm sure you know this already. But if not… well, I'm pretty sure the man in that photo is the brother of one of my researchers. I think you know her. Susan Pearce?"

CHAPTER 5

om awoke before first light and brought a cup of coffee to the back porch where the sunrise was slowly transforming a distant misty puddle into a bright metallic disk that was Coldwater Lake. He got no farther than the top rung of the split log steps, before the dawn air exploded with two hundred decibels of ear splitting siren and a blinding flash of red halogen light. The mug of coffee slipped from his hand and tumbled down the steps. Then Joe burst through the back door with a twelve gauge shotgun angled across his chest and a pair of boxer shorts sliding toward his ankles. Tom raised his hands above his head. "I forget to say 'May I?'?"

Joe let the firearm slide to his side and reached inside the sliding door to press an electronic touch pad. The horns died and the lights faded. "Should have warned you about the toys, I guess."

"Anything else besides noisemakers?"

Joe pointed the barrel of the rifle toward the slim black rectangles bolted beneath the eaves. "Cameras, so I can watch it later with popcorn."

Tom clenched his hands to keep them from shaking. "What if Mom wants to go out for a walk?"

"She can't. Her leg's broke. That's why you're here."

Even as a kid, his smart-mouth younger brother had a quick retort for everything.

"What if *I* want to go for a walk? Do I come back in one piece? And what about the kids?"

"The place is only rigged at night when everyone's inside sleeping, or when we're all out."

"How about giving me the code, in case I want to break curfew while I'm here."

Joe hesitated. Then without expression, recited, "0 4/ 0 1/ R I P."

It was a moment before either brother spoke.

"You're expecting trouble?"

Joe shrugged. "It comes with the job. This place is empty most of the time. If it's not, I like to know before I walk in the front door."

"And that code?"

"A reminder not to get careless."

* * *

Kate grabbed a pancake, folded it like a crepe and bussed her mother's cheek before disappearing into the bathroom. In fifth grade, she was already eye-to-eye with her mother. Meghan, who appeared next, had her father's height and coloring as well. She took the stool next to Tom, opened a book and hovered over some last-minute homework. Joe entered the kitchen last, resplendent in Sam Brown boots and wide leather belt. He poured a cup of coffee and motioned to Tom to join him outside.

The noise of boots on gravel mixed with the calls of morning song birds and the rustle of autumn leaves. Joe sipped from a ceramic cup that was clearly a homemade present from one of the girls. "We need to find that NeuroGene guy's former partner and check his story. He got kind of squirrely when you started with the money questions."

"He'd have gotten squirrelier if I'd recognized him sooner."

Joe spilled the coffee onto the ground and pointed the empty mug at Tom's chest. "Quit being a smart ass, Tommy. You busted my beauty rest and I'm in no mood for guessing games. You recognized him? How? When? From where?"

"Coldwater High School. Fall semester, twenty years ago. New chemistry teacher, straight out of college. Girls were all over him and vice versa. That is, until he pissed one of them off and she got him fired by telling the principal he promised to show her how to make LSD in the high school Chem lab."

Joe frowned. "I don't remember any of that. Why didn't you say something last night?"

"You don't remember because it wasn't your girlfriend who was Mr. Wizard's main admirer. And because you were too busy terrorizing visiting team quarterbacks the whole ten weeks he was there. I didn't tell you last night because I only placed the face this morning when you came busting out with your drawers around your knees. The visual must have jarred something."

Joe shook his head. "You're a piece of work, Tommy. What makes you think it's the same guy?"

"The photos on the bookshelf in his office. He kept looking at them. One was himself with a guitar, long hair and a Fu Manchu—Don Juan d'Chemistry, but without the teacher haircut. Same size, same big choppers, only they're yellow now. I don't think he was using the name Willow back then, but you could look it up."

Joe unfolded his arms and relaxed. "Nice detective work, brother."

"If it's him. He's got balls coming back here."

"Big ones, if it turns out he's missing a sleeping bag." Joe slid behind the wheel of the patrol car where the girls were waiting for their ride to school. Bonnie stood at the cabin door and watched her family head down the mountain. Tom joined her. She looked exhausted.

"Sorry for waking everyone."

Bonnie turned toward him, eyes hard and arms folded tight across her chest. "You have to tell him to quit."

"Bonnie, it was me who set off those alarms."

"Three times this month. Every petty criminal in Coldwater knows that Joe's lost his deputies and has no backup now. They're testing him."

"He told me that he'll have help again in the New Year."

"Bullshit!" She turned and walked into the house. He followed her into the kitchen to where she stood looking out the window toward the lake. He put a hand on her shoulder. She brushed it away.

"What's going on, Bonnie?"

Pulling a chair from the kitchen table, she pointed to the one opposite. "Sit. Listen. Then talk to your brother."

Tom poured a cup of coffee and tried to think of what his brother might have done to require fraternal intervention. The possibilities were endless. He took the chair and waited. "Coldwater is changing," Bonnie began. "But your brother refuses to recognize it, or do anything to protect himself or us." Tom wrapped his hand around the cup and concentrated on maintaining eye contact. "The State has all this federal money since 9/11. Supposedly to protect the border. But they're using it mostly to revisit old battles. They want to roll up all the small town police departments and make them part of the State Troopers."

Is that what you're worrying about? "The state troopers have been trying to rein in the small town cops since MadDog's time. The pitch back then was computers. It's nothing new."

"Well they've got a better pitch now, and money to go with it. They're dangling budget relief in front of all the little town governments. And the town council is more than ready to offload any costs the state is willing to pick up."

Tom put down his cup. "Joining the Troopers might not be the worst thing for Joe. It would mean a bigger paycheck and a state pension. I know my brother values his independence…"

"Oh, Tom, the troopers aren't going to give Joe a job. They hate his guts. They hate the whole Morgan family!"

Tom looked away. "And you think Coldwater's going to let Joe go?"

"No one's delivered a pink slip yet. But the troopers have already lured away Joe's deputies. The town council took away his dispatcher. The

27

scuttlebutt is they're waiting for the State to fund a Border Patrol barracks on that vacant lot next to the Grange Hall, so they can put one of Joe's' old deputies in charge and have everyone on the state payroll instead of the town's. Even your mother says that firing Helen, who'd been there thirty years, was the writing on the wall. She says Joe needs to get out before it gets ugly."

"And do what?"

Bonnie's eyes brightened. "There's an opening for a math teacher and football coach at Coldwater High School starting in the spring. Joe would make a great coach, don't you think?"

No. And imagining Joe as anything other than the Coldwater County Sheriff was like thinking of Tarzan living in Manhattan.

"Have you talked to him?"

"Your mother and I both have. She says it's like talking to you about grandchildren."

Ouch. "Look, Bonnie, I've been away for a while. Give me a few days to digest the local politics and then I'll talk to him."

She reached for his hand. "Don't put it off, Tom. The longer he waits… " The phone next to the cupboard began to trill, interrupting whatever consequence she'd intended to bring to his attention. She lifted the receiver from the wall. "Yes? No. I would try him at the Grange.. . I really don't… I've given him your messages, Miss Pearce." She'd slapped the receiver back into place.

"Susan?"

"That woman's a pain."

"In pain, I imagine. Her brother just died."

Bonnie looked away. Her expression was hard and unsympathetic. Tom would have liked to ask why, but could sense this was another no-fly zone. Instead, he said, "I'll talk to him. And I'm sorry about that Pig Latin stuff with Luke. I wasn't thinking."

Her face grew tighter. Then tears fell. Tom looked for a box of tissues or other prop that might substitute for opening his mouth and making things worse. Bonnie raised her head and looked over his shoulder, wiping her eyes with her fingers. Tom turned and saw Luke standing in the doorway, holding a pair of fishing rods.

"Hey, Buddy. They make you catch your breakfast around here?"

"Blueberry Pancakes," said Bonnie, choking the syllables.

Luke rested the rods against the kitchen island and hopped onto a stool. He looked at the two adults.

Tom grinned. "You ever catch a salmon?"

The boy turned his head from side to side.

"Would you like to?" Tom held his palms a yard apart. "They're about this big."

Luke jerked his head up and down.

Tom turned to Bonnie, "Is it okay?"

Her face resumed its mask of worry —- the mom's version this time, not the wife's. "That's a big lake, Tom. Those are huge fish."

Luke moved his head up and down again, a giant grin stretching his face.

"I'll make him wear a life jacket. I promise."

Bonnie hesitated.

"Trust me."

CHAPTER 6

Luke sprinted to the end of the dock and dipped a bare hook into the blue/black water, staring expectantly after it. Tom checked the marina office and found it locked and shuttered. The only sign of life appeared on the deck of a thirty foot Penn Yan tied to the end of the dock. Tom walked over and asked the man mopping the stern if they were too late to rent a boat.

"Season's over," he said, spilling soapy water from a bucket onto the deck. "I'm just getting ready to haul this one."

Tom admired the oiled mahogany and polished bright work. "She's a beauty. Ever take her out for salmon?"

The man brushed the soapy water toward the stern. "Don't have the time. I've got an old downrigger in the locker, if you're looking for used tackle."

Tom laughed. "I need a boat first. I made the mistake of telling my nephew here about this place where the fish are as big as he is."

"That'd be out past Pocket Island in about a hundred feet of water, if they're there today."

Tom touched the pocket that held his wallet. "Anyone who could get us there could name his price."

The man smiled. "What's the boy's name?"

"Luke Morgan."

"Any relation to our sheriff?"

"His son. My brother."

The man's face grew thoughtful. "We might be able to work something out, Mr. Morgan. I'm Jack Thompson, by the way."

Tom held out his hand. "Tom Morgan."

"That's right. Tell young Luke there to step on board. We'll see if one of those monster fish is out there cruising around."

Tom felt the flush of relief. He'd been cooler in the face of a busted mega-deal than in the prospect of disappointing Luke on their first outdoor adventure. "What do I owe you for saving my life, Jack?"

Thompson grinned. "I'll let you know later."

The Penn Yan kept to the middle of the channel until it cleared the cove, then Thompson opened the throttle for the twenty minute run to the trench west of Pocket Island. Over the noise of wind and motor, he shouted to Luke, "Go below and say hello to Brutus! He likes company!" Luke disappeared into the cabin and emerged with his arms wrapped around a large black Labrador. Thompson handed the boy a biscuit. "Give him this."

Overhead, long, v-shaped lines of geese and mallards dotted the pale blue sky. It was good that the lake was calm. Luke wasn't big enough to take a pounding, and the deep water beyond Pocket Island could get rough.

When the depth-finder registered an abrupt drop from thirty to a hundred forty feet, Thomson eased the throttle. "We're here." To Luke he added, "Take Brutus up front. He likes to sun himself up there. Take these, too." He handed Luke a baggie of dog biscuits. Then he turned to Tom. "Do you know how to set up a downrigger?"

"It'll come back to me."

Thompson disappeared into the cabin and came back with an old Cannon hand crank, a seven foot Loomis rod and a single red and white J-plug. It took Tom longer than he remembered to get the drag and clip set right. But eventually everything was ready. Thompson held the boat in the center of the trench and kept the throttle at one and a half knots. Tom took the mate's chair and turned it to face the rod. If a salmon hit, the line would pull free from the downrigger, and the rod would snap upright signaling a fish was on.

Thompson turned the captain's chair to face his passenger. Soft and matter of fact, his voice blended easily with the throaty murmur of the inboard engine puttering just above idle. "So, who killed William Pearce?"

Tom looked at the Lowrance. Depth 120 feet, water temperature 51 degrees Fahrenheit. "You a good swimmer, Jack?"

Thompson smiled. "Coldwater hasn't gotten any bigger since you left, Tom. Everyone knows the sheriff's business."

Tom looked toward the bow where Luke lay curled with the dog. At one and a half knots, the boat moved through the water at the pace of a brisk stroll. He calculated the permutations of possible trouble with Thompson. None worried him, as long as Luke kept out of the way. "What makes you think I know who killed Billy Pearce?"

Thompson smiled. "My niece is the receptionist at NeuroGene. She called to tell me her boss recognized the picture in the Gazette of the man they pulled from the lake yesterday, and that our sheriff and his brother were out there asking questions."

"Your sheriff would say that's police business."

"It's also news."

"Are you a reporter, Jack?"

"Reporter, photographer, printer, publisher. I own the Coldwater Gazette." He raised his chin toward the boy and the big black dog dozing in the sunlight. "You said I could name my price. I just did. An interview. About the murder of William Pearce."

Tom released a stoppered breath. "You should really talk to my brother."

"Maybe I should do an article about him?" Thompson's voice was mock thoughtful. "That would be some juicy reading."

Tom assumed his boardroom face, alert and expressionless.

"Do you know how hard it is to keep a weekly newspaper alive on a diet of school events and county politics?" Thompson asked. "A home-town murder is a gift from the gods. Pardon my cold heart. I've got a stack of bills on my desk that'd choke a moose. A juicy local murder could mean a couple of months of extra readers and ads that could put a dent in that pile of bills."

Tom looked up at the bow where Luke lay with his arms around the Labrador. It was dead calm and there were no boats in any direction. "How much revenue could you get from the story you're looking for, Jack?"

"You're changing the subject."

"No. You were talking about unpaid bills. How much revenue?"

"Enough to keep the doors open."

"And your biggest cost is payroll?"

"Ha!" Thompson spat. "I'm it. The paper can't support more than one person, even if he is getting kind of long in the tooth. Printing and newsprint are the big tickets."

"Suppose you could cut those bills in half?"

"I'd sell my soul... for that or a Pulitzer."

Tom reached for the binoculars tucked into the pocket on the back of the captain's chair and focused them on the horizon. Ten miles away, the dark shoreline of Quebec was broken by the thumbnail smudges of Sainte Foy, Pont Rouge and Grand-Mere. He handed the glasses to Thompson. "From here you can see three towns with newspapers just like yours. If it were clearer, you could see more."

"So what?" said Thompson, not bothering to look. "That's Quebec."

"And the papers are French," said Tom. "So they don't compete with you for the same readers. If you went to any of them and offered to co-buy and co-publish—paper, ink and everything else, you could all cut your operating costs by an amount a whole lot larger than a temporary bump in ad revenue from a one-time murder story. You could even print cheaper over there and bring the papers across duty free under NAFTA."

Thompson looked at him hard. "Is this what you do for a living?"

"On a different scale. Yes."

Thompson handed the glasses back. "The brain drain around here..." He shook his head. "It's a wonder this town survives. Every one of you bright boys should be made to come back and do a year of public service to repay the free education that launched you."

Tom laughed. "Take this as a down payment. A six-month ad bump from a murder story is just that. But the savings from co-publishing with one of the French papers across the lake would be permanent. And you don't have to compromise a murder investigation to get it."

"So it is a murder?" Thompson leapt.

Tom shrugged. "Unless Billy Pearce put himself into that bag and tried to play Houdini."

* * *

Thompson turned the boat at the end of the trench, shifting the sun to the stern. The big Labrador followed the sunlight and Luke followed the dog. Thompson whistled and waved at Luke to move to the stern. "Go sit behind the rod, son. If you see it pop or if Brutus starts to bark, crank the reel as fast as you can. There's fifty feet of slack and you'll need to get all of it back before the salmon throws the hook."

Luke nodded and climbed into the chair behind the downrigger. The dog sat on the deck and watched the rod. Tom took a turn asking questions. "So what do you know about Billy Pearce? You must hear things in your line of work."

Thompson shrugged. "I do. But why should I tell you, if you're not going to help me?"

Tom waved toward the shoreline of Quebec. "I just balanced your checkbook for the next ten years. I could give some thought to that Pulitzer, too, if you let me know what you left out of the obituary."

Thompson's eyes widened, but his mouth remained firm. "Rumor and innuendo. None of it news. I played bridge regularly with the father years ago. Hell of a card player. But always whining about his idiot son. Of course, the boy got in trouble when he got older: shoplifting, graffiti, that kind of thing. I take it you never met him."

"I used to coach his little league team. He was a bright kid. No idiot at all."

"Well, the father had some pretty high standards." Thompson checked the depth finder and turned the wheel to bring the boat about. A hundred feet below, the J Plug slowed to a halt as the bow swung to port, then accelerated as the stern swung back in line. As the wheel straightened, the dog barked and the rod popped. "Fish on!"

Tom wrapped his hand over Luke's on the handle of the fishing reel as the rod tip plunged and line began to tear off the reel. "Crank, buddy, crank! He's hooked!"

Luke churned his arm. The bail spun like a fist-sized dynamo. Tom squeezed the boy's hand. "Wait. When he's taking line like that, just hold tight and keep the rod tip up. When he stops, start cranking."

Luke nodded and kept his eye fixed on the reel.

The rod began to straighten. "He's coming up," said Thompson.

Thirty feet behind the boat, the blue/black water erupted in foamy spray and rainbow prism. A gray cylinder the size of a man's leg broke the surface and whipped the water into foam with a tail as wide as a catcher's mitt.

Thompson whistled. "That'll go forty pounds."

Don't jinx it.

Tom held out a hand. "You got a net?" Thompson disappeared into the cabin. The rod plunged again and the reel began to scream. "Let it run," whispered Tom. "He'll tire himself out."

Luke nodded.

The fish rose and the boy took line. It sounded and he gave it back, the drag putting pressure on the fish. When the reel stopped turning, Luke cranked again, Tom's whisper steady in his ear, "Crank, buddy, crank."

Then a boy-sized fish rose to the surface, tailing behind the boat, momentarily exhausted.

"I'm going to take the rod out of the downrigger and hand it to you," said Tom. "I want you to stand and grip it above the reel. Tuck the butt into your hip, then crank and lift steady. The rod will bring the fish to the net and then Mr. Thompson can grab it."

Luke nodded.

"You ready?"

He nodded again.

"Here goes." Tom took the rod out of the holder and placed it in Luke's hands, putting one above the reel, settling the butt on the boy's left hip and placing his other hand on the handle. "Okay, lower it. Slowly."

Luke dipped the rod with Tom's hand underneath acting as a brake. "Reel in the slack."

The boy turned the big, knobbed handle while Tom guided the rod from upright to nearly horizontal.

"Now lift again. Slowly."

"He's coming," shouted Thompson. "Keep it up!"

"Lower and lift," said Tom. "Lower and lift."

Luke nodded and did what Tom said.

Thompson leaned over the stern and waved the net over the water. "Closer," he shouted. "Two more feet."

Luke lowered the rod and reeled in the slack. Tom held a hand under the rod and placed the other on the boy's back.

"Six inches," shouted Thomson. "God, he's the size of a duffel bag!"

"Just a little bit more," Tom whispered.

Luke lowered the rod, reeled in the slack and lifted steadily. Thompson thrust the net into the water. "Got him!" he shouted. "Got him!"

As Thompson shouted, the Loomis plunged. The rod ripped from Luke's hand, slapping him across the face and then disappearing over the stern. A small white tooth landed on the deck.

"Oh shit!" said Thompson. "Oh, God."

Tom moved his hand to Luke's shoulder. Blood oozed from the boy's chin and the skin around it turned the color of eggplant. He didn't notice the tooth until later. "Are you okay, buddy?"

Luke moved his head up and down.

"You're going to have a shiner. Me too, when your mom and grandma get a look at you."

Luke stared at the spot behind the boat where rod and fish had disappeared into the blue-black water. His right arm trembled at his side.

"You okay?"

The boy nodded slowly.

"So what do you think about salmon fishing, now? Like it?"

The boy made a sound, but Tom couldn't make it out. He rested his chin on top of Luke's head and stared at the spot where the big fish had disappeared.

"I didn't catch that, buddy. What did you say?"

The boy whispered again.

Tom kept his chin on the top of Luke's head. "That's right, buddy. That's right."

CHAPTER 7

Billy Pearce's funeral was held at the local United Church, a merger of the former Methodist, Baptist and Presbyterian churches whose congregations and collections had dwindled over the years to the point of overlooking doctrinal differences. It was Tom's first time inside the simple clapboard structure and, he suspected, the first for Billy as well. The dark wood and white plaster interior was eerily Spartan compared to the lakeside Catholic church where the Morgan family had spent the soporific Sundays of Tom's youth. There were no statues, no pictures, no candles and no gold. The attendance that morning was equally sparse: fewer than a dozen mourners, including himself, Joe and the minister.

Susan Pearce sat alone in the front pew next to the closed casket, her charcoal tailored suit and silver jewelry more understated than severe, and her shoulder length hair the golden focal point in an otherwise colorless gathering. Her small straight nose, thin upper lip and rounded cheekbones were exactly as Tom remembered. He couldn't see more without changing seats, and Joe's orders had been to remain inconspicuous.

The lone occupant of the pew on the other side of the casket was a dark complexioned, forty-ish looking man wearing an expensive herringbone suit. Tom guessed Armani and noted, too, that despite the absence of other visual distractions, the man never looked in Susan's direction. Or if he did, he was extremely discrete. When the service began, his movements copied hers, with a second or two delay at the kneeling parts as if he was unsure whether these might be gender specific.

The heavy, brooding figure at back of the church came from the other end of the fashion spectrum. The feet were hidden, but muddy boots most likely completed the outfit. Tom had no trouble putting a name to the pugnacious profile. The extra forty pounds on Frankie Heller did nothing to soften the menacing image seared on Tom's memory.

One of the more painful and humiliating incidents of Tom's youth had been a confrontation with Frankie Heller at a Coldwater High School dance. Tom had spent most of the evening on the basketball court turned dance floor, absorbed in the company of a vivacious young woman who he had known casually for some time and who he hoped to get to know better, as occasionally happens at high school dances. The only impediment to his plan was another dancing couple who kept crashing into Tom and his partner, and who neither apologized nor seemed to make any effort to avoid doing it again. By the end of the evening, Tom had had enough. When the dervishes careened into Tom and his partner one more time, Tom planted a polished wingtip in the backside of the twirling trousers, connecting solidly.

Before his foot returned to the ground, Tom realized he'd made a mistake. The butt he'd kicked in a moment of pique looked, on quick assessment, to be easily capable of kicking him back and then some, thoroughly, and over a long period of time.

Frankie Heller's assessment was the same and quicker. Before Tom had even finished his pirouette, Frankie crashed into Tom's torso, knocked him to the hardwood floor and mounted his chest. Grabbing a hunk of hair, he bounced Tom's head on the parquet floor like one of the basketballs the hardwood was meant for. For what happened next, Tom had to rely on the account of others, because by then, he was out cold.

Some accounts had Joe and a few of his teammates from the Coldwater High School football team pull Frankie off, drag him out to the parking lot and beat the bejeezus out of him. Other accounts had Joe doing it all by himself right there in front of everybody. In any event, alone or with help, Joe did a thorough job. Tom recovered his senses in a few minutes and the softness and ache at the back of his head disappeared in a few days. But Frankie Heller lay in the Coldwater Hospital for a week and did not return to school for a month. Joe escaped assault charges only because the sheriff who investigated the incident (their dad) claimed to be unable to find a witness.

After that night there was an unspoken realignment in the Morgan family constellation. Tom began to draw away from his former circle of friends, from sports and everything else that had defined him until then, including his family. Joe grew closer, rapidly becoming their sheriff father's heir apparent and, as between the brothers, the acknowledged muscle. Frankie Heller made no move to exact revenge, demonstrating a wily intelligence generally thought to be absent. The girl Tom had danced with at the dance that night was Susan Pearce.

Blinking his eyes as if emerging from a troubled sleep, Tom tried to banish the painful memory by turning to survey the rest of the assembled mourners. Two pale young men sat quietly on the center aisle nearest the exit, gripping the hands of a third who sat sobbing between them. A head shop's inventory of cheap metal jewelry sprouted from the distraught youth's ears, eyebrows and lips. The two young men on either side were less dramatically skewered, though clearly of the same urban tribe. That was the total attendance: six mourners, plus Joe and himself.

Toward the end of the service, Joe slipped quietly from the church. When a gust of wind blew open a side door, Tom could see him squatting behind a silver sedan copying license plate numbers into a leather covered notebook.

* * *

When Tom returned to Joe's cabin, Mary told him that he'd just missed his old friend Father Gauss. "Came to visit the sick and stayed to finish a pitcher of gin and tonic. He said for you to stop by the rectory while you're in town."

Tom's face lifted in surprise at his mother's friendly tone. Growing up, he had the impression that she didn't much care for the worldly, ultra-liberal Father Gauss.

"Go ahead," said Mary. "Call him. Take him out to dinner. He might know something that could help your brother with this Billy Pearce business."

The suggestion was even more surprising.

"How would Father Gauss have known Billy Pearce?"

"I didn't say he did." Her voice was firm. "He might know something, that's all. Priests get to know all sorts, and they hear a lot."

"You're being mysterious, Mom."

"Not intentionally. Just careful not to be spreading rumors."

"Rumors?"

"Don't cross-examine me, Tommy. Just have dinner with the man. The subject of Billy Pearce is bound to come up. How could it not?"

"Did it come up while Father Gauss was here?"

Mary smirked. "Why do you think I had him make a pitcher of gin and tonic? I hate gin. Priests seem to thrive on it."

"And?"

"That's all you're going to get from me, young man. You and your brother find out the rest for yourselves."

* * *

Joe came home before dark and announced that he and Tom were going to pay a nocturnal visit to Frankie Heller's junkyard.

Tom groaned, and not in jest. Joe laughed. "I should have warned you to wear your Depends." He led Tom to the garage behind the cabin where a black monster truck with wheels as high as a man's chest took up an entire outsized bay.

"This must have burned a few paychecks," said Tom.

"Makes up for all those hand-me-down bicycles."

"We're not going to sneak up on anybody in this."

41

"That's the point, brother. Black and white's for handing out speeding tickets. This is for reminding assholes who's in charge around here."

Tom rested a hand on one of the chest high tires. "You planning on crashing this thing through the front door of everyone who came to Billy's funeral? Maybe scare a confession out of one of them?"

"Got to start somewhere."

Tom took a deep breath. "I'm asking, Joe, because I've got a job I have to get back to, and you've got a history of dragging me into things that are more trouble than I've got time for."

Joe drummed his fingers on the steering wheel as he gunned the truck down the steep, two lane road that wound around what he liked to refer to as 'his mountain.' "Your old girlfriend came into the station house this afternoon with a story about Frankie Heller and her brother Billy getting into some sort of dust-up down at the Pearce's boathouse the week before Billy got killed. That's why we're paying Frankie a visit tonight."

Tom felt his bowels stir. "Did Mom tell you Susan phoned yesterday, looking for you?" He watched his brother's face and hands.

"Complained about it. I went to the Pearce house after the ambulance took Billy to the morgue and I left you off with Mom. Miss Pearce didn't want to talk then. Guess she's had time to pull herself together."

"Does she think Frankie had something to do with Billy's murder?"

"All she's got is that they had some sort of shouting match down at the boathouse, loud enough for her to hear up at the main house. She thinks I should find out what they were arguing about."

"She heard them all the way up at the main house, but didn't hear what it was about?"

"She says not. But she claims to have heard Frankie screaming that Billy was too stupid to live."

Tom felt his pulse jump and his stomach drop. "And on that load of nothing, we're going to sneak into Frankie Heller's junkyard in the dark?"

"I am. You're coming to watch my back. Frankie can still be a handful if you come up on him wrong."

Tom had no trouble conjuring the appropriate image.

Joe eased the truck to the side of the road along the ridge above Heller's junkyard. From there they had a clear view of the garage, outbuildings and a couple of acres of weathering automobiles surrounded by a chain link fence. As they waited for darkness to fall, a gray four-door Taurus drove up to the garage, and a metal door rose to let it in. A few minutes later, two men exited the back of the building and walked toward the rows of junked cars.

Joe put the binoculars on the men and then handed the glasses to Tom.

"Frankie," said Tom squinting through the lenses in the fading light, "and maybe that guy who was sitting across from Susan at the funeral."

"Indian, do you think?" asked Joe. "Something like that?"

"Could be. Did you get a non-Anglo name off one of those license plates?"

"Didn't get anything. Mounties are taking their sweet time these days on any requests from this side of the lake."

The brothers passed the binoculars back and forth while they watched Frankie Heller lead his visitor to one of the junkyard wrecks, open the trunk and stand aside while the man stuck his head in the trunk. Then the visitor got behind the wheel and Frankie leaned through the open door and did something that neither brother could make out in the fading light. Finally, Frankie heaved himself out of the car and the other man started the engine and drove the junker out of the yard through an open gate in the back of the chain link fence.

Tom handed the binoculars back to Joe. "Okay, I give up. What's going on?"

Joe shook his head. "Don't know. But whatever it is, it's not what we're here for."

"You're not curious?"

Joe shrugged. "I said I don't know. That doesn't mean I don't have a pretty good idea."

Tom waited.

Joe tilted his head and grinned. "You really don't know?" His tone managed to imply some fundamental breakdown in the natural order of things, like you should not be learning about the birds and the bees from your adult younger brother.

"Should I?"

Joe smiled. "Do you remember Frankie's dad?"

"Scariest looking human being I've ever seen. The size of you and me put together."

"And did you ever know anyone who brought a car to his garage to get it fixed? Or went looking in his junkyard for spare parts?"

"No one in their right mind went near here."

"So how do you figure the Hellers' garage stayed in business, if nobody ever came here?"

Tom hesitated. "Look, if it's about Dad...." His voice dropped and his eyes shifted to an unfocused middle distance. "Maybe we should drop it."

Joe smirked as if they were boys again and Tom had just said something unmanly like he didn't really enjoy gutting frogs. "It's not. At least not what you think."

Tom braced for the unknown and likely unwanted.

"A hundred fifty years ago, or so, there was a farm down there where the garage and junkyard are now... with Hellers on it same as now. Dad said that it was a stop on the Underground Railroad before the Civil War. Abolitionists hid runaway slaves in the barns before taking them out to Pocket Island and then across to Canada. The Hellers weren't abolitionists or anything. They were just making money, like always. With Canada so close, people around here have been bringing stuff back and forth for generations."

Tom looked through the windshield, trying to avoid his brother's gaze.

"Frankie's great uncle or someone got the idea of turning the farm into a garage during Prohibition. The way Dad put it... what's the perfect cover for strange cars coming in and out of town without attracting a lot of attention? A commercial garage. Right?"

"That was then," said Tom. "This is now."

"Right. So in the twenties it was liquor. In the seventies it was marijuana, and a little later cocaine. Since then, it's been a bit of everything."

"And you let it go on? Just like Dad did?" It was an accusation, not a question. Tom sometimes wondered if the fuel for his outsized ambition wasn't simply the need to demonstrate to his ethically challenged family that you could make money honestly.

Joe rolled down the window and spat the four feet to the ground. "I'm not the DEA, Tommy. My job is to keep Coldwater safe. Period. That's all I care about and that's as far as I go. The Hellers are just weeds in my garden. I pull up the worst—the violent and ambitious. But the rest I leave alone, unless they get out of hand." He paused to let the nuggets of homespun philosophy sink in. "If that seems lazy to you, or even suspicious, think about it. Coldwater isn't big enough to have more than one or two full-time cops. If I go locking-up everybody who deserves it, what comes along to take their place may not be so easy to keep in line."

Easy or not, brother, that's the job.

As if reading Tom's thought, Joe added, "Dad thought he could do it all. But look what happened to him that year he put away Frankie's dad, the Flynns and Eddie Cashin all at the same time. Their pals from across the lake were here before Christmas, and they took care of Dad's ass real quick."

Tom had been in his final year of law school when their father's body was found in the front seat of a Coldwater patrol car with his tongue pulled through a semi-decapitating gash in his throat. It was April Fools' Day. The State Bureau of Criminal Investigation and the Drug Enforcement Administration sniffed around for a while. But they never discovered who did it or why. Tom and Joe stumbled onto *why?* even before the body was in the ground, and knowing that, they left the *who?* unmolested.

Mary had given the funeral parlor one of her husband's seldom-used suits for his body to be buried in. Hours later, Joe got a call from an agitated funeral director who had found stacks of hundred dollar bills in the jacket lining. When Tom arrived the following day, he found Joe hunched over a pile of cash in the middle of the family's kitchen table, with a look on his face like he'd swallowed something rotten.

Their mother had showed little concern over her husband's unusual form of banking. A child of parents for whom the Great Depression was a fresh and vivid memory, she'd grown up with cash-stuffed mattresses and fruit jars full of everything but fruit. Her husband had been the same, she insisted.

But her sons were not that naive. They talked for days, finally agreeing that sharing their discovery with the state police or DEA would only bring pain and humiliation to a woman who deserved neither, and that it would be unlikely to result in the killers being identified and brought to justice. So they kept the money-stuffed jacket a secret.

Joe, who had been working in the Sheriff's Department since finishing junior college, ran for his father's job in the next election, and the Coldwater's voters who may have forgotten by then that it wasn't the same Sheriff Morgan that they'd always voted for, gave Joe the job. The brothers never spoke again about the hidden cash, and the iconic hero of their pastoral youth was buried along with his emptied piggy bank.

Tom could accept the logic of Joe's compromise, if that's what it was. It didn't make him feel good. But he had to acknowledge the difference between picking your battles and taking cash to avoid them.

In the silence of gathering dark, they watched a wandering light trace a firefly path from the Heller garage to the farmhouse behind it. Then a brighter light appeared in what Tom guessed was the farmhouse kitchen. "Frankie lives by himself?"

"Sometimes," said Joe. "There've been a couple of Mrs. Heller wannabe's. Runaways mostly. They get younger every year. Sooner or later they head out. Or at least nobody sees them anymore."

"You mean nobody's found any body parts."

"Or looked for them." Joe stepped down from the truck. "Stay put. There's a gun and a camera in the glove compartment. If you have to shoot something, take pictures. But don't get jumpy and put a bullet up my ass."

Tom strained to follow the sounds of receding footsteps. Manhattan's never-ending chorus of sirens, horns and squealing tires never seemed as loud as the cacophony of the rural night when you're suddenly alone in the dark. While he waited and listened, Tom found himself conjuring thoughts and images of his deceased father—something he had not done in a long time.

Most boys are imprinted by their dads. But when yours wears a uniform and carries a gun, impressions can be exaggerated. When such men fall, as theirs had, the plunge can be even more exaggerated. Growing up, Tom had overheard many of his parents' arguments about the demands and temptations of his father's job. They were frequent and almost ritual. Tom realized early that his father was one of those men who lived his job and whose family was at best a collection of secondary planets around his own central sun. So when the end came, it was no surprise that their father had died with his boots on. But it was a profound disappointment that the boots were in effect stolen, and that their larger-than-life father was simply another cop on the take.

Howls from the woods beyond the junkyard yanked Tom's thoughts back to the present. An orange moon rose over the back of the garage and wandered across a winking sky. The elongated shadow of a trailered bass boat made Tom think of the pen and ink drawings of pirate ships in his childhood copy of Peter Pan. Scary book. Mary said that coyotes were making a comeback in the Coldwater hills and that domestic pets had become a popular snack. Some of her fellow seniors refused to go out at night, worried that they might be next on the food chain.

Sitting alone in the shadowy dark listening to howling predators didn't feel to Tom like watching someone's back. It felt like abandonment. Joe had said to stay put. But could he have meant this long?

Then somewhere in the symphony of night sounds, he heard the crunch of gravel on gravel. A few minutes later he heard it again, this time closer. Moving his hand to the latch of the glove compartment, he stretched his fingers through the maps, pens, batteries and tissues until they found a hunk of metal that ancient memory identified as a gun.

A chorus of cicadas fell suddenly silent, as if responding to the flick of a maestro's baton. Tom listened to his breath and felt the throb of pulse at his neck. Then a sharp rap on the window next to his ear nearly made him wet his pants.

"Drop the gun, Morgan."

CHAPTER 8

S mall choking noise escaped from Tom's throat. "You sca...cared the shit out of me."

Joe opened the door and climbed behind the wheel. "Been doing that for years." He glanced at the gun in his brother's hand. "You can put that away now."

Tom slid the weapon back into the glove compartment and tried to still the tremor in his hands. "You and Frankie find anything to talk about?"

"I told him that I was surprised to see him at Billy's funeral. That I didn't know he and Billy were buds. He claimed he was just driving by and saw a hot blond standing outside, so he stopped to take a closer look."

"I'll bet the new Mrs. Frankie, or whatever, loved that. Did you get anything else worth nearly giving me a heart attack for?" Tom crossed his arms to hide his hands.

"Nothing from Frankie. Though the new lady friend volunteered he was up at the stock car races Saturday night."

"Volunteered?"

"Yup."

"So she thinks he needs an alibi?"

"Apparently."

* * *

Tom got up early, made coffee and went out to the porch to watch the sunrise. He remembered to punch the code into the pad before opening the sliding door, so when Joe joined him an hour later, he was wearing pants and carrying a cup of coffee instead of a firearm.

"So what did we learn last night that was worth scaring the shit out of me?"

"Don't know yet." Joe dropped into an Adirondack chair and sipped his coffee. "The girlfriend seems to think Frankie needs an alibi for Saturday night. But that may not be related to Billy. He could have been up to anything."

"So we got nothing?"

"Working our way down a list, brother. Next is for you to visit that priest pal of yours. Find out what he was up to Saturday night."

"What could Father Gauss possibly have to do with Billy?"

Joe blew a cooling breath over his hot coffee. "He was outside the church when I went to check on those cars. I don't suppose he stopped on account of the hot blond, too."

"Did you talk to him?"

"He scooted when he saw me. I want you to find out where he was Saturday night and what he was doing hanging around Billy's funeral."

Tom grimaced. "I haven't seen the man in years. I'd rather not catch up by insulting him."

"It's a lead, brother. We have to follow it… or I do. You don't have to insult him. Just find out where he was Saturday night."

"Come on, Joe. What are the chances that an old priest stuffed Billy in a sleeping bag and dumped him in the lake?"

"If you believe the newspapers, some have done a lot worse."

* * *

Bonnie took the girls to school, and Joe left to collect the results of Billy's autopsy. Luke appeared with the fishing rods as soon as both parents had left the house.

"Sorry, buddy," said Tom, taking the rods off the counter and pouring a bowl of cold cereal. "You and I are grounded." It had been the trick question about life jackets rather than the black eye or the missing front tooth. Though neither had gone well with the moms.

Luke took the carved whistle from his pocket and gave it a blast.

"I know! I know!" Tom raised a hand in surrender. "But you had your chance to back me. Now we're grounded."

Luke remained silent. Other than the whisper on the boat, he hadn't said a word since losing the big salmon. Tom was tempted to turn him upside down and shake him until more came out. But his mind was yanked from thoughts of therapeutic child abuse by the appearance of a slim young woman in a form-hugging biker's outfit peddling past the kitchen window on her way to the front door. "Girl alert!" Tom shouted.

Luke scowled and scooped a spoonful of cereal.

"Did you see her, buddy? Do you know her?"

Luke moved his head from side to side, not bothering to look.

"Come on, she's a fox. Let's go see. If we can't go fishing…"

Luke shook his head again, ignoring the soft knock at the door.

"I'm going." Tom glanced at the front hall mirror and raked a fist of fingers through a mop of untidy hair. Then he opened the door onto a vision of glossed lips, even white teeth and a cascade of wheat colored tresses falling over slim rounded shoulders. "Hello, Tom."

His throat spasmed. "Hello, Susan. Plain as ever."

Luke appeared and tugged Tom's pant leg, trying to haul him back to the kitchen. "This is Luke," said Tom. "Grounded fisherman."

"Hello, Luke." The woman held out her hand.

"adic-I d-adic-on't l-adic-ike g-adic-irls." The boy hauled on Tom's trousers, digging into the floorboards with his heels.

"Pig Latin?"

"It's a long story. This is actually a pretty exciting development."

Luke released his grip on Tom's pants and slunk back to the kitchen.

"Would you like to come in?"

"I'm not sure that I'm welcome." She laughed, gesturing at the face scowling from behind a cereal box. "And you don't look prepared for company. What male mischief have I interrupted?"

Tom rubbed an hand over stubbled chin. "Joe had me out all night playing cops and robbers. If you're looking for him, you might try his office. But I don't think he's there now."

"Actually, I came to see you." Some words you hear with your ears, others with your mind. These he felt in his shorts. "Why don't we walk, if your companion will allow you to go outside with a girl for a few minutes? It's a beautiful day."

"Sure. I'll let mom know that Luke's in charge until we get back."

Mindful of Joe's security gizmos, Tom returned and escorted his long ago love down the center of the gravel drive until they reached the dirt road beyond it. Small birds called from the canopy of green above the lane and insects buzzed among pink spotted knapweed beside it.

"I'm sorry about Billy and your parents. I just found out."

Susan lowered her eyes and turned her head toward the greenery at the side of the road, content to let the silence gather, although Tom felt overcome by an almost adolescent awkwardness.

"I should apologize for Luke. But I'm also pretty excited. That's only the second time he's spoken, that I know of."

"In Pig Latin?"

Tom explained. "Mom and Bonnie weren't too keen on the experiment. But I think they'll come around now."

Susan laughed. "Don't count on it. Mamma bears don't like bachelor bears experimenting with their cubs. You'd make a good dad, though."

It was an offhand compliment, probably meaningless. But it made him uneasy. "Don't say that to Mary. It'll encourage her."

"She knows. She saw you often enough with Billy."

That made him even more uneasy. He picked up a stone and threw it into the woods.

"I used to think that you and Billy were variations on the same theme: too

51

much directionless brain power. But you eventually found something to do with yours. Billy didn't. He became a 'bad boy,' hung around people who weren't half as smart as he was, and got his kicks out of making *them* feel stupid."

"The kind of kicks that might have made someone angry enough to kill him?"

Susan shuddered. "I don't know, Tom. Somewhere along the way Billy developed a talent for pushing people to the edge. I overheard him and Frankie Heller having a knock down drag out argument a few days ago. I told ST about it."

"Who's Estie?"

"Oh, dear." She shook her head, and the flow of tresses made Tom's heart skip. "S. T. Super Trooper. Your brother." She grinned. "That's what people around here call him now. Didn't you know? I think it kind of fits." Tom folded his arms across his chest. She tried to console him. "Mother once told me that if Billy had had your looks, some girl would have come along and done a make-over on him, too."

"I thought your mother didn't like me. She always acted like I was going to steal the spoons."

"I don't think that was what she was afraid of." In the branches overhead a dove began to coo.

Time to change the subject. "So what have you been doing since you left Coldwater?"

"College, graduate school. Married for a while. Working mostly with a bunch of biotech start-ups. It's where the interesting science is right now."

"So how did you end up back in Coldwater?"

"Billy called with the news about our parents. Their lawyer needed to meet with me."

The birds stopped twittering and a cool breeze blew dust devils across the road. "I'm sorry," said Tom. "I heard it was a boating accident."

Her face tightened and her mouth turned down at the corners. "Dad bought a forty-foot Sea Ray with some of his retirement money. Maybe it was too much boat for him. They found it smashed on the rocks in Wilson

Cove."

"I'm sorry."

He had said that already. But an invisible censor stopped him from saying more.

"He was so excited when he bought it. He and Mom were going to cruise the Canadian side of the lake during the summer and then go out the St. Lawrence and down to Florida for the winter. It was something they'd been talking about for years."

"It must have been a shock."

Can you think of any more clichés?

"It still is. Then coming home for their funeral after being away all those years, and staying in that house I grew up in. I just couldn't leave it again right away."

He and Susan had once shared a passion for the hills above town, and the lake that stretched for fifty miles in either direction. It had been hard for him to leave, too. But without more to do than frolic in the woods, it would have been harder to stay. "It was lucky NeuroGene was here," he said.

She smiled. "I suppose. After the funeral, I spent weeks riding my bike along the shore trails and hiking in the hills. When I was finally ready to leave, I ran into someone at Skippers who I worked with in California. She told me that she'd come here to help a biotech start-up with some grant work, but that they'd found private financing, so she was going back to California. I gave them a call, they gave me a job, and here I am. It's hard to believe something like NeuroGene exists in Coldwater. But I guess it was meant to be."

Tom picked up a stick and held it behind his back. "Where did Billy work?"

"He didn't. He lived off my parents. After they died, he lived off the money they left him."

"Did he live *with* them too?"

"Practically. Dad turned the loft above the boathouse into an apartment. Billy did whatever it was he did from there. Sleep mostly. Every once in a while he'd pick up an odd job, like feeding a couple of dogs on Pocket Island for an owner who's never there. I've been staying up at the old house since the funeral. Billy would go out in the evenings, but I have no idea where. By the time he'd crawl back into the boathouse at night, I was in bed. I hardly ever saw him."

Tom listened for tone as well as substance, taking gentlemanly inventory whenever pace or turn in the road provided the opportunity to do so. Susan had changed little in a decade. Five foot seven in bicycle flats. Her hair hung loose in a ponytail today. But at the funeral, it had been as he remembered: shoulder length, thick and the color of brushed gold. The bicycle outfit took the guesswork out of the rest: slim and curvy still. He remembered the girl on the dance floor laughing, "If you've got it, flaunt it."

Susan turned to face him. "You have that funny look on your face, Tommy Morgan."

"Just thinking."

"I can see that. So what have you been doing that I don't already know from Googling Thomas J. Morgan about once every six months? You're not married, either. Is there someone hoping to change that?"

He smiled. "My mother. And you're toying with me. There are a gazillion Thomas Morgans in the English speaking world. What did you turn up besides pirates and rum makers?"

"Congressional staffer," she said brightly. "Cornell Law School, Clerk for a New York federal judge, I forget which one. Pictures in 'The American Lawyer' on a bunch of corporate mega-deals."

"Must be one of the other Tom Morgans."

"Pictures with the eyes my mother warned me about?"

He laughed.

"And that you're not happy."

BOOM! It was a statement, not a question. An irritating echo of Joe's: "Lot more than you get out of yours."

"Google says I'm not happy?"

"No, some other research I've been doing. Your life sounds large. I'm impressed."

Tom folded his arms, hoping the posture said skeptical rather than defensive. Every emotion except anger seemed to have surfaced in the last ten minutes. He felt as if he were wading through treacherous waters and needed to concentrate to keep his footing.

"It's not personal," said Susan. "It's just science."

"Which requires explanation, don't you think?"

"Alright. But it's that biochemistry stuff that used to put you to sleep."

Tom smiled. "I could never hit Bobby Cashin's knuckle ball, until I heard your father's explanation of chaos theory. You used to have his gift. Tell it to me so I stay awake."

She shrugged. "I'll try. But let's sit. This takes a bit of talking."

They had arrived at a spot where two shallow streams came together and crossed under a stone bridge. A rough rock wall ran thigh high along either side. Susan sat on the wall and swung her legs over the water.

* * *

"All right. Imagine two cavemen: Fred Flintstone and Barney Rubble. Barney tries to lead a balanced life. He kills only what he and his family can eat. The rest of the day he spends in quality time with Betty and Pebbles. Fred, on the other hand, is driven. He's got to have the biggest cave, dried mastodon carcasses piled to the ceiling and curvy cave girls on the side in little animal skin outfits who regularly produce more little Freddies. For Fred Flintstone, enough is never enough."

Not just for Fred.

"Then comes the flood, famine, epidemic disease…whatever. Who do you think survives? Balanced Barney? Or Insatiable Freddy or one of dozens of little Freddies? Then repeat that process again and again over millions of years. The theory, basically, is that Balanced Barney's genes never made it out of the Stone Age, and that we're all the great, great, great grandchildren of Insatiable Freddie."

Tom hauled his gaze away from distraction. "That may explain my lust for pizza. But what's it got to do with me being happy as a lawyer?"

"It has everything to do with your inability to be permanently happy with any achievement. As a linear descendant of Insatiable Freddie, your brain is hardwired so that it can't be permanently satisfied with any accomplishment, no matter how spectacular. You can enjoy them for a while. But you can never be happy resting on your laurels. If you want to get happy again, you have to go out and do something new."

"So are *you* happy being a biochemist?"

"Good question. And no, I'm not. Being something or having something can never make one of Insatiable Freddy's descendants permanently happy. To get that, you have to fool your genes and manipulate your brain chemistry."

"How?"

"By manipulating your brain into giving you a dopamine or endorphin kick for things that you choose, rather than for things that might have made sense for Insatiable Freddie."

"Like what?"

"You pick. That's where intelligence and personal choice come in. You know what's good for you and what's not. You know what goals inspire you."

"So goals are important?"

"Having them. Not accomplishing them. And it doesn't matter whether you're trying to eat your way across a dessert table or trying to find a cure for cancer, the Insatiable Freddie gene keeps you on course by doling out dopamine and endorphins in small increments as you go along—not in one big blast at the end."

"So *'it's the journey not the arrival that matters?'*"

"Exactly. Though whoever first said that probably thought he'd had some great insight into the human soul. But what he really did was make a forensic discovery about the evolution of human brain chemistry."

He swung his legs in time with hers, but could not keep them in sync, so he stopped.

"Did you ever talk to Billy about this? It seems like something that might have helped him."

Her voice faded, as if the bell ending class had just rung. "Once. Down at the boathouse." She pulled her legs back over the wall and stood.

"What did he say?"

"He laughed, pulled opened a desk drawer, took out a baggie filled with white powder and threw it at my feet. *'Dope o'Mine,'* he said."

CHAPTER 9

The troubled look on Tommy's face confirmed Mary's fears. But she didn't get to quiz him about his encounter with the Pearce woman, as his brother chose that moment to wrench Tommy's mind someplace else.

"I should get paid for this," he said, putting down the phone. "Joe wants me to find out if Father Gauss has an alibi for Saturday night—as if a priest might have something to do with Billy Pearce ending up in a sleeping bag at the bottom of Coldwater Lake."

"Not that anyone would blame him," said Mary.

"What?"

"If you're going to stay away for years at a time, Tommy, you're going to miss a few things."

He folded his arms and waited.

"One of Father Gauss's pets...."

"His what?"

"All right. One of his protégées. You weren't the only one. Or the last. The newest was the Frazier's boy Maurice. He got himself mixed up with that Billy Pearce, and Father Gauss tried to interfere. Pearce's charms, whatever they were, won out."

"And that makes Father Gauss a suspect in Billy's murder?"

"The young man died, Tommy. Drugs or something. But Father Gauss…
well, you'd think he lost a child."

"When did all this happen?"

"Three months ago. Not even."

"And Joe thinks Father Gauss might have done something to Billy?"

"It's your brother's job to look past the collar."

Footsteps in the hallway signaled the end of Luke's self-imposed exile. A
fishing rod in each hand made it clear what he had in mind. "You might as
well go," said Mary. "He won't stay with me as long as he's got you to play
with." The boy nodded and ran out of the house. "But no boats, hear me?
And teach your brother that silly language, or you'll be leaving a mess when
you go."

"Luke will be talking fine before then. One more adventure should do it."

Mary wrapped her fingers around her son's arm. "It's wonderful you're
making connection with the boy, Tommy. But don't go making the uncle
bigger than the father. No good will come of that."

He nodded.

"And be careful not to insult the other Father, too. I may need him to
forgive my sins one of these days."

A smile spread across her handsome son's face. "Got any good ones?"

She turned away before the color flooding her cheeks gave an incriminating answer. "Go!"

* * *

Tom left Luke and his fishing poles down at the church dock and walked
up the lawn to the rectory. Mrs. Flynn, the housekeeper, answered his
knock. Her hair had turned white since his last visit. The shapeless form in
the flowered print house dress and blue apron was a size smaller than he
remembered, as if she had shrunk as well as aged. She showed no sign of
recognizing him.

"Hello, Mrs. Flynn. I'm looking for Father Gauss. Is he here?"

"Out in that rowboat of his, I should think. He should be back for confessions at three."

"Is it all right if I wait down at the dock?"

"Suit yourself. The geese have made a mess of it though."

Tom watched his nephew cast a silver Rapala into the clear blue water and retrieve it over the patches of discolored mud and sand where the blue gills and rock bass had fanned their spring nests some months ago. "This is where your dad and I learned to dive. Monsignor De DiMaggio stood in that water with one arm out stretched. Your dad and I would run down the dock and jump over his arm. Then he'd back up and we'd do it again. After a couple of steps back, the only way to get over his arm was head first. Your dad did it before me."

Luke smiled.

Father Gauss had arrived a half dozen years after that long ago diving lesson. Without a vowel on either end of his surname, he was received with caution by congregation and fellow clergy alike. It didn't help that he was a thin, chain-smoking, Vatican-trained intellectual with little tolerance for superstition masquerading as theology. Rumor had it that he had been dismissed from his previous post for insubordination.

Like everyone else, Tom had found the new priest a little strange and even somewhat intimidating—especially when he seemed to take a personal interest in Tom's academic and social development. Tom had been one of those boys who refuse to accept the Darwinian pecking order of the schoolyard, where older boys monopolize the only basket with an unbent rim and bully the younger kids away from the flat, shady spot near the Monsignor's garage that was the only decent spot for flipping baseball cards. The result was more than the customary number of schoolyard fights. Long stretches of effortless B's, randomly broken with inexplicable D's, were equally maddening to the black-robed nuns who ran the school; and Tom's was a regular presence on the hardwood bench outside the principal's office. But all that ended with the arrival of Father Gauss. Sister Judith, Principal for Life of Our Lady of The Lake School, simply handed Tom over to a higher power.

If Tom did poorly on a test, Sister Judith sent him to the rectory to review it with the new priest. Any nonsense in the schoolyard and she sent him straight to the rectory, where the new priest would have him sweep the parking lot after school, write an essay and then walk home. Nor did the special attention end when Tom left for the local public high school a few years later. Every few months, Father Gauss would invite him to stop by the rectory and give him a book he thought Tom should read, or invite him to see a play or classical music concert in the city. Over time, Tom came to appreciate the priest's thoughtful reflections on the world around him and to enjoy his company. Father Gauss was a genuine intellectual, the first and only in Tom's life until he entered the orbit of the Pearce family a few years later.

It never occurred to Tom to ask what Father Gauss might be getting out of the association, as his mother once did, in a strained and convoluted conversation with the priest one Sunday after Mass when Tom was thirteen. Tom got the story from his mother's friend, Dorothy Ryan, years later.

One of the truths of parochial education, Gauss had told Tom's mother, was that the curriculum was designed to impart basic academic and religious ABCs to the student of average intelligence. For someone as bright as her son, the glacial pace and lack of substance could be suffocating. The sad result, was that once out of the church's academic classrooms, many of the brighter students abandoned the church itself. What he was trying to do, Gauss explained, was expose her son to a world of ideas and culture that might compete for his attention with the sex, drugs and other temptations he would soon encounter in the larger world. The same had been done for him when he was Tom's age, and it had made an important and timely difference.

Mary undoubtedly felt she had little choice but to accept the priest's explanation and, if true, to be grateful. But she had heard the unkind rumors, and she kept a close watch.

Luke broke into Tom's nostalgic reverie by waving his fishing pole at a rowboat coming around the point. A hollow faced man with thin white hair sat in the middle of the boat, pulling on sun bleached oars. A solemn-faced passenger sat in the back, staring fixedly toward Pocket Island. Sensing that an intrusion might not be welcome, Tom hustled Luke up to the church and waited on the steps. From there, they could see the boat pull alongside the dock, and a slim youth with wispy sideburns jump out and stride up the hill. When the boy disappeared behind the school, Tom and Luke walked back to the dock and Tom introduced his newest friend to his oldest.

"Hello," said the priest. "Are you a fisherman, too? Should we see if they're biting?" Luke nodded sharply. "Thanks for making yourself scarce, Tommy. Some of my penitents are shy about being seen."

"It might be easier if you saw them in the rectory."

"That wouldn't be wise in some cases. Besides, water seems to have a soothing effect on troubled minds. The stubborn ones have no choice but to sit still and listen to what I have to say, unless they want to swim home."

The priest surrendered the oars and took the slat bench in the stern. Luke sat beside him and let the fishing lure skip behind the boat.

"So how's your soul, Tommy?"

Tom laughed. "Restless. Though I've just been told it's supposed to be." He recounted his recent conversation with Susan Pearce and her new twist on Darwin's old theory.

"I've heard that one before," said the priest. "But it really doesn't get at the heart of things, does it? Misses it entirely, if you ask me."

"Go on," said Tom, pulling at the oars. "I can't escape."

"All right, then. The theory, if I understand it correctly, is that temptation is nothing more than the normal operation of healthy brain chemistry."

"So I'm told."

"And I say, so what? It's still temptation. We still have free will to fight it. And that's what the whole game is about, as I'm sure you remember."

Tom laughed. "I haven't had time to give it much thought, Father. But speaking for myself, I find it comforting that my lust for coffee ice cream may not be an inherent flaw in my character."

"Ah but it is! And if Miss Pearce is correct, it's hardwired right into our brains. Imagine that! Original sin may actually exist after all."

"They'll burn you at the stake, if you talk like that from the pulpit." It had been years before Tom had come to appreciate how much of a renegade

Father Gauss was in his chosen field, and to understand what that must have cost him.

"Yes, that would be imprudent. But it's interesting, don't you think? That the devil may be with us all the time. Only he's hidden in our genes!"

"I'll have to ask Miss Pearce what she thinks of your twist on her research."

"I'm sure you'll have that chance."

Tom smiled. "You don't miss much."

"And you hide very little, Tommy." Gauss leaned forward and placed a calloused hand on Tom's where it rested on the oar. "Now why are we out here in this boat, when we could be up in the rectory having a sip of scotch?"

Tom gestured at Luke. "Got a serious fisherman on my hands."

"So I've heard. Jack Thompson's telling your 'one that got away' story all over town. But you didn't come here to go fishing. Not in this leaky tub."

Tom saw no point in evasion. "My little brother wants to know where you were on Saturday night."

"On my knees praying for skirt-chasers in Smokey the Bear hats."

Tom looked at Luke, whose attention was fixed on the rod tip and the line trailing in the water. "So I can tell him to take you off his list?"

Gauss lifted his face as if seeking guidance in the wispy clouds that drifted overhead. "Does your brother's curiosity have anything to do with the dead man fished out of this cove the other day?"

Tom nodded. "He's checking up on everyone who was at the funeral. You didn't go in, but you were seen outside in the parking lot."

Gauss remained silent.

"I'm sorry, father, but there's not much else to go on. Anything you know about the deceased could be helpful."

Gauss leaned back and rested his forearms against the thwarts. "There may be things I know about Mr. Pearce that your brother doesn't. But nothing that would be useful to your brother's inquiries. Idle gossip, on the other hand, has a way of harming the innocent."

Tom wasn't sure what to make of the comment. "But you knew Billy Pearce," he pressed.

"Oh, yes. His name had a habit of coming up in the conversation of certain parishioners who came to me for counseling over the years. I always suggested that they drop him. Mr. Pearce took umbrage at that advice when he heard about it."

"What did he do?"

"Showed up at the rectory one evening… to 'seek counsel,' he said, 'on the recommendation of a mutual acquaintance.' But what he really had in mind, and got, was an opportunity to come on to me in private and then make trouble."

Tom opened his mouth and left it open.

"Oh, don't be naïve, Tommy. It's an occupational hazard. Comes with the territory. Pearce should just have headed into the big city and found his way there. He was too smart for the crowd he hung out with here. The pack always knows when you're not one of them. In his pack, that could be dangerous."

"What happened after he *took offense?*"

"A little trouble with His Eminence. Nothing more."

"Did you hear from Pearce after that?"

"Nothing from him… a little about him from time to time. Tittle-tattle, mostly."

"Like what? If you can say."

"Like that he murdered his parents and made it look like an accident, and that he was terrorizing his sister to try to get her to agree to sell the family estate. That sort of thing."

CHAPTER 10

Father Gauss wondered if he should have told Tommy Morgan the rest, just to be done with it. Better than having him figure it out for himself; and he would, with God knows what consequences. Gauss paced the Bishop's conference room, stifling the urge to light a cigarette and blow the smoke under one of the tapestries. The Bishop's assistant had given no reason for the summons. But it wasn't hard to imagine what it might be. Gauss read the newspapers, and he knew he wasn't the first to get the call.

The last time he'd been inside the Chancery had been thirty years ago on a tour for recent graduates of the diocesan seminary. It looked much the same now as it had then, except for the pox of *don't do this* and *don't do that* signs and the absence of ashtrays—heavy mahogany furniture, ancient oil paintings of ancient prelates, clunky metal candlesticks and cut glass bowls crammed with wilting flowers. The décor was largely unaltered since the Edwardian period of the Chancery's construction, and the atmosphere was even older. It was feudal.

Gauss fingered a pack of menthol cigarettes and eyed a dusty umbrella stand near the framed oil of Pope Pius XII. It would have to do. Vacuuming the minty smoke into his lungs and tapping the ashes into the umbrella stand, the distracted priest sought to clear his mind. But it was an hour before anyone entered the room. A plain young woman in non-ecclesiastical black—boots, jacket, hair and lipstick—came in first. They call it *Goth*, he reminded himself. She dragged a luggage trolley with a couple of machines strapped to it, also black, and plugged them into an outlet beneath the conference table.

"Got a card?" she mumbled, fumbling with wires and knobs.

"A what?"

"A business card," she elaborated.

Gauss made an impatient gesture toward his roman collar, which was as much as a card might have said had he had one.

A young man in a navy blue Brooks Brothers suit came in next and introduced himself as Francis Dolan, Special Counsel for the Diocese. Gauss wondered if "special" was a euphemism for "junior", as the young lawyer seemed hardly old enough to vote. "Has your attorney arrived yet?" he asked.

"My what?" Gauss blurted for the second time.

Dolan allowed the question to speak for itself.

"Monsignor Marchetti didn't say anything about bringing an attorney," Gauss grumbled. "He didn't say anything about a meeting with one, either."

The lawyer folded pencil arms over a narrow torso made gaunt by the vertical piping of his shirt and suit jacket. "The Diocese is investigating allegations of priest misconduct," he said. "You've been asked to appear here today to respond to several that concern you."

"Christ!" Gauss muttered.

"Would you like to have an attorney present to represent you?"

"No."

"Would you like to speak with Monsignor Marchetti before we start?"

"About what?"

The lawyer shrugged and turned to the girl in black. "We'll start then, Miss Kelly."

The Goth flexed her lacquered nails over the keys of the steno-machine. The lawyer removed a thick accordion folder from the briefcase at his feet. "I'm going to start with some background questions," he began. "Your education, parish postings and so on."

Gauss looked toward the open window and caught a whiff of burning leaves. He wondered what would happen if he got up and lit a cigarette. *Offer it up for the souls in Purgatory, if there is such a place.*

While the young attorney cross-checked dates and degrees, Gauss stifled a mounting urge to get up and walk out. He understood why they had to do it, but there was a miasma of witch-hunt about the whole procedure that made the remains of his breakfast churn.

When the legal inquisitor had finished with the brown folder, he picked up a yellow one. Gauss wondered whether the distant smell of burning leaves had anything to do with the cigarette he'd flicked out the window earlier.

"I'd like to take you back to the time you were at St. Agnes," Dolan said.

"My first parish," said Gauss. "I taught Philosophy at the Seminary before that."

"Do you remember a parishioner there named Francis Anderson?"

"No."

"He would have been about eleven years old back then."

"What year was that?"

"Nineteen sixty-eight."

"That was a busy year. I did a lot of draft counseling back then. Miraculous how pious some of my parishioners became once they turned eighteen and got their draft numbers."

"Mr. Anderson says that you touched him in the sacristy."

Gauss rolled his eyes. "My anatomy is a little rusty, Counselor. Is that above or below the belt?"

The Goth giggled.

Dolan snapped, "This isn't a joke, Mr. Gauss."

"<u>Father</u> Gauss," Gauss snapped back. He lifted his chin toward the handwritten document beneath the lawyer's folded hands. "Is that a letter from Mr. Anderson?"

"It is."

"Looks like it was painted by Van Gogh. It's recent, I take it."

The lawyer ignored the probe.

"Thought so," said Gauss. "With a psychiatric hospital for a return address?"

"The protocol here, is that I ask the questions," said Dolan, "and that you answer them." He turned a page in the yellow folder and squared another document. "Do you recall a Kevin Burke? St. Bartholomew's, nineteen seventy-one."

"No."

"He says you molested him on a camping trip."

"I'm a city boy, Counselor. I've never been camping in my life. Perhaps Mr. Burke's troubled mind has confused me with a scout master."

Dolan turned another document. "Timothy Ruark. St. Francis, nineteen seventy-nine."

"Him, I remember. But it was the father who was the wacko."

"He says you molested him, too."

"Says?"

"Yes."

"Then someone's pulling your leg. Timothy Ruark took his own life twenty-five years ago. I said the funeral service. The father pitched a fit that it wasn't a High Mass."

The attorney fumbled the next few papers but continued doggedly. "Kevin McCarthy? Saint Francis, nineteen eighty-two?"

"Doesn't ring a bell."

"Patrick O'Hara, Saint Agnes, nineteen sixty-nine?"

"Another wacko. Mr. O'Hara asked me to go with him to his draft board hearing. When the board didn't buy his cockamamie pacifist act, he seemed to think it was my fault."

"He says you molested him, too."

"A prison letter I suppose."

"You know that?"

"Mr. O'Hara's habit of fabricating grievances didn't stop when he got drafted. Unless the army has started paroling pacifists who shoot their officers, I assume he's still there."

"And if he is?" Dolan pressed. "Does incarceration mean his accusations

68

are unreliable? Is that what you're saying?"

"It means he reads the newspapers. And that he keeps bad company."

Dolan continued to turn pages and documents, but Gauss' answers were all of a piece.? Either he didn't recall, the evidence was suspect or the accuser nuts. But it took nearly an hour for the diocesan lawyer to work through the entire file, and Gauss could sense that the young man found it unlikely that they could all be making it up. But he waited until the session was over and the lawyer had begun to pack away his files before launching his counter.

"Are you a criminal lawyer?" he asked when Dolan paused in his packing.

"Insurance defense."

"Ah, yes. I can see how the church must be needing your services these days. But you're a member of the bar, are you not?"

"All practicing attorneys are required to be."

"And there's an attorney disciplinary body that hears complaints from disgruntled clients?"

"There is."

"And would you happen to know if that disciplinary body receives more complaints, say, from clients of criminal defense attorneys, than it does from clients of insurance lawyers?"

"No I wouldn't."

"Any guess?"

"No."

"But you see the point."

Dolan snapped his briefcase closed. "I didn't know you were making one."

Gauss's gray-flecked brows compressed into one. "Then let me make it clear for you, Counselor. Specialist practices attract special clients and troubles. You with me so far?"

The church attorney moved his head from side to side like a bobble-head doll.

"Your friend, Bishop Mczynski, has what you might call a fund-raising practice. His clients are well-heeled contributors and their troubles, if any, are financial. They don't become his. Your colleagues in criminal defense, on the other hand, have clients that are not only morally challenged, but emotionally damaged as well. My <u>point</u> is that the criminal defense lawyers who serve such troubled people no doubt have complaint files a lot thicker than the ones for their peers in insurance defense."

"I wouldn't know," said Dolan.

"But you see the sense of it."

Dolan shrugged.

"I don't have Bishop Mczynski's gift for fund-raising," Gauss persisted. "My specialty is counseling troubled teenagers. They come with problems, not cash; and their problems aren't spiritual. Their lives are messed-up. They come from broken homes. They're depressed or schizophrenic, but their families don't believe in mental illness and refuse to get them treatment. Or they're gay and trying to come to terms with that in a church that labels them sinners."

"You said you had a point," Dolan interrupted, visibly uncomfortable with being on the receiving end of an interrogation.

"And I think you get it," said Gauss. "Priest or attorney: a file like the one you just drooled through is about what you'd expect of a professional who's been working with troubled minds for thirty years."

The young lawyer looked away.

"Look," Gauss pressed, "I hope you find the misfits you're after. They're there, and they're probably more of them than the Bishop wants to know about. But there should be some integrity to the process, don't you think? There aren't many of us left in the vineyard, and we're getting old. Harassing old plow horses on their way to the glue factory isn't just wrong, it's pointless. If you've done more than a few of these *investigations*, you must know that by now."

The young attorney's expression had not changed, but Gauss could sense that his point had at least grazed the untested armor.

"And how would <u>you</u> go about finding these… *misfits?*" Dolan sniffed.

"I'd start with Bishop Mczynski," said Gauss. "There's a first-class mind behind all that glad handing and baby kissing. Not much gets by him, and he's the one who keeps the report cards around here."

"I've spoken with His Eminence. He's the one who directed me to you."

Gauss's mind paused, but his tongue kept moving. "Then if I were you, and investigation was *my* specialty... then I might ask myself *why*?" Dolan pressed his fingers together as if he were about to respond, and touched them to his mouth as if to signal himself not to. "Have you been to the seminary yet?" Gauss pressed. "Have you talked to some of the delicate young men they're taking in there these days?"

Dolan shook his head. Gauss' eyes shone like Paul's on the road to Damascus. "Ha! I get it. The seminary's off limits, isn't it?" When the lawyer still said nothing, Gauss took it as an admission. "Then your *investigation* is a fraud, Counselor. It's not going anywhere, and it's not meant to."

Dolan's lips buckled at the corners. "I wouldn't count on that, *Father* Gauss."

CHAPTER 11

Joe made it home in time for dessert, then apologized that he had to leave again. The girls pleaded for him to stay. "We're practicing for a play! You have to hear our lines."

"Your father's got a job to do," said Mary.

Bonnie stood to clear the table.

"Sorry girls. I'll be back before bedtime." Joe motioned for Tom to join him outside, where the sound of dishes crashing like percussion instruments was muffled. "Did you find out where that priest friend of yours was on Saturday night? Or where he says he was?"

"Quote 'On my knees praying for skirt chasers in Smokey the Bear hats' unquote. That would be Bonnie's skirt, right? PDA in the back pew?"

"Knock it off, Tommy. He wouldn't say where he was?"

"I don't know about wouldn't. He didn't and I didn't press. He pulled me up short with that skirt chaser line. Is everything okay with you and Bonnie? I'm sensing a certain *tension*."

Joe sighed. "Bonnie's pissed about the no help, no time off drill, that's all. I've got to get back to the Grange Hall to deal with the troopers from DuBois who want in on the Billy Pearce investigation."

"Good. You need help."

"Don't be naive, Tommy. They don't want to help. They want to take over. No one in Coldwater is going to talk to an outsider. They know that.

But they've got Paulie Grogan, my former deputy, with them now and they think that's going to make a difference."

"Joe..."

"Tommy, I've got to go. Don't worry about the skirt chaser crack. People say all sorts of things to priests just to stir the pot."

* * *

Tom escaped in Joe's truck after everyone had gone to bed, intending to unwind from an eventful day by revisiting the watering holes of his youth. Instead, and within minutes, he found himself idling at the columned gates of the private drive leading to the Pearce estate. The question that buzzed in his head was one of those that are answered just by being asked. *"What are you doing here?"*

The main house was a three story, double winged Adirondack chateau with acres of slate roof, miles of copper gutter and sweeping lawns that undulated in triple terraces down to the edge of Coldwater Lake. How many times had Tom driven his clapped-out VW Beetle up that long, tree-lined driveway, never entirely certain if the rickety car would make it to the top? On summer weekends, the house would be ablaze with lights, like a small European hotel at holiday time. Music would drift gently from the piano room, and guests would stroll the lawns amidst the sounds of tennis balls being thwacked smartly under outdoor illumination. Weekdays, there would be a glow from the kitchen wing when Tom brought Susan home from their date, or if Dr. Pearce were up late, a single shaded lamp glowing from behind the six-paned glass of his study.

Tonight the house was dark. Tom leaned out the truck window to look for signs of occupancy. But all he saw was darkness and all he heard were crickets. Leaving the truck in front of the house, he followed a brick path through the hemlocks and around the kitchen wing to the back. No lights shown from the upstairs windows. Both wings and all three floors were pitch. Below the sweeping lawn, Coldwater Lake glistened like polished pewter under pale moonlight.

Making his way by a remembered path to a stone bench at the end of the upper terrace, Tom's eye found Pocket Island, a dark mushroom cap on silvery liquid a mile offshore. His mind conjured memories of summer afternoons where he and Susan would tie a canoe to the branches of centuries old beech trees and swim in the privacy of the narrow inlet that gave the island its name. Surprised and embarrassed at the unexpected surge of nostalgia, he pulled himself short: *Okay, Tommy. The woman is smart, sexy and she's been keeping tabs on you. But you let each other go a long time ago because neither would follow the other, and she says she's happy with the path she chose.*

A wobbling flicker of light at the water's edge disappeared into a shaft of moonbeam, reappearing for an instant before disappearing into the boathouse. Leaving the bench, he picked his way across the dewy lawn, his heart racing as it always had when he approached this place in darkness. Though in the past it had been with passion, not apprehension. A light most certainly meant that someone was in the boathouse—someone who had heard the truck, or spotted Tom's silhouette when he came around the back of the house.

Placing his hand on a cold metal knob, wet with evening dew, he eased the door open. Moonlight shone through the arched boat entrance and reflected off the water of the empty boat slip. Above it, an old mahogany runabout hung cradled in canvas straps, and an equally ancient cedar canoe lay covered in dust against the far wall. Tom moved toward the stairs that led to the loft overhead. Old boards squeaked a greeting. Or warning.

A door that had not been there years ago, blocked the top of the wooden steps. Opening it and confronting what lay beyond was arguably imprudent. As was being there at all. But as the pugilistic philosopher, Billy Conn, once opined, "what's the point of being Irish, if you can't be stupid?" Tom turned the handle, opened the door and stepped into the darkness.

"AWK! AWK! AWK!"

A tattoo of pointed blows peppered the crown of Tom's head. A deafening thut, *thut, thut,* pounded above him like an unbalanced ceiling fan.

"AWK! AWK! AWK!"

74

Milling his arms, as much in confusion as defense, Tom felt one of them connect with something solid. "Shit!"

As if to a password, a lamp flickered on. A large, white bird landed on a headboard beside it. Pressed against the headboard, covered to the neck in a bright, patchwork quilt, was a vision he might have expected.

"Tom!"

Motionless, speechless, and for the moment without a coherent thought, he put his hand to the top of his head and removed it covered with blood.

Susan threw off the quilt and hurried to him. His attention automatically shifted from his hand to the short, green nightshirt that was the only thing between them.

"I saw the headlights coming up the driveway," she said. "I didn't want to see anybody, so I came down here."

He watched her walk to the small half-bath and return with a handful of tissues. He felt lightheaded.

"Sit," she ordered, taking his hand and leading him to the bed.

"AWK! AWK! AWK!"

Tom threw his arms in the air and covered his head. "Shush! Roger!" Susan hissed. Tom tried to laugh, but it came out a groan. She sat him down on the bed. "You remember Roger?"

How could he forget? The sly Dr. Pearce had given each of his children a large, white cockatoo as a high school graduation present. As Tom and others had quickly discovered, cockatoos are unshakably loyal and fiercely protective. No one came into Susan's dorm room unless Roger was safely in his cage. He learned the hard way never to touch, much less crawl into bed with, Susan without putting a heavy cloth cover over Roger's cage. Even then, the bird would often go batshit in there. He had often thought that the worldly Dr. Pearce knew exactly what he was doing with that unlikely gift. The damned things could live eighty years.

While Susan worked on his scalp, Tom tried to keep his head still and his view unobstructed.

Susan laughed. "Look, if you must. But there's no cage down here for Roger." She pulled his head forward so that she could apply tissues to the back of his skull. Her breasts massaged his forehead. The ripple went straight down his spine.

"This isn't going to work." She sat back and surveyed his bloody scalp. "You're going to need stitches."

He placed a hand on her thigh to steady himself.

"AWK! AWK! AWK!"

Throwing his hands in the air, he gasped and swiveled his head. "Billy had one of these things, too, didn't he? Where is it?"

Susan climbed from his lap. "I haven't seen Ruby since Friday. I don't know where she is. Let me take Roger to the house and get some gauze and disinfectant. I'll be back."

Tom held the bloody tissues to his head and watched Susan leave, thoughts and feelings hopelessly fragmented. A small voice in the back of his mind whispered caution.

He tried to bring order to jumbled impressions by taking mental inventory of the loft's contents: a queen sized bed, a kitchen table that served as some sort of work desk, an elaborate video and music system, one large, overstuffed chair and a small, cramped bathroom. On the narrow porch on the other side of a sliding glass door, a pair of beach chairs faced the water.

Susan was away long enough for the wounds on his scalp to begin to throb and for the brain beneath it to demand an answer to the question it had posed when he first turned into the Pearces' driveway. *"Why are you here?"* The possibilities were finite, but what he knew for sure was that he didn't want to leave.

When Susan finally returned, it was with gauze, disinfectant, a thermos of hot cocoa and several disappointing layers of clothing. She handed him the disinfectant and sat across the room in the overstuffed chair, looking away. An awkward silence filled the space between them until she broke it. "I'm sorry. I can't."

He didn't need to ask: 'Can't what'?

"It's too late," she whispered.

He closed his eyes and poured disinfectant on his scalp, pressing a wad of gauze into the wet mess.

Susan squared her shoulders and held her hands in her lap. "I just can't get involved with you again, Tom. I won't do that to myself."

"You don't owe me an explanation." Though he was at a loss to provide one himself. A grown woman in a flimsy nightshirt does not usually allow herself to straddle a man to whom she is not, at least momentarily, attracted. That much he knew, even before the Ivy League education.

"No, I don't. But I don't want to mislead you, either. Or lose you as a friend now that we've reconnected."

The word "friend" stung as much as the gouges on his head and arms.

"I'm still attracted to you," she blurted. "I always have been."

Nor did he need a degree in English grammar to know that the next word was going to be "but."

"But I'm getting uncomfortably close to forty. All the smart men I meet are geeks. The hunks are intimidated by my intelligence, and I can't spend the next couple of years..." She let the sentence trail away unfinished.

He kept his features expressionless.

"Say something!" she demanded.

He waited.

"Then I'll say it. I'd love to pick up where we left off... spend the next few years with you rutting like rabbits. But I refuse to spend forever with someone who is basically unhappy."

He didn't know what he'd expected to hear. But it wasn't that.

The silence lasted a long, painful minute. "You have no idea what I'm talking about, do you?"

"No. But I have a hunch that you're going to tell me. And that it involves more brain science."

Her mouth formed a smile and then a frown. "Do you know what makes people attracted to each other?"

"Blond hair, green eyes and soft curves. Not necessarily in that order."

"Non-overlapping immune system markers."

He felt a groan and suppressed it.

"Opposites attract," she explained. "—genetically speaking. Do you know what turns them off?"

He spread his hands.

"Opposing energy levels."

"Meaning what?" It was an expression of wounded pride more than confusion, but she chose to treat it as the latter.

"Meaning people don't change. The best predictor of how someone is going to be ten years from now, is how they were ten years ago. You weren't happy when I met you. You're not happy now. That means the probabilities are high that you won't be happy ten years from now. And, regardless of how good he might have been in bed when he was younger, I'm not looking to spend the rest of my life with someone who is basically unhappy."

Clouds of confusion escaped with shortened breath. "Susan! The time I spent with you was the happiest I've ever been."

"Me, too." Her voice was sad and soothing. "And I think we might have a good time again, for a few years. But highs and lows aren't permanent. The base we return to is what counts in the long run. Mine's high. Yours—unless you've got your clothes off—is low. We're not compatible over the long haul."

How had they gotten here so fast from where they had been just minutes ago? Defensive and stubborn, he asked another one of those questions which answers itself. "This is where I'm supposed to say you're wrong and fight for you, isn't it?"

Her voice was the hard side of weary. "But we both know that you won't."

And they both knew she was right.

CHAPTER 12

Tom got back to the cabin just as the household was beginning to stir. Joe stumbled into the kitchen, winked at Tom and asked him how he had slept. Bonnie came in next, said nothing, and started making pancakes. Luke and the girls drifted in once the aromas were airborne, and then the phone rang.

Bonnie glared at the wall clock. It was six thirty a.m. Tom answered the phone. "Morgan residence."

"Tom? This is Tanner Hartwell." Hartwell was the senior managing partner at Tom's law firm. The sound of Hartwell's name blew away whatever fog remained from Tom's sleepless night. "Sorry to disturb your family at this hour, Tom. But your cell has been off for two days, did you know that?"

It's called vacation.

The voice didn't wait for an answer. "I'm afraid we have a problem that requires your attention."

Fatigue swept Tom's body. "Is it the thing Stu Bailey called about the other day?"

"That's right. We need you to look at some old documents and walk us through what they mean. It's not something we can do over the phone."

Tom felt suddenly like he was in one of those childhood dreams where you get caught cheating on the big test and get kicked out of school. There's nothing you can do. "When do you need me there?"

"Today."

Five pairs of eyes watched him replace the phone. "I've got to go." The girls groaned. Luke slunk from the room.

"Oh, Tommy," said Mary. "Why don't you tell them to go stuff themselves?"

"Will you be able to come back?" asked Bonnie.

"I don't know."

"Let me drive you," said Joe. "If we leave now, we can be there by late afternoon. You take care of what you have to, and we can be back here before sun up tomorrow.

"That's too much trouble, Joe. I'll just fly."

"Look, Tommy, I called that guy whose card the NeuroGene owner gave us—the one who used to be his partner and lives in Manhattan. He's willing to meet as long as he can bring his lawyer. I was going to make him come up here. But if he can do it today, we might as well make it a road trip."

Bonnie and Mary looked at him pleadingly.

"Alright brother. But keep it under 90 miles an hour, okay. My stomach's churning already."

As soon they turned onto the Northway, Joe started. "You're pissing me off with this Super Uncle shit. Secret languages, monster fish... Next thing I know, you'll be getting him laid."

Tom glanced at a speedometer fanning clockwise as if it were measuring the driver's blood pressure instead of the car's speed. "Afraid he'll beat your record?"

"Don't be funny. I'm serious."

"Then be serious. You don't have time to be a dad. No Coldwater Sheriff in living memory has. MadDog wasn't around when we were kids. You and I had each other. But all Luke's got is two older sisters. It's not the same, and it's not enough."

"You're setting the bar too high, Tommy."

"By taking the kid fishing and playing an old family word game? Come on. He's dying for some guy time, that's all. Put a couple of fishing poles in the trunk of the patrol car and take him on your rounds, if that's all you've got time for. It doesn't matter what you do. The kid just needs to hang with men every once in a while, preferably his dad."

"What do you know about children?"

"I was one."

Joe glared at the windshield. The patrol car gradually decelerated.

"Sometimes you're too fucking smart for your own good, Tommy." Joe bit his lip and glanced sideways. "So how do you speak this Pig Latin gibberish? I forget."

Tom put Joe through his remedial language paces until he could carry on a simple conversation without misplacing half the nonsense syllables. Then he dozed the rest of the way down the Northway and Thruway until they reached Manhattan.

"There's something else I need to talk to you about." Joe slowed the car for the 'Cash Only' toll both on the George Washington bridge. "I ran into Susan Pearce a few months ago out on Watermelon Hill, near one of Cashins' dope patches." Tom sat up and rubbed his eyes. "She was sitting on a picnic blanket. With her shirt off."

Tom groaned. "I'm not sure I want to hear this."

Joe kept his eye on traffic. "I go up the Hill every spring just to see where the new dope patches are. But I leave the plants alone until just before harvest. That keeps the Cashins busy and out of trouble weeding and guarding their turf all summer. Then I go back a few weeks before the plants are ready and I pull most of them up."

"No booby traps?"

"Simple stuff. I think they all read the same Mother Jones handbook. Besides, I don't even think they know it's me. They probably suspect the competition."

The cash lane line was a hundred cars deep. *Couldn't the town spring for an EZ Pass?*

"So there she is, lying half-naked in all that greenery, little khaki shorts, blond ponytail, hiking boots and a smile. Reminded me of Jane Goodall in one of those old National Geographic magazines. Only topless." Joe grinned. "I know she heard me coming. She must have seen me too. But she didn't even look up. Cool as a cucumber."

"I definitely don't want to hear this."

"How do you know what it's about?"

"Non-overlapping immune system markers."

"What?"

"Opposites attract."

Joe lifted a hand from the wheel. "No. Listen. Your ex is up there planting something. I'm certain she took her shirt off just to distract me. Quick thinking, too. It nearly worked."

Joe had Tom's attention now.

"But it was still early enough for the grass to be wet, and I could see tracks that led from the blanket to a couple of spots across the clearing. So being a good little 'do be,' instead of going first to where she was all sprawled out on that blanket grinning at me, I started over to where the tracks came from. And as soon as I did, she sat up. 'Hello, Sheriff,' she says to me. 'Come over here and sit.'"

Tom felt his stomach clench.

"I waved. But kept following the tracks in the wet grass. So then she stood up. God, what a body! Forget what I said about Jane Goodall." Joe grinned. "Anyway, what do you think I found there?"

"A personal dope patch. So what?"

"That's what I expected. But no. There's a bunch of rocks scattered around there. And the clearing sort of slopes south a bit. So it's an okay spot for growing something. But not great, unless you're trying to hide it too. The rocks make good cover, and you'd have to look hard to see the one or two seedlings she put in front of them and behind some sort of little shrub she put in, too."

"Not dope?"

"Not dope."

Tom's curiosity began to replace the initial urge to turn on the radio and find some loud music.

"So after I checked out the plants, I go over to where she's sitting. Only now she's got her shirt back on."

"I'm glad to hear it."

"I did ask her if we could start over again. This time I'd stop at her blanket first. 'You made your choice, Sheriff,' she says." Joe laughed and shook his head. "That's some woman you let get away, brother."

Tom could feel his patience waning. "All right. Now that she's got her clothes back on, what happened next?"

"Naturally I asked her what she's doing. And does she know that she's just a hundred yards downhill from a couple of semi-commercial dope patches? She's got this sketch book out and she's making penciled drawings of her plants and not even looking at me. 'Yes,' she says. She'd noticed them. But her plants would be ready at different times from the *cannabis sativa,* so she doesn't think she'll run into any trouble. Cool as you please."

"Did you offer to help her harvest, just in case?"

"I did. But she said, 'No thank you, officer. There are just a few of them and they're very delicate.'"

"What did she say they were?"

"Brain food, I think. Now that we've talked to that guy from NeuroGene, I understand what she said better than I did then. She went on and on about brain chemicals, keys and locks and stuff. It sounded a lot like what Willow was talking about. But since it was coming from someone who'd just ripped off her shirt to keep me from noticing her stash, I had a hard time concentrating."

Tom tried to drag the narrative to higher ground. "So what kind of plants were they?"

"She told me some names, but I wasn't really listening. I figured I'd just pull a few of them up when I came back to rip out Cashin's stuff, and then send them to the lab for identification."

Tom gestured at the fresh gouges on his brother's arms. "And you did that just a few days ago?"

It was a simple question. But instead of answering it, Joe pulled a sheet of paper from the glove compartment and handed it over. Tom read the note clipped to the front:

'You're losing it, Sheriff. Looks like you've staked-out an amateur herbalist. Attached is a full report. But the bottom line is you can get this stuff, or its active ingredients, in any health food store. Actually, you could get better and cheaper there. The only thing you can't is the rosary pea. It's an ornamental, but it grows wild all over Florida. It's also a poison. Your gardener probably added it to the mix to keep animals away. Is she pretty?

Max'

Tom skimmed the report:

Plant **Common name**

Scutellaria lateriflora - Quaker bonnet
Valerian Officinalis - Valerian
Tabernanthe iboga - Iboanine
Abrus precatorius - Rosary pea

Tom read the list twice, but could see no connection between the innocuous herb garden it described and his former girlfriend's sudden impulse to disrobe for his younger brother. "Did she explain why she was going to all the trouble planting her garden way out in the boonies?"

Joe shrugged. "Sort of. She said that everybody in research tries to keep what they're working on secret until they publish. Otherwise other people glom onto it. She said something about there being four different brain chemicals that influence behavior, and that each of the plants had a different 'uptake inhibitor.'" He laughed. "I remember that phrase 'uptake inhibitor.' I asked her if she was working on some sort of anti-date-rape drug."

Tom groaned.

"Yeah. You laugh, smart guy. But do you want to know what she did then?"

"No."

"She just about took all her clothes off again. Gave me a big, wet kiss and started blabbering about Newton and his apple and about great discoveries usually being some sort of accident."

"But she didn't."

"What?"

"Take her clothes off again?"

"You figure out what I'm missing in that report and I'll let you know."

CHAPTER 13

J oe found a garage in mid-town where it cost more to park for three hours than it did to rent a car in Coldwater for a month. His meeting with Sharp was at two o'clock. Tom's was across town at four, and he agreed to sit in on Joe's and keep his mouth shut.

The bronze elevator doors opened as smooth as a mother's hand on a baby's butt. A 30-something receptionist in a smoke gray skirt and white silk blouse open to the sternum led them down a hallway lined with worker bee offices to a conference room the size of a small house. A few million dollars of exotic hardwoods and 19th century oil paintings covered three of its walls. The fourth was floor to ceiling glass with a panoramic view of lower Manhattan, New York Harbor and the Statue of Liberty. It was all designed to impress and intimidate. It cost bucks to step in here, it said, and sometimes more to get out.

Joe ran a hand over the intricate inlay of the maple and anegre conference table and fiddled with the seat height adjustment on his leather chair, practicing his hick cop act. Tom didn't doubt his brother's abilities, but he hoped Joe understood that this was no place to get cute.

A young man arrived pushing a cart of soft drinks and water, followed by the former NeuroGene partner, and his lawyer. Michael Sharp stood about five foot seven and carried close to three hundred pounds. His lawyer was a head of thick silver hair taller and country club lean. His perfunctory introduction segued into a twenty-minute ramble about his own advisory role, his client's rights and the limited purpose and scope of the meeting. To Tom it was the familiar drone of an airline attendant's canned speech about keeping your seat belt buckled and noting the nearest emergency exit – impossible to listen to after you've heard it a million times.

Joe caught his eye, his expression openly contemptuous. *This is as phony as it gets, brother. How can you stand it?* When the lawyer finally finished, Joe announced that Tom was there to help with some questions on the corporate structure of NeuroGene and that otherwise he would be keeping his mouth shut. Then he spoke directly to Sharp.

"I'm not sure I understand all that mumbo jumbo about limited scope and so forth. I came here as a courtesy so that you didn't have to come back to Coldwater. I'm going to ask what I came to ask, and you can answer, or not, as you please. But if I have to get a warrant to haul your ass to my home turf, I will."

Sharp's lawyer started to speak, but his client raised his hand. "That's all right, Walter. We've been over this. I've got nothing to hide from the Sheriff and I'd like to be helpful, if I can. I'd also like to get this over with as quickly as possible."

"All right then," said Joe. "Why don't we start by you telling me how you came to be associated with NeuroGene and how and when you came to leave it?"

The lawyer shrugged. Sharp began to talk. "Fair enough. I don't know how much you know about biotech start-ups, Sheriff. But the vanilla profile goes something like this: scientist with a bright idea hooks up with his buddy the sales guy. If the sales guy can keep the cash coming in long enough for Mr. Wizard to get his idea out of the lab, you've got the beginnings of a company.

"But even with money coming in the door, most start-ups don't survive; because often neither the science guy nor the sales guy have ever heard of a budget, cash flow, burn rate or any of the other boring stuff that goes along with keeping a business afloat. Add a financial guy to the mix and then the company may have a chance. Mr. Salesman brings in the clients, Mr. Scientist cooks up the next wonder drug in the lab and Mr. Finance makes sure that ends meet, so that the company doesn't have to fold in a fire sale when it can't make rent or payroll."

Tom nodded to confirm Sharp's synopsis. Joe looked away.

"NeuroGene is a variation on that basic theme. I was the finance guy. Dave Willow was, or is, a kind of combo science/sales guy. We had a bunch of rent-a-scientists working on some of his ideas. Paid them as little as possible and kept them around by promising them a piece of the action, if we succeeded."

"And why did you leave?" Joe asked.

"Dave triggered the shotgun."

"He threatened you?"

Sharp's lawyer snorted. "A 'shotgun' is an exit mechanism in a partnership agreement," he explained. "One partner proposes an amount at which he is willing to sell his interest in the company or to buy his partner's. The other partner gets to choose which it is: buy or sell."

Tom nodded again. "And you sold?" asked Joe.

"That's right. I don't know if Dave had stars in his eyes about the future of the business, or what. But my bean-counter's brain told me that the price he put on the table was way too high."

"Or he knew something you didn't," said Tom.

Client and attorney swiveled to face each other, their expressions like opposite sides of a drama mask: Pissed! and Surprised! Joe looked annoyed.

"That's possible," Sharp admitted. "Though I think it more likely that Dave just got frustrated with my financial controls. But you're right. He could have downplayed something on the research side that I might not have known about." He turned to his lawyer. "I don't remember you mentioning that possibility, Walter."

Tom smiled.

Joe produced a copy of the photo he had shown to Sharp's former partner, Dave Willow, and asked if Sharp recognized the man in it. Sharp held the blown-up copy of Billy Pearce's New York State driver's license close to his face. When he looked away, his eyes moved up and to the right. His head moved from side to side.

"Are you sure?" Joe asked.

"Pretty sure. This guy looks kind of scruffy."

Joe put the photo back in the folder. "Do you know a Susan Pearce?"

"Dave's girlfriend?"

"What!" Tom blurted.

Joe glared again.

"Maybe that's a bit strong," said Sharp. "Before the entrepreneurial bug bit him, Dave was just another randy junior professor at Stanford. Miss Pearce was one of his graduate students, I think. They had something going on back then. Whether Dave managed to revive it at NeuroGene, I don't know. He sort of let on that he did. But that could have been wishful thinking."

Though the conference room air conditioning was balanced to perfection, Tom felt his shirt absorb sweat like a sponge.

"Do you know if Miss Pearce has any brothers or sisters?" Joe asked.

Sharp looked up and away. "Not really."

"Does NeuroGene sell only its own products or does it sometimes act as a reseller or distributor for third parties?" Joe read from the list of questions that Tom had scribbled in the car.

"Only its own products," said Sharp.

"Does it sell any of its products outside the United States?"

"No."

Joe ran through the list, his mouth occasionally contorting over a legal term-of-art, like a schoolboy struggling with a vocabulary assignment. But Sharp's answers were consistent and Joe didn't follow-up. Sharp's lawyer seemed ready to suggest that they finish. At the risk of stepping too boldly on his brother's turf, Tom interrupted and started to ask the follow-up questions that Sharp's answers suggested. "Did NeuroGene have any non-research income?"

"Once in a while we'd scratch some extra revenue by renting our mailing list and providing access to our distribution network. To keep the cash coming in, we basically leveraged what we had by making parts of it available to smaller companies in the same field."

"And which companies did you deal with on that basis?"

Sharp paused. "HGP Associates rented our customer list. The owner invented a piece of testing equipment that he hoped might catch on in the Human Genome Project. It didn't. He went belly up before I left. U- Labs used us every once in a while for secure mailing."

"What's that?" Joe interrupted.

Sharp shrugged. "There are a lot of paranoid researchers in our space," he explained. "They put their whole lives and piggy banks into the contents of one little petri dish. Then they try to keep their colleagues and competitors from finding out what's in it until they can prove it works and lock in commercial rights. But it's a community of very bright people, who keep close tabs on who's doing what with whom and where. In this crowd, something as simple as an address on an envelope can be a tip-off to what a colleague or competitor is working on and with whom."

"So this U-Labs used NeuroGene as kind of a post office box?" Joe asked, trying to nail it down.

"Basically, yes."

Sharp's lawyer interrupted. "Sheriff, I thought you were here to get my client's assistance in your investigation of a homicide. I don't see the relevance of this line of questioning."

"Noted."

"It's okay, Walter," said Sharp.

Joe nodded at Tom to continue.

"Did this rent-a-mail-room bring in any meaningful revenue?"

"Not at first," said Sharp. "In fact, it was hardly worth the trouble. But remember, I was the finance guy. So I did what finance guys do with a marginal supplier, I raised prices."

Joe asked, "Did you ever consider that one of these outfits might have been using NeuroGene to distribute controlled substances?"

"You mean narcotics?" asked Sharp.

"Yes."

Sharp's lawyer interrupted. "Sheriff, is this a murder investigation or something else?"

Sharp waved a hand. "We're talking about a few dozen petri dishes here, Sheriff. A couple of boxes of stoppered lab glass, that sort of stuff."

"Did you ask?" Joe demanded.

"I didn't have to. Every time I raised our handling fee, I got a call from Dr. Hassad with some new sob story. The next big cancer breakthrough... an off-license AIDS cocktail for some friend's sick son. Whatever he thought might get me to hold the price down for one more shipment."

"Did it?"

"Sometimes. But he always paid if I made him wait, so it was a question of how badly we needed the cash. In the end it's a judgment call on how much the market will bear. I never felt like I squeezed him all that hard. It was more like he just enjoyed haggling."

"Did Dave Willow participate in these negotiations?" Tom asked.

Sharp started to wag his head. Then he stopped. "At first he did. But then he always wound up chasing his own tail about who we should help and who we shouldn't. There's a lot of competitive jealousy in the research business. A couple of times we wound up turning away business when we really needed the cash. That's no way to keep the doors open. So in the end, I just made those decisions myself."

Sharp's candor was making his lawyer visibly uneasy. "Why don't we take a break for a few minutes?" he suggested. "I need to hit the men's room and have a chat with my client."

Sharp remained at the table. "You go ahead, Walter. I'm fine. I'd like to get this over with. Go on, Sheriff."

"Tell me where you were last Saturday evening between the hours of ten P. M. and midnight?" Joe's voice was steady, almost bored.

"What!" Sharp's lawyer bleated. "My client isn't a suspect here. And you have no jurisdiction to be asking those types of questions."

"Home in bed, Sheriff, watching the Yankees on television."

"Alone?"

"Alas."

"Sheriff Morgan, if you're going to pursue this line of questioning, I'm going to have to end this interview. Mike, I really have to insist."

"Where is U- Labs located?" Joe continued.

"Somewhere near Montreal," said Sharp.

"Mike!"

"It's okay, Walter."

"And how did these petri dishes or whatever arrive? Were there customs declarations and so forth?"

"Actually, the stuff usually just came in the mail."

"From Canada?"

"No, from this side. Sometimes right from Coldwater."

Sharp's lawyer was perspiring visibly.

"How's that?" asked Joe.

"Canada is only about thirty or so miles from Coldwater, right? Dr. Hassad probably just had someone pop over on a lunch break and put it in the mail."

"Isn't that somewhat... irregular?" Joe asked.

"No. I'd say VIP posting is the norm in our business."

Joe lifted an eyebrow.

"'Vial-in-pocket'," Sharp explained. "Look, Sheriff, scientists are just like everybody else. They don't like paperwork and they don't like hassles."

"You're telling me that there are vials and petri dishes being walked across the U. S. /Canada border and just dropped in the nearest mailbox?"

"All the time. Occasionally, Dr. Hassad sent someone over, if it was something he thought needed special handling." As he said this, Sharp paused, closed his eyes and tilted his head up and to the left. When he opened them he said, "Let me see that photo, again, Sheriff."

Joe removed the blown-up copy of Billy Pearce's driving license from the folder on his lap and handed it to Sharp.

"This guy came, once. I remember him now. He was a real prick. Parked his truck in the handicapped parking spot. Came in with a boom box blasting. Told everybody to get the hell out of the mail room. And he smelled, too. I called Dr. Hassad after that and told him to send someone else next time or find a new distributor."

While Joe scribbled a note, Tom asked, "You said that you thought your partner wanted to buy you out so he could get back to basic research?"

"That's right. The burn rate on our cash was pretty steep and I think Dave was getting kind of tired of the nonstop fundraising gig. He was on the road three days a week at least. We had a bunch of arguments about scaling back research to meet cash flow. I think Dave just got tired of the whole profit and loss side of the business.

Maybe he found an investor, or maybe he hooked one of the big drug companies. But at the silly price he was offering, I wasn't going to ask."

* * *

Tanner Hartwell, the senior managing partner at Tom's law firm, and two other lawyers were waiting in a conference room when Tom arrived. A row of fat document boxes covered the table in front of them. Hartwell was a slightly stooped six foot one, the same as Tom though a quarter century older. He extended a long fingered hand, bound at the wrist by a slim Cartier tank watch. "Thanks for coming," he said. "I believe you've already met Stuart. This is his associate, Charles Adams." Tom shook hands with the balding compliance partner and the young associate who looked like he might have passed up a career in professional football. "Charlie, why don't you show Tom those documents."

The associate opened a series of red wells and velo-bounds stamped with the logo: Greater Cairo Infrastructure Project. He handed Tom one of the volumes, opened to the signature page and pointed to Thomas Morgan, Esq., attorney-in-fact.

"Do you remember this deal?" Hartwell asked.

"Vaguely," said Tom. "That must have been fifteen years ago. I would have been a young associate, like Charlie here, working on pieces of fifty different deals. But if I recall correctly, it was an Egyptian public works project funded by the U. S. Agency for International Development. The partner in charge got me involved because Egyptian commercial law turns out to be based on the Napoleonic code."

"Because you read French?"

"That's right. Egyptian civil courts don't publish judge-made case law the way American courts do. They look to the French code and cases the same way we sometimes look to British common law."

"And how did you wind up signing for this Societia de Electrification Cairo?"

Tom examined Hartwell's face for a sign, but the senior partner waited patiently with pen poised over notepad, giving away nothing. "The closing was supposed to be at some air-conditioned hotel in downtown Cairo. At the last minute, the Egyptian sponsor decided to do the signing as a photo-op at the job site, two hours out into the desert. A couple of the older guys weren't up for that, so I offered to stand-in with a power-of-attorney. Professional courtesy."

"So this company you signed for wasn't a client of the firm?" Hartwell asked.

"No. All of the equipment manufacturers supplying the project had offshore construction subs. That one belonged to one of the others. Not our client."

"I see," said Hartwell, making a bold box and check mark on the yellow legal pad. "Stuart, Charlie, you can leave Tom and me here to chat. We may not need to go through the rest of these boxes, after all."

The two men left the room quietly. Tom felt the cloth under his arms dampen with sudden sweat. "So what's this all about, Tanner? I'm not getting a good feeling."

"Politics," said Hartwell succinctly. "There's a mid-term election next year. The parties are starting to look around for mud balls to sling."

"And there's mud in those boxes?"

"There might be." Hartwell pressed a hedge of large upper teeth into a thin lower lip. "I got a call from a source in the Manhattan DA's office who owes the firm a favor. Our Democratic governor's instructed his appointees in Albany to jump on this Eurocon thing to see if they can snare some down-state Republicans."

"With a decade-old subcontract on a Middle East construction project?"

"You can dig clear through to China if you've got enough shovels."

"What did they dig up here?"

Tanner paused, as if deciding what, if anything, to reveal. "You're right about the ownership of that construction sub you signed for. Charlie looked into that already. At the time of the project, it was owned 51% by Siemens and 49% by Perini. But Eurocon still held a small amount of Perini stock from some lending they did back in the '70's."

"That wouldn't make it Eurocon sub, or even an affiliate."

"For most purposes. But according to Charlie's research, under federal procurement regs, any ownership interest counts, no matter how small."

"And let me guess. This indirect minority interest did something it shouldn't?"

Hartwell nodded.

Shit. Tom stared out the window hoping salvation might be staring back from the reflecting glass of the tower across the street. "Any chance of it being a six year statute of limitations?"

"Ten. So they have to get cracking, if they want to use it."

"What does your source say?"

"That one of our people is on their list."

"Me?"

"I'm afraid so."

"Because fifteen years ago I did an older colleague a favor and saved him a two hour trip out to the desert?"

"Because this is an election year and you're a photogenic, downstate sometimes Republican fund raiser who'd make a perfect poster boy for a timely government procurement scandal."

"You're shitting me."

"I wish I were. Something like this happens every ten years or so, when one of the parties gets the taste of blood in its mouth and decides to take the gloves off."

Tom pressed his fingers to temples. "Is this a problem for the firm, Tanner? Or just for Tom Morgan?"

Hartwell's answer was all the more depressing for its thoughtful diplomacy. "I've got a call in to Morris Silverstein. He's the top white collar criminal defender in New York. I'm not sure what the firm can do if this construction company wasn't actually our client. But I think you should engage Moe to represent you personally."

"At what? Nine hundred fifty dollars an hour?"

"This isn't something you can handle yourself, Tom."

The old advice that a lawyer who represents himself has a fool for a client, didn't make Tom feel wiser for following it. It made him feel poor.

"I'm due back from vacation next week. Will <u>that</u> be a problem? I'll need money coming in, if I'm going to be pumping it back out through a fire hose to Moe Silverstein."

"Let's play that by ear," said Hartwell. "You're on vacation. Let me talk to Moe first and we'll take it from there."

CHAPTER 14

Traffic heading out of Manhattan toward the George Washington Bridge was backed-up almost to midtown, making a typical New York sound soup of angry horns, blaring radios and multi-lingual curses. Street vendors worked the aisles between the stalled vehicles, hawking shopping carts full of fake Rolex watches, faux designer purses and cheap electronics of no known pedigree. Joe turned on the patrol car's bubble light to cut through the traffic. The New Yorkers ignored him.

Tom decided not to say anything right away about the Eurocon mess. He needed to sit with it first and sort through its implications. None seemed good. It was the nightmare he'd never allowed himself to entertain. The one where the gold cup is snatched away within sight of the finish line.

He had always tried to be rational about money. Rejecting the prejudice of his upbringing and the excesses of his peers, he'd come to view it neither as an evil nor an end to itself, but as a tool. Good, bad, happiness or unhappiness, came from how you used money, not from the fact of having it. Though he had reservations about many of the sacrifices necessary to acquire it: the ridiculous hours, busted romances, and years devoted to things of no apparent value other than how well they paid. But he kept going.

Now what? If Tanner was right, fifteen years of single-minded pursuit of financial independence was headed straight for the toilet. The bromide of being able to start over was an illusion. Spend another decade pushing the rock back up the hill? Suppose the gods rolled it back again? That's the flaw in your tool theory, smart boy. The sacrifices are worth it, only if you get to the finish line. If you don't, you could have been doing something else. With Susan. *Is it really the journey, not the arrival, that matters?*

He felt a jab in the ribs and opened his eyes.

"You're talking in your sleep," said Joe.

Tom unfolded his body from a dashboard/seat back fetal position, sat up and rubbed his face. "Need a pit stop."

"We're ten miles from home. You slept the whole way."

"Still need to stop."

The multi-colored canopy of fall foliage had come and gone while he was sleeping. It was dark now and the strobes of oncoming headlights forced him to look away.

"Who's Camille?" Joe asked.

"What?"

"You were talking to her in your sleep."

He closed his eyes again. "French co-counsel on an anti-trust case."

"'*Je t'aime?* ' Is that how you address fellow lawyers these days?"

"In my dreams."

Joe pointed to a roadside billboard. "We can stop at Trudy's? Might as well eat, too, while we're there."

"Let's go. I haven't been to Trudy's in…I don't know when. Can't believe it's still there."

Joe yawned. "I need fuel or something. Feel like crap."

Tom stretched. "Manhattan is an acquired taste."

Joe rolled down a window and let in a blast of cool air. "You can keep it." He stuck his forehead into the breeze. "So what were you trying to get out of Sharp with all those arithmetic questions, if you don't mind my asking? That was no criminal lawyer he had, or he would have thrown us out."

"He's a corporate lawyer," Tom said. "Probably represented Sharp when he sold out his NeuroGene interest to his partner, Willow."

"So what were you after?"

"Trying to find out if he's a liar. If he cheated his partner in the buyout. And if he did, did Billy Pearce play a role and did he get whacked on account of it?"

"Ambitious, aren't you?" Joe's voice sounded relieved and disbelieving at the same time. "So how did any of that gobbledygook get you there? Because I sure as hell had no idea what you and he were fan-dancing about. And I'm sure his lawyer didn't either or he would have stopped you."

"Yes, yes, yes and maybe."

"Quit showing off, Tommy. Put some meat on it."

"Okay, first, the guy's a liar. Every time you asked him for a significant memory, like the first time you showed him Billy's picture, or when you asked him if Susan had any siblings, he lied."

"How do you know?"

"I'll show you when we get to Trudy's."

"Tell me now."

Tom turned his face away from the oncoming headlights. "You need to be looking at me. And right now I'd rather have you looking at the road."

"All right, but tell me how you know he cheated his partner."

"Cheat's probably overstating it. Let's just say he took advantage of Willow's financial naiveté."

"Cooking the books?"

"Nothing that crude. Like he made sure to point out, everything was on the financial statements and accounted for properly."

"So how did he cheat him?"

"By making the business profitable."

"Quit busting my chops, Tommy. I'm tired."

"You don't look so good either." Joe's face looked like dead fish belly in the strobe of passing headlights.

"Just tell me."

"All right. Sharp knew what I was getting at when I asked him if the buyout was a multiple of earnings. Do you remember he asked if I thought he was going to be next? He meant the next corpse."

"It's not getting any clearer."

"Listen. It's simple. A business is basically worth a multiple of its future earnings. You noticed that Sharp never mentioned how much this petri dish sideline brought in. That wasn't an oversight. My guess is that Willow and whoever backed him thought they were buying a marginally profitable research business with some potential upside, not a sinkhole propped-up by a sideline business in cross-border, no questions asked, sealed packages. You noticed something too, when you asked him about illegal substances. They may not have been sending recreational drugs across the border. But I'm certain that when we look at the NeuroGene financials, we're going to find this U-Labs was paying more for its U. S. mail room than can be explained by a need for scientific secrecy."

"You sure about that?"

"Pretty sure. It looks to me like Sharp was doing what's called a 'pump and dump.' When he figured out that his partner was looking for an angel investor, he pumped the company's earning with this 'no questions asked' distributor scheme, and then dumped his stock at an inflated price when Willow exercised the shotgun."

"You're making my head ache, Tommy."

"You're tired, that's all. I'll write it down for you when we get back."

"Good, Watson. Stick around. I always thought there were more shenanigans going down in Coldwater Park, than there were up in the woods with the Cashins and the Dooleys. You should come home and specialize."

"What's the pay?"

"What do you care, you're rich already. The job can be anything you want to make it."

Don't think about Susan. "How about I just help you find Billy Pearce's murderer."

"Okay, but I'm not through with you on this. Now what's the connection between this financial sleight-of-hand and Billy getting dumped in the lake?"

"I don't know yet. But tell me that a legitimate scientific research outfit entrusts some loser like Billy Pearce with its ultra-secret whatevers. Forget about trusting him, how would a legitimate Canadian biotechnology company even come to know a small-town punk like Billy Pearce? It's not like he hung with the scientific jet set."

"Okay. But unless there's a connection between Sharp cheating his partner and Billy getting dead, this is just a distraction."

"Is there a way to check on Sharp's story of where he was Saturday night?"

"Don't need to," Joe yawned. "We already know he wasn't in bed watching the Yankees."

"How?"

"Because he's no more of a Yankee fan than you are. The Yankees don't play on Saturday night. Weekend games are in the afternoon."

* * *

Trudy's Diner hadn't changed since the Morgan family used to go there after Sunday church when Tom and Joe were boys. The diner was a 1950's era converted aluminum Airstream, sixty feet long and eighteen feet wide, with a cigarette-scarred Formica counter down the center and a row of swivel stools covered in red plastic facing it. Four bench booths lined the windows on either side of the entrance, with a cash register, candy counter and cigarette machine just inside the door. Two shelves of pies and cereals clung to the back wall above the toaster and drink machines.

Tom sat in the booth across from the cash register and flipped through a juke-box menu of unfamiliar titles while he waited for his brother to come back from the men's room. *When had Coldwater gone country?* Outside, an old Buick Park Avenue inched into the gravel parking lot and unloaded a quartet of senior citizens out past their bedtimes. Behind it an equally ancient Camaro fishtailed to a stop and ejected a pair of leathered-up teenagers. The skinny one slithered through the oldsters like a rat through a cane field. The other hung back with a posture and expression like he was having a gastrointestinal moment. The door to the diner flung open and a blast of chill air hit Tom in the back of the neck.

"Shut it, please," said Tom, not bothering to turn his head.

"Shut yours," said a voice, at once insolent, adolescent and unmistakably high. Only the high part didn't piss Tom off. He pointed a finger at his reflection in the window and through it to the Coldwater patrol car parked outside. "See that car with the bubble light? I leave in that. You can, too, if you don't shut that door." Tom spoke to his reflection in the window and to the pasty, cadaverous face above and behind it.

The face lifted and scanned the row of empty booths in either direction. "Bullshit."

Tom pointed his chin at the plate across the table. "He's in the can. That's his meatloaf you're freezing. Go ahead, keep standing there."

A spike haired moon-face appeared above the deaths-head in the window refection. "Wassup, Cashin?"

"Nothing, Mulvey. You stink."

The draft on the back of Tom's neck disappeared and sound of metal heel taps receded. Joe reappeared, looking colorless, clammy and ill.

"You okay?"

Joe put his hand on the edge of the table and eased himself into the booth. "Threw up in there. That city of yours can have that effect on people."

"You look like death."

"Don't say that, Tommy. Not even in jest."

"Sorry. I'll drive home, if you'll let me do that siren and bubble light thing."

Joe grunted, "Don't touch the toys. I need to get to bed soon. Feels like I'm coming down with something."

"You look like you're going to fall over."

"Enough!" The *"Look"* was their mother's. Only flashing out from under a buzz cut, the similarity gave Tom the creeps. "Tell me how you think you know Sharp was lying."

Tom smiled. "You're going to like this. It's a trick one of my litigation partners taught me. One I'm glad Dad didn't know." Joe lifted the palm of his hand to his forehead and squeegee-d a line of sweat into his hair. "What color was the tuxedo you wore at your Senior Prom?"

Joe leaned his head back and appeared to search for an answer in the far left-hand corner of the diner where the ceiling and walls converged. "John Travolta, 'Saturday Night Fever' white."

"And what song did the band play when King and Queen danced?"
He closed his eyes, tilted his head to the right and his face to the left. "Can't
remember."

"And if the Coldwater High School varsity football team played the
Jefferson High School cheerleaders in a bowling tournament, and you had
to design the bowling shirts, what would they look like?"

Joe closed his eyes and this time turned his head up and to the right.
"See-through," he grinned.

"True. True. And not true," said Tom.

Joe grunted. "Okay, smart boy. Explain it to me."

Tom smiled. "I'm kind of fuzzy on the science and so was the guy who
explained it to me. But it has something to do with different kinds of
material being stored or created in different parts of your brain."

"You and your ex have got brains on the brain."

Tom grinned. "Yeah, well you're going to thank me for this. Think about
the questions I just asked. One asked you to retrieve a visual memory, one a
sound memory and one asked you to make-up an image."

"Okay."

"When you were searching for the visual memory, your eyes went up and
to the left. When you tried to remember a sound, your eyes went sideways
to the left. And when I asked you to make-up an image, they went up and
to the right--the opposite of where they went when I asked you a question
where you had to retrieve an actual memory."

"'The eyes are the windows of the soul'?" Joe quoted.

"Exactly. Eye movements track the part of your brain that you're accessing
in response to a question. Sights, sounds, and feelings are stored in different
areas of the brain and they're made-up in different areas, too."

"And how does this tell you when someone is lying."

"It doesn't. But if you ask somebody for a memory and their eyes go to the
left, it tells you that they're accessing a real memory. They may not tell you
the truth about the memory, but they're accessing something they've actually
stored. For a sound, the eyes and face go to the side, for a feeling, they go
down and the chin comes in. If the eyes go to the right, they're creating, not

accessing. Like your see-through bowling shirt. They're making it up."

"You get paid for this?" Joe snorted.

"It's not foolproof like fingerprints and lie detectors. My partner's a litigator. He uses it in depositions and cross-examination to let him know if he's on the trail of something or not. He says it only works about 80% of the time. The signals tend to be reversed in lefties: and some people are mixed dominant—you know, throw righty and bat lefty. But if you establish a baseline by asking them for an obvious memory that they have no reason to make up, like the prom tuxedo question, then you can figure out what their signals are."

"Forget Dad. We're lucky Mom never knew this."

"Amen."

"So what did Sharp let slip? And how did you keep track?"

Tom moved some dishes and rested his hands on the table. "When you showed him that photo of Billy, Sharp made a big show about peering at it closely and then looking up and away, as if he was really trying to search his memory. But when he did it, his eyes went up and to the right. When you asked him if Susan had a sibling, they went the same way—up and to the right. But when you asked him where U-Labs was, his eyes went the opposite way—up and to the left. That doesn't mean he was telling the truth when he said Montreal, but it does mean that he was searching an actual memory."

"But he told us about Billy. He brought it up."

"Eventually. I think one of the questions spooked him into thinking you were going to find out anyway."

"And why would he lie about knowing if Susan had any brothers or sisters?"

"I don't know. But it was after he didn't recognize Billy's photo when you showed it to him the first time, and before your questions jogged his memory."

"Sounds like mumbo-jumbo."

"It's not what lawyers call admissible evidence. But if I ask you now whether Susan took her clothes off again when you gave her the anti-date rape idea, are you going to look me in the eye?"

Joe didn't answer. He didn't seem to be listening. His mouth hung open and beads of sweat oozed from the pores of his face. His breath came shallow and rapid.

"Hey,brother, are you okay?" *Stupid question.*

Joe tried to stand, but his legs buckled and he fell backward into the booth, anointing the linoleum with undigested meat loaf special.

CHAPTER 15

Joe kept heaving long after there was nothing left to expel. Tom gave him water but it didn't stay down.

"Sheriff's drunk!" Howls of derisive laughter erupted from the punks in the corner booth. Joe didn't seem to hear. The waitress hovered briefly and then disappeared. The four gray heads in the booth near the bathrooms exchanged hushed whispers.

Tom lifted Joe onto a clean stool and propped him there while he fumbled with the keypad on his cell phone. Joe's hand gripped Tom's shoulder, and his head snapped forward retching foul air.

"Drunk as shit!"

Sliding from the stool, Joe fell to the floor and lay there breathing hard and fast. Tom dialed 911. As soon as the line opened he started talking. "Trudy's Diner Route 6. We need an ambulance. The Coldwater Sheriff collapsed here a few minutes ago... vomiting. Can't catch his breath... Yes, he conscious, but he can't talk... Right. What? How soon?" Tom closed the phone and squatted next to his brother. "There's an ambulance on the way, Joe. The waitress called already."

Joe didn't look up or respond. The skin on the back of his neck was a slick, clammy and white. His breath between heaves came like a collapsed sprinter's.

Tom put a hand on the back of Joe's suddenly soaking shirt. He didn't look up. The hooters kept their distance, but not their tongues. "Sheriff's shitfaced!"

The paramedics arrived before Tom's teeth ground to stubs. They lifted a padded cart up the steps of the diner and parked it next to the cash register. One put a paper mask over his mouth and latex gloves on his hands. He took Joe's wrist and pulse while the other asked questions.

"Has this man consumed any alcohol?

"No," said Tom. "Nothing."

"What did he eat?"

Tom pointed to the floor. "Meatloaf, mashed potatoes, string beans, Diet Pepsi. Same thing I did."

From the end of the diner came a taunting duet. "He's drunk!"

Joe opened his mouth and sucked in rapid, shallow breaths.

"He said he was feeling something in the car before we got here."

"When did he start vomiting?"

"About ten minutes ago. He hasn't spoken since. I don't think he can."

The paramedic kneeling beside Joe took a metal cylinder from his backpack, cut open a sealed bag containing a plastic mask and tube, connected the tube to the cylinder and put the mask over Joe's face. Joe clamped a hand over the plastic and lifted his head. His breathing began to slow. Then he yanked it away, bent over and heaved air.

"Let's load him," said the paramedic who had given Joe the mask. He and the other paramedic scooped Joe under the arms and eased him onto the cart, then pushed and pulled, one at each end, through the door, down the steps and into the back of the ambulance. The one who had asked all the questions got behind the wheel while Tom and the other climbed in the back with Joe. The siren echoed in the closed space while the vehicle sped down the road.

Tom watched the paramedic unload boxes and bags from a cabinet on the metal wall beside the door, strap a blood pressure cuff on Joe's arm and shine a penlight into his pupils which were now the size of dimes. Pressing a button on the plastic box strapped to his shoulder, the paramedic began to speak crisply. "Vomiting, hyperventilation." He looked at the dial on the blood pressure cuff. "75 over 40".

The box cackled. The paramedic took a baggie containing a pair of wires with jacks and buds at either end and plugged them into the radio. He put one in his ear and let the other dangle at his throat. The cackling stopped. "Does he have any food allergies?"

"I don't think so," said Tom.

"Would you know?"

"He's my brother."

The paramedic lifted the wire at his throat and repeated Tom's answer into the bud. "Was he in any industrial facility today? Near any noxious chemicals or fumes?"

"We spent the day in Manhattan."

The paramedic's eyes flashed and his mouth tightened. "This isn't a joke."

"Neither is my answer. That's where we were. All day. There and in a car."

The paramedic relayed what Tom had said and then asked, "Did you stop anywhere?"

"No. We left Coldwater this morning at about six a.m., drove to New York City, had a two hour meeting in a midtown law firm; he took a walk while I had another meeting and then we drove back. The only place we stopped is that diner back there where we both ordered the same meal."

Joe stopped heaving and for the moment he was still. When he opened his mouth it sounded like a shake being sipped through a straw. The paramedic dropped to one knee and moved his ear close to Joe's mouth. "Can you breathe?"

Joe made eye contact, sipped a breath and moved his head slowly from side to side.

The paramedic spoke into the bud. "Tracheal blockage. Deteriorating. Possible anaphylactic shock." He opened the door-side cabinet and removed another plastic box. Inside was a row of labeled ampules and half a dozen disposable syringes. He selected one of the ampules, loaded a syringe and then did the roll up the sleeve arm wiping drill while Joe made straw sucking noises and his eyes followed the needle as it disappeared into the muscle of his shoulder.

"What are you giving him?"

"Point three cc's of epinephrine"

"Which is what?"

"A bronchodilator and antihistamine. Your brother's breathing tube is closing. This may open it."

Tom found himself counting silently like in a game of touch football before the ball is snapped: one Mississippi, two Mississippi, three Mississippi.

"How soon?"

"Ninety seconds, if it works."

Tom counted ten Mississippis. "What if it doesn't?"

"Another three cc's, then Benadryl, if he can swallow some pills. Though that doesn't look likely."

Joe's mouth hung open, his breath was a guttural stutter.

"Then what?"

"Then we open it." The paramedic grabbed another box and extracted a sealed bag with a finger sized tube and scalpel visible through the clear plastic. "Manually."

Joe's eyes widened and the pores at the edge of his scalp began to leak like a garden hose.

* * *

Bright florescent light and jarring sounds filled the Coldwater Hospital Emergency Room. A mix of sour and astringent odors assaulted Tom's nostrils. The paramedics lifted the padding beneath Joe's limp body and slid him onto a white metal gurney. Two women in pale green scrubs took it from there, pushing the gurney like a bob-sled down the hall and through a swinging door labeled: No Admittance.

Tom had been inside the Coldwater Hospital only once since his baby brother was born. Now he felt like he was taking him back like he was under warranty or something. He had not seen Joe so sick since the Christmas they both had measles and chicken pox at the same time. *What the hell could it be?*

Tom found a men's room and applied wet paper towel and hand soap to remove the congealed vomit that had splattered his pants and shoes. What he couldn't remove, he patted dry and left feeling damp and pungent. At the end of the hall he found an alcove of vending machines and traded a pocket of change for a cup of something scalding. Then he found a waiting room and sat in it.

Coldwater isn't a big town; but Saturday night in its only emergency room seemed to draw a crowd. Among the families and friends of the night's unlucky, the fugue of anxiety, fatigue and mindless fidgeting made a viscous soup. No one paid attention to the blaring television mounted half way up the wall; but no one moved to replace it with silence either.

For the first time in nearly an hour, Tom felt his heart decelerate and his lungs relax from sucking air as through a snorkel. But his senses remained quickened as if they knew this was a pause in the action, not the end of it.

Leaving the vending machine swill on a stack of magazines, he went for a walk down the hall beyond the nurses' station. When the hall abruptly ended, he took the branch to the left, counting on the finite possibilities of building construction to eventually bring him back to where he started. Wandering past rooms filled with smells and groans, he tried to distract himself from the puzzle of Joe's collapse by turning to the puzzle of that afternoon's interview with the former NeuroGene owner.

The signs of financial fiddle at the small biotech company were neon. The only surprise was that Sharp and Willow had cheated each other and not some innocent buyer. Sharp was lying about not knowing Billy Pearce and about where he was when Billy was killed. Though that didn't make him Billy's killer, or even tie him to Billy's death. But why lie? There was more digging to do than there had been a few hours ago, and Joe was in no condition to pick up a shovel.

That happy thought led to another and another, until Tom realized that while he was asleep in the car, Joe had probably called home to let them know when they'd be back and that by now they were long overdue. He found a corner with a cell signal and punched in Joe's home number. The line opened on the first ring.

"It's about time, young man."

"He... llo mother. Psychic as well as beautiful?"

"It says 'Tom' right here on the machine."

"Right." His eyes sought the ceiling. "I'm afraid we're going to be late."

"You're already late," said Mary. "Everyone's gone to bed." An exaggerated sigh punched through the ether. "You're not still in New York, are you?"

"No we're...."

"If you are, you might take your brother to one of those clubs. He could use some fun. He works too hard."

"We're in Coldwater, Mom. Joe got sick when we stopped for a bite at Trudy's Diner."

"What? That's a greasy spoon? He should know better."

"I had to take him to the Emergency Room."

"Why? Just bring him home and roll him in bed. He'll be fine in the morning."

"He has to stop vomiting first." The revelation was met with silence. Tom filled it with, "Maybe he's got a bug, Mom. I don't know. But I thought it was better to bring him here and let a doctor figure out what he's got, than bring him there and maybe give it to you and the kids." The silence continued. Tom sensed a quiet dusting of a lifetime's experience weighing the fibs of small boys.

"I'm not getting a good feeling, Tommy."

"You're tired, Mom. I should have called earlier."

"What aren't you telling me?"

"That's all I know, Mom. I haven't spoken to a doctor yet. I'll come home when I've done that. With Joe, if they let him."

"Call me as soon as you know."

"It could be hours. I'll catch up in the morning."

"Call me."

"Yes, ma'am."

As he folded the phone, a short, round man in a doctor's white lab coat approached carrying a clipboard and a stack of blue cardboard files. Tom noticed the sign on the wall showing a cell phone inside a circle with a line through it. He dropped the phone in his pocket. "Sorry".

The doctor shook his head. "No. No. I'm looking for Sheriff Morgan's brother. Nurse Mulvey said someone who might be him was wandering the halls."

"Right. That's me. How is he?"

"He's spoken about you."

"At least he's talking. How is he?"

"No, no. Before." The doctor tapped the stack of files in his arms. "Our sheriff is a frequent visitor to our small hospital. Nothing life threatening—contusions, lacerations, that sort of thing. He takes his job seriously."

"Doctor." Tom read the name tag pinned to the white coat. "Sayed. How is my brother? Is he all right?"

"He's quite ill, I'm afraid."

"What's wrong with him?"

The physician moved his head from side to side, but kept his face forward. "Dehydration. Upper respiratory trauma. We'll have to wait for lab results to determine what from."

"Can I take him home?"

"No. He needs to remain on an I. V. for a while. We've stabilized his breathing. But without knowing what's causing his symptoms, it would be dangerous to discharge him."

Bonnie's going to freak. "Could it be the flu or something?"

The doctor pressed his lips together, but didn't answer. Tom could sense that the hesitation had nothing to do with giving serious thought to the suggestion of flu. "It could, yes. But I don't think it is."

"Why not?"

The doctor shrugged. "For one, the symptoms are too severe for someone as robust as our Sheriff."

"And for another?"

The doctor shrugged again. "The lab results may tell us more."

Tom suppressed a sudden surge of adrenaline—something he did not need more of now. "But that's not what you tracked me down to tell me, is it?" He tried to keep the annoyance out of his voice and off his face.

Sayed seemed to hesitate.

"What has he got, doctor? Or what do you need from me to help you figure it out?"

"So very much like our Sheriff."

"I'm sure you mean that well. Now tell me what he's got, or what you need to know in order to find out. What you tracked me down to find out."

Sayed seemed to make up his mind. "I listened to a recording of the paramedic's transmission. And I understand from it that you and our sheriff spent the day in Manhattan, in a car and at the diner where he became ill."

"Right. But I think he was already ill before we stopped to eat. He said in the car before we got there that he felt like crap."

"Do you know where your brother was in the twenty-four hours prior to starting your day together?"

"Some of it: home in bed before we started, say from midnight last night until six this morning. Before that, his office and around town."

"Do you know where, specifically?"

"No. There was a body recovered from the lake the day before yesterday. He's been running around looking into that."

"Running?" Sayed asked. "To where? Please, if you know."

"I don't. Other than the office we visited today. And the diner where he collapsed."

"I see." The muscles around the doctor's mouth tightened.

"So it's not the flu?"

"No. It's not."

"But you've got a theory that had you hustling the halls looking for an answer to the question of where your patient's been in the last twenty four hours."

Sayed shrugged.

"And you're disappointed that I don't know."

Sayed offered a weak smile. "So very much alike."

"So what is it?"

"Sorry?"

"Your theory."

"The lab results…"

"May tell you nothing. You wouldn't have tracked me down if the information you hoped I had wasn't just as important—or more."

"My, my."

"So what's your theory, doctor? What fits these symptoms you've either seen before or read about, that works or not depending on where my brother may have stuck his muddy boot in the last thirty six hours?"

The doctor put his hand to his chin, partially covering his mouth. His eyes met Tom's. "His arm, I think."

"What's he got, Doc? And how did he get it?"

Sayed looked into Tom's face. "I can't yet tell you how, Mr. Morgan. But I believe that sometime in the last thirty-six hours your brother was exposed to some kind of chemical toxin."

"Accidentally?"

The doctor tapped the stack of files in his arms. "Your brother's job can be physically demanding. But unless it also involves experimentation with lethal compounds…."

"Let's assume it doesn't."

"Then someone exposed him."

"Exposed?"

"Poisoned."

CHAPTER 16

Mary waited for the crunch of tire on gravel, the pop/whoosh of front door quietly opening, or the heart-jolting trill from the silent phone at the end of the couch. But the only sounds that broke her night-long vigil were the creaks and groans of an empty house, the hum of a dying fluorescent light and the rattle of a wind-teased chimney. Bonnie and the children were asleep when Tom called, and with this silly broken leg, she hadn't been able to get up and let the poor woman know her husband was in the hospital. When she tried Tom's cell phone, she got his voicemail. When she tried the hospital, she got the run around. Finally, as the sky began to lighten over the hill above the cabin and the nuthatches began to appear at the kitchen feeder, she pulled herself to the end of the couch, picked up the phone and called Herbert. He had a car. And if he wasn't awake yet...well, he should be.

"They're boys, Mary," the sleepy voice soothed. "They get busy and they don't think."

She assumed her friend's soothing voice and patient demeanor had more to do with living in the Coldwater Senior Center, a place where women outnumbered men six to one, than it had with his Southern upbringing. But it was wasted on her. "Fine. I'll get a cab."

"There's no need, Mary. Just give me an hour."

An hour? "It's not the Senior Prom, Herbert. How's your back?"

"Depends what you have in mind, Mary."

"Don't be fresh. Can you carry a suitcase?"

"Of course! Too much family?"

The hearty bravado might have charmed some, but she was in no mood. "Joe's in the hospital."

"Oh dear." His voice lost the banter. "I'm sorry. Is it serious?"

"I don't know yet. That's why I called. He got sick at Trudy's Diner last night. Tommy took him to the emergency room; but I haven't heard from either of them since. She and the girls will be up soon. I was hoping you could drive me to the hospital so I can find out what's going on."

"Be right over. He won't need a suitcase just yet. Pajamas and razor should be enough for a while."

"The suitcase is for me, Herbert. If Joe's sick, I can't stay here."

"I thought your daughter-in-law was there, and your other son, too."

"She has children, Herbert, and now a sick husband. Tommy has to go back to work in a few days. I don't want him doing double duty or thinking he has to stay longer." *And getting involved with that Pearce piece of work.*

"Give me twenty minutes."

* * *

By the time Mary hobbled to the polished green sedan and arranged her plastered leg under its dash, it was more like an hour. Bonnie had looked frightened when Mary told her Joe was in the hospital. Bonnie hurried the children through a quick breakfast, saying she'd drop the girls at school and go on with Luke to the hospital.

Attempting to suppress her irritation at Herbert's geriatric driving, Mary looked away from the gnarled fingers that gripped the steering wheel at precisely ten and two o'clock and at the watery blue eyes that scanned the rear and side view mirrors every fifteen seconds. The cream colored slacks held razor creases and the Hugo Boss blazer was spotless. Thick white hair streamed from a tanned forehead and small, groomed ears lay flat against a wide skull. Herbert Ball was a handsome old peacock. But he was infuriatingly precise in everything he did. Mary stared out the window as the lake shore houses drifted past at a soporific thirty miles an hour.

She briefly considered placing a flirtatious hand on Herbert's bony thigh and asking him to speed it up. But then she wondered whether an eighty year old man who takes a full day's rest before and after every excursion might overreact, now or later; and she decided that she didn't need another complication right now.

A half hour later, the Buick rolled to a stop in front of Coldwater Hospital and Herbert wheeled her inside. At the end of a hallway lined with open doors and noisy family gatherings, they found Tom talking to a doctor in a white lab coat. "Where's your brother, and what's wrong with him?"

Tom planted an air-kiss on the top of her head. "Hello, Mother. Joe's asleep. Bonnie and Luke are up in his room. Dr. Sayed here gave him something to knock him out. He was up all night."

"Looks like you both were," said Herbert.

Mary lifted her face to the man in the white coat. "What's wrong with my son, Doctor?" She saw Tommy move his head slightly left and then right.

"Dehydration, arrhythmia, gastrointestinal distress. I was explaining to your son that we're running tests to try and isolate the cause. I've already spoken with his wife."

"I thought it was food poisoning," said Mary.

"We haven't ruled that out."

She looked at him suspiciously. "Do you think it's something else?"

The doctor looked at Tom, who shrugged and nodded. "Food poisoning doesn't usually last this long, Mrs. Morgan."

Mary ran her fingers across the top of her scalp. "He was in here a month ago, throwing up and all the rest. He said he'd been exposed to some kind of weed killer."

"Yes, I treated him then as well."

"Could it be the same thing?"

The doctor lifted his shoulders. "There are gouges on his arms that I haven't had a chance to discuss with him. But they're clean and seem to be healing. I'm afraid we just have to wait for your son to stabilize and for the lab results to come back."

"Hellers," said Mary, turning to Tom. "Your brother said they put something on their marijuana plants now. You two were up there the other night, weren't you?" She searched Tom's face, and he looked away like he was ten years old again and she had asked him if he had brushed his teeth. "He took his gun, Tommy. You weren't out for pizza."

"We drove to the junkyard, Mom. Lots of rust. No crops."

Dr. Sayed interrupted, "Could your brother have been exposed to an industrial chemical at this junkyard?"

"Actually, he went into the house next door, not the junk yard. He told me later that he was in the kitchen the whole time, talking with the owner."

"He left you outside?" asked Mary.

"To watch his back."

"This is more of that Billy Pearce business, isn't it?"

"Joe getting sick?"

She waved the back of her hand and turned to the doctor. "When can I see my son?"

"He should be awake this evening."

"I'll take you home," said Tom. "We can come back tonight."

She looked at him closely. "You need to be in bed, too. Then helping your brother, not waiting on me."

"How about your leg?"

"I'm taking it to my apartment."

Tom looked at the man behind the wheelchair.

"Herbert's driving me," she added.

The old man showed a pair of gleaming dentures and passed an index finger alongside his nose.

"Okay," said Tom. "Looks like you're in good hands."

She pressed her lips and stifled a retort.

"I was going to stop and see Father Gauss this evening," said Tom. "If you want, I can come by the Center and pick you up after that?"

"Well, there's some news there, too."

"What?"

"Father Gauss has left. Mrs. Lynch says that he wasn't at Novena last night, and that when she called the rectory to find out why, the housekeeper said he'd been transferred."

"To where?"

Mary shrugged. "She didn't say. And then that Pearce girl phoned again. If you don't mind my saying so, that girl is the 'r' in relentless."

"Was she looking for me?"

Mary frowned. "For your brother."

CHAPTER 17

Tom collected the Coldwater patrol car from the parking lot in front of Trudy's Diner, where the Cashin kid and his sidekick had surprisingly left it undamaged. *Punks must be scared of you, brother.* He drove toward town, feeling the breeze through the open windows dry the stale film of sweat on his arms and face and ripple the front of the pungent shirt he'd had on since yesterday morning.

The last and only time Tom had driven the Coldwater Sheriff's patrol car, was the summer he got his driver's license, when Mary had twice sent him to collect her husband passed out behind the wheel across the street from a house where he had no business being. Tom had no idea what was going on in his parents' lives that summer, though it was obvious in hindsight that something had been. The vicissitudes of his own rocky romance pulled his attention elsewhere. Then as now.

Memories clamored for daylight, but he forced the shutters tight. The distraction of ancient mysteries was just that. He had to get back to New York soon and rescue his career, or give it up. Pissed was fast replacing confused, and worry was gaining on them both.

Sayed's file on Joe's prior hospital visits was as fat as a phone book. The doctor had made light of the broken fingers, facial lacerations and other occupational hazards of small town law enforcement. He had even dismissed two prior herbicidal poisonings that he and Joe had concluded were due to ripping up treated marijuana plants. But this was different, beginning with the severity of the symptoms. Tom had asked the doctor point-blank if his brother could end up with some kind of permanent impairment.

"He could die," said Sayed bluntly. "A weaker man might have already."

Tom didn't believe that Joe was going to die. Though admittedly, that was a non-expert opinion. But he also knew that short of death, Joe would have to function in at least some limited capacity soon, or all hell was going to break loose. Shit happens fast when the teacher is out sick and the class learns the substitute is clueless.

Tom parked the patrol car in front of Our Lady of The Lake rectory and sat for a while watching a soft northwest breeze ripple the blue black water across the street. Father Gauss had made it clear he wasn't going to violate a confidence—even if it might help lead to Billy's killer. But other than finding Gauss and having another go, what was there to do until Joe was coherent enough to direct next steps? Tackle Frankie Heller and his stock car alibi? Mike Sharp and his phony Yankee game?

Tom left the car and walked to the rectory, whose three stories of weathered clapboards were unlikely to see fresh paint any time soon. The single pane windows were as old as the structure itself, swollen shut in the summer heat and rattling and porous in winter when the winds from the north swept across the frozen lake. The paint-crusted button beside the door made a tinny hum when he pressed it. No one answered. He thumbed the bell again, tried the door handle and then pressed the unlocked door until it swung open.

"Mrs. Flynn! It's Tom Morgan."

A pear shaped figure, topped with braided white hair and scowl answered from the second floor landing. "Yes?"

"May I come in?"

"You're already in." said the housekeeper. "He's not here; he's gone away"

"Do you know where?"

"No," she said, firmly. "But wait here; he left something for you." She disappeared up the stairs and returned a few minutes later carrying a fat leather bound book, stamped along the spine in faded gold lettering with a single word: *Ethics,*. "He said you'd be around sooner or later, and to give it to you. At least I think he meant this one. He's got a lot of books up there."

"He didn't take his books?"

"Only what fit in that old travel bag of his."

Father Gauss had once remarked on the church's abrupt and sometimes arbitrary personnel assignments. But this sudden disappearance felt more like a rent skip than a transfer.

Tom carried the book to the patrol car and propped it open on the steering wheel. A folded letter fell from its pages onto his lap.

Dear Tom,

I don't know if you've read Spinoza's Ethics. If not, it's time you made the author's acquaintance.

Despite what you may have been taught across the street, most modern thinkers don't consider science, philosophy and theology to be fundamentally opposed. Plato claimed that man is a puppet pulled on strings by the gods, but that he has one string of his own that he can pull back on: Reason.

The ancient Greeks didn't have what we would call a theology. But their philosophers understood that some things are not susceptible to knowledge through reason and that it was essential to understand the difference.

It seems to me that you've started down a very old path. Some who have gone before you have left useful markers for others to follow. The author of this book is one of the better ones.

By all means test your theology – if your education has left you any – with science and the other arts. If a theology can't stand up to the scrutiny, chuck it. Though I encourage you to remain open to what science and logic cannot explain and to allow for the difference.

I wonder if we in the church do a disservice to our young by feeding them a watered-down theology in the form of Catechism and then ignoring the polishing stone of reason. Man has puzzled over the same basic questions for thousands of years: Who are we? Why are we here? What are we supposed to do while we're here and what, if anything is next? If you're not careful, you can disappear into your own navel trying to answer such questions. But if you're inclined by nature to ask, as you seem to be, then it's helpful to know the location of the stones in the path that others have tripped on before you.

Give me a call if you want to chat. I can be reached at the number on the back.

Kind Regards,

Father Gauss'

Tom flipped through the pages of the well-thumbed volume, noting the penciled underlinings and marginalia. The letter didn't sound like a man in serious trouble had written it. But it did sound very much like all of the serious communications Tom had had from Fr. Gauss over the years: kindly, but pointed—with an undertone of challenge. Prepared to be patient if the challenge were not immediately taken up.

He put the book and letter in the glove compartment, and drove back to Joe's cabin. "Okay," he muttered to himself. "But not now."

* * *

Bonnie handed Tom the phone as soon as he walked in the door. She looked as worn out as her husband.

"Tom? This is Moe Silverstein. Tanner gave me this number and filled me in on your little problem."

"Glad to hear you call it little."

"Poor choice of words. Look, when can you get back to New York?"

Tom glanced at Bonnie. "I'm kind of up to my ass in alligators right now, Moe." He explained briefly about Joe being in the hospital and Mary with a broken leg.

"You can't catch a break, can you?" Moe sympathized. "Well I hate to add to your troubles, but there's going to be a line in tomorrow's New York Post, Page Six gossip column about a rising star at a certain white shoe Manhattan law firm who's got himself tangled in a nasty government procurement scandal. No names. But that's how our DA works: soften the ground with strategic leaks to friendly columnists so there'll be good coverage when the indictments come down."

"What do you need me to do?"

"I need you to get back here so we can get to work. You've got to find everyone who was with you on that Egyptian project and get them to give affidavits that you weren't counsel to that Eurocon subsidiary. Then you need to do an interview with a reporter I've got lined up who's agreed to do a piece about your charitable fundraising. Basically, you need to get back here and get in the fight."

Tom hesitated. "Can you give me a few days, Moe?"

"It's your ass, Tom. But they're already chewing on it."

"I'll get back to you."

Tom looked at Bonnie. She looked beaten. "Do you have to go?" she whispered.

"I'll put if off as long as I can."

* * *

Joe lay on his back with an IV dripping into his arm and a thin, damp sheet stuck to his chest. A wallet and cell phone held down a pile of papers on the table next to the hospital bed. Someone had removed the line from the hospital phone and plugged it into the back of a lap-top computer. "You look like ten miles of hard road, brother."

Joe pried open an eyelid, "Crank me up."

Tom moved a night table that held a stack of files, and pressed a button on the side of the bed. "You moving your office in here too?"

Joe slid his torso upright. "I asked Bonnie to grab the stuff on my desk. I can't keep my eyes open to read it, though."

Tom pulled a plastic chair up next to the bed. "Do they know what you've got yet?"

"If they do, they're not telling me."

"Your pal, Dr. Sayed, asked me where you'd been over the last forty-eight hours. I told him what I knew, but it didn't seem to mean anything to him."

"They'll figure it out."

"He says you might have been exposed to some kind of 'toxin.' And Mom

124

threw in something about the Hellers and homemade weed killer, and you being in here last month with basically the same thing."

"Shit." It was a sigh, not a curse.

"I didn't tell her about you pulling more crops a few days ago. But I did tell Sayed."

"What?"

"That you were out in the woods pulling up marijuana plants the day before I got here. You told me on the way in from the airport, remember? Before we found Billy."

"Oh."

"And the doctor said that one of those cuts isn't healing."

"Tommy..."

"What?"

"I'm not processing too well right now."

Tom put his hand on Joe's sheeted thigh. "Sorry. Maybe I should come back later. Go back to sleep."

Joe took a breath, started to nod and then fumbled for the button at the side of the bed. "I need help."

Tom reached for the side of the bed. "Up or down?"

"No. Shit. Leave it." Joe waived at the laptop and stack of files. "I mean help with this."

"Your mail?"

"Finding Billy's killer."

Tom didn't respond—with enthusiasm or anything else.

"I can't do it alone, Tommy. Not now, lying here puking my guts out. I can't even keep my eyes open."

Tom folded his arms and spoke to the uncurtained window that framed the distant view of Coldwater lake. "I have to get back to New York, Joe." He explained about the Eurocon mess and the phone call from the white collar criminal lawyer telling him to get his ass back to Dodge.

Joe's voice was a hoarse whisper. "Does this mean you might end up living like a normal person?"

"Only if I can keep my ass out of jail."

"Are they serious?"

"They're acting like it. In the meantime, you're laying here worthless and whoever killed Billy is out covering his tracks. I need to get back to New York and you need to hand this over to the state troopers before whoever killed Billy gets too big a lead."

Joe lifted his head and wheezed, "Can't."

"Why not?"

"Oh for God's sake, Tommy. I let a pack of strange dogs in here and they'll go sniffing down every trail they find—not just the ones that might lead to Billy's killer."

"They'll sort it out."

"Don't be a Boy Scout."

"What are you worried about, brother?"

Joe pressed his forearms into the bed. "I thought maybe you and I could do this together, now that the gods have cut you loose."

"I have to get back, Joe. The state troopers will be here sooner or later, regardless of what you want. As soon as they find out that Coldwater's only cop has been lying in a hospital bed for two days with a murderer running loose, they'll swarm you. Snarling and pissing on the high bushes wont' scare them off, either. Not with you lying there in just a paper nightgown."

Joe glared. "Then we have to act fast, don't we?" He waved a hand at the stack of papers, as if the matter were decided. "There should be an address in one of those files for the lab in Montreal that Sharp mentioned. I want you to drive up there, find this Dr. Hassad and find out if there's a connection between him and Billy."

Tom riffled the stack of papers. Halfway down were copies of the letters he had seen in the boathouse, and beneath those, an autopsy report. He started to read it.

"Hey! Not that one! Put it down."

Tom dropped the folder onto the bed. "You want to do this alone?"

Joe looked like he was about to say something rude, but thought better of it. "I want you to be objective when you talk to this Hassad character, keep your ears open and stick to the script. The more you know the harder that will be." Joe sank into the pillows. "I need your help, Tommy. Hell, I can't do anything without it now. But letting you do this without direction makes about as much sense as you letting me do the same on one of your gazillion dollar business deals."

"You just sounded a bit too much like the old man for a second. That was never my favorite tone."

Joe lowered his chin. "Point taken. Look, if you're feeling ambitious, remember the three lovelies who were sitting at the back of the church at Billy's funeral?"

"Hard to forget them."

"They drove down from Montreal in a rented car. There's a copy of a driver's license they used to rent it at the bottom of that stack and a business card with the same name as the license. How's your French? Other than *je t'aime.*'"

Tom suppressed a salacious image of French co-counsel. "Making us work summers in Québec was one of the old man's better ideas."

"If you get a chance, you might also stop by and see if Billy's friends along the rue La Fontaine have any idea who might have been angry enough to want to stuff him in a sleeping bag and dump him in the lake."

"La Fontaine?"

"Just south of *l'Université de Quebec* near that place where you waited tables that summer. *Le Village.* Can't miss it. Biggest gay neighborhood in North America."

"You're full of surprises, brother."

Joe gestured toward the door as his head slumped into the pillow. "Watch their eyes."

CHAPTER 18

Though Tom regularly enjoyed the hospitality of the world's financial capitols, the city where he had spent the young-man-loose-in-the-city-summers of his late teens and early twenties was the place that still made his heart weightless. Youthful memories of summertime Montreal were his emotional touchstones: waiting tables in le Quartier Latin, sweating buckets in a third floor walk-up off the *l'boulevard St-Laurent,* and practicing French with a friendly mademoiselle when the opportunity arose. The corporate mega-deals and dollars that followed came a distant second.

Map Quest located the address Joe had provided somewhere in the rat's nest of side streets off *l'boulevard St-Laurent*—the main route north from the harbor and the de facto dividing line between Anglophone and Francophone Montreal. Tom tucked the rental car behind a construction dumpster, stuffed Joe's scribbled address in his jacket pocket and began to walk a pattern of expanding polygons from the last cross-street on the Map Quest directions.

Two long loops through a handful of neighborhoods killed a quick thirty minutes. One brought him to the environs of *l'Université du Québec à Montréal.* The other pushed into a neighborhood of head scarves, beards and covered limbs, as if the plunging temperatures soon to come had arrived there early. Signs in Roman script were at a premium. Friendly faces did not exist.

A few unmarked streets south of *l'rue Coloniale,* he stopped at a table piled with dried fruits and nuts, and shaded by a green and white awning that might have been new when Pierre Trudeau last campaigned through the neighborhood. The number above the door behind the table, and the name carved in stone forty feet above the street, matched the address Joe had given him.

Light behind the door seemed to promise that the shop was open for business; though there was no activity inside. Patrons wandered in and out of a coin laundry next door. A lone customer waited outside the Curry-in-A-Hurry shop on the corner. Tom picked up something that looked like a dried apple and looked around for a scoop or a produce bag. But no one came out of the shop to close the sale. He put the fruit back and tried the door.

He'd once been a frequent patron of Le Main's neighborhood shops and eateries, ripe with exotic smells, vibrant with primary colors, jammed with boxes covered with unfamiliar writing and wallpapered with posters and calendars of dark pretty faces in modest attire. But nothing like that met him here. A few dusty boxes covered with squiggly writing lined the painted wooden shelves, and the simpering face on the Bollywood calendar behind the counter had been there for months.

"Allez! Ferme!" The shout came from a doorway that lead to a lower level. The shouter wore a salt and pepper beard and mouth full of crooked teeth. Behind him came another man waving a short piece of pointed metal. Both wore flip flops and stained off-white garments which covered them from neck to ankle. Tom focused on the one waving the piece of pointed metal. That it had an electric cord dangling from the handle didn't make it less threatening.

"Nous sommes ferme!"

"Hello to you too," said Tom, his voice deliberately calm and nonthreatening. "I'm looking for Dr. Hassad."

"Closed," said the other, switching to a thick, guttural English.

Tom shrugged. "He gave this as his address. Also something called U-Labs.

I have a message for him."

The shopkeeper's thick, dark eyebrows compressed into one. For several seconds his flat brown eyes held Tom's. *"Nous sommes ferme,"* he repeated.

Joe might have dragged the pajama-boys into the back room and taught them some manners. But Tom had already achieved what he came for--the address, the layout and a couple of warm bodies to go with it. What more was he going to get by getting into the *mine is bigger than yours* confrontation?

Taking a card from his wallet, he scribbled his cell phone number on the back and held it toward the one whose hands were free. "Dr. Hassad is going to want this."

The two men looked at the card, but neither moved to take it.

"Suit yourself." Tom laid the card on the counter with the NEUROGENE logo and the name of the company's owner, Dave Willow, face up. Then he backed slowly out of the store.

* * *

Once outside, Tom paused to get his bearings before heading back toward the street of patisseries and internet cafés he'd passed earlier. As he got closer to *l'Village*, the scenery began to change from scarves to halter tops and his mood lightened with the couture. At an internet café near the Berri-UQAM metro, he passed a half-hour sipping latte and Googling variations on the names Hassad and U-Labs. The computer spat out the same address that Joe had found, plus a short list of other Hasads and Hassads with Montreal addresses. The one at *L'Université de Québec a Montréal* seemed a logical place to start.

Tom knew that UQAM did not have a central campus in the Anglo/American model. Like the urban universities of Europe, its buildings cluster in connected neighborhoods, with maps mounted outside the principle buildings to guide disoriented visitors and new matriculates. He stuffed the Hassad addresses in his pocket and went in search of an outdoor map that would show him where to find *L'Académie Biochimique*.

Joe's instruction was simple: find out if there's a connection between Dr.

Hassad and Billy Pearce. But Tom wondered about Joe's assumption that his lawyer brother could conduct a meaningful investigation. Tom knew how to examine a witnesses under oath, prepared and represented by competent counsel. That was a bloodless chess game where the moves are known in advance and the outcome is a matter of who uses them more skillfully under pressure. But the cop game could be the antithesis of bloodless, which Tom well knew from having grown up around it. Sometimes preparation wasn't possible and trouble could come from any quarter. The minor standoff in the grocery store was a reminder of the difference between a corporate game and a genuine blood sport. The skills needed to excel in one might overlap the other, but they were not identical. Then, as if in response to these directionless musings, came the memory of one of MadDog's early hunting pointers. *You don't sneak up on rabbits, Tommy. You stomp on the brush pile until they run.*

L'Académie Biochimique turned out to be a four story, white brick office building on the south side of *boulevard de Maisonneuve* about five blocks from the St-Laurent metro. Tom positioned himself across the street and observed several groups of students enter the building past a lone security guard sitting behind a desk with his head buried in a newspaper. When the guard didn't look up, even to observe a trio of UQAM hotties, Tom crossed the street and entered the building, feeling like the proverbial dog who had chased a car and caught it. Now what?

He gave the third floor receptionist's one of Willow's business cards and announced that he had a package for hand delivery to U-Labs. She picked up the phone and punched a few buttons. *"Il-y-a quelqu'un ici a vous voir professer."* She read from the card. *"Monsieur Willow de NUROGENE."*

She looked Tom up and down. *"2 mètre. 85 kilo. Cheveux brun."*

"Black," Tom muttered to himself.

She gestured toward a corner office at the end of the hall where an unsmiling man stood behind a desk just inside in the doorway. Hassad stood about six feet tall, hollow cheeked with jet-black hair combed back from a high forehead, and was wearing a pressed, charcoal gray suit and Hermes tie that looked absurdly out of place in a cramped academic office.

He did not hold out his hand for a package and did not ask Tom to sit. *"Qui est vous?"* he demanded.

"My apologies for the subterfuge," said Tom. "I'm here in connection with a police matter in the United States."

Hassad switched to a crisp British-accented English. "Do you have any identification?"

"None that would mean anything to you."

Hassad lifted the receiver from the desk phone and murmured into it.

"You're going to want to talk to me, Professor."

Hassad held the phone to his ear and waited for the campus operator to retrieve the phone number for university security. "You Americans are a global pestilence."

"Suit yourself. But you've obviously taken care to obscure the connection between you and the names that got me in here. Make that phone call and that obscurity is history."

Hassad tucked the receiver against his shoulder and scribbled some digits on a pad. *"Merci."* He replaced the phone, but remained standing. "And what is this police matter?"

"A homicide investigation."

"And why do you think I might be helpful?" The voice was snotty, but wary.

"It's a long-shot. But it starts with your telling me what U-Labs has been sending to a company called NeuroGene."

Tom watched the professor's face, but it gave nothing away.

"And how would that be helpful in a homicide investigation?"

"Truthfully? I don't know. It depends on what you have to say."

Hassad moved his head slowly from side to side. "I can't help you, Mr. ? Your real name, please."

"Morgan."

Hassad's head lifted slightly, as if an invisible hand were tugging upward on his left ear. "I hold a position of confidence in the academic community, Mr. Morgan. What you are asking is unlikely to be of any use to you. But to answer such a question would betray confidences and jeopardize valuable

132

scientific research. I must decline."

Tom ignored the little speech and handed Dr. Hassad a blown-up copy of the photo from Billy Pearce's driving license. "Do you recognize the man in this picture?"

Hassad studied the photo for a few seconds and then handed it back. "No."

"And if I told you that the owner of NeuroGene Research identified this man as having brought materials from U-Labs for repackaging and distribution in the U.S.?"

"I still do not recognize him. Nor would I recognize the man who delivers my post here at the university."

"Do you know a Dave Willow?"

"Yes."

"And a Mike Sharp?"

"Also yes."

"In what capacity do you know them?"

"As the owners of that company you mentioned."

"Do you deal with them both, or only one?"

"Both," said Hassad.

"And what do you send them?"

"As I told you, these are not matters I can discuss."

"Why not? Aren't you U-Labs?"

Hassad shook the paper on which he had written the number of the campus security, as if the ink was still wet and he wanted to accelerate the drying. "Mr. Morgan, many members of the scientific community conduct research under conditions that you might find hard to imagine: government censorship, military and religious interference, commercial and academic espionage. They are not free to simply pick up the phone or use the mail to exchange ideas with other scientists in their fields. Even in the West, which prides itself on the open exchange of ideas, there are many obstacles to free communication. Not a few of them tied to so-called government 'support.' I could go on, but presumably you see the point. Like any oppressed group, the scientific community has its own, informal ways of obtaining uncensored information and basic resources."

Tom waited until the canned speech was finished, then asked, "So where were these basic resources that you funneled through NeuroGene supposed to end up?"

Hassad sighed, "This isn't going anywhere. If you've spoken to the NeuroGene owners, then you understand the confidential nature of our relationship. Specific scientific information can't possibly be relevant to your investigation. Assuming you could understand it any more than the man in that photo. Or are you going to tell me he was a scientist, too?"

Tom made a mental note of the tense before responding. "I did speak with the owners. And I put to them the same questions I'm putting to you. It's not necessary that I fully understand their response or yours. I just need to hear it."

"That makes no sense."

"Sure it does, Professor. Put it this way, if Sharp and Willow say that you and NeuroGene have been doing confidential research on a new brand of Canadian chutney, and you can corroborate that story, then I can go home. I don't need the formula for the secret sauce."

"And what if I can't, or won't?"

"Then one of you is lying."

Hassad took a step toward the tall, narrow window that overlooked *l' boulevard de Maisonneuve* and remained there for some minutes, arms folded in thought. Sounds of passing voices and chimes from one of Montreal's many neighborhood churches filtered through the airless room. "It troubles me," he said still staring out the window, "that the NeuroGene principals have violated the confidences they promised to protect. What they have done may already have caused significant harm. I wonder if they realize that."

"A man is dead," said Tom.

"I understand that," Hassad snapped. "But you need to understand something, also. The purpose of biotechnology is to save, or at least improve, human life. Unfortunately, much of that work and the people who do it are constantly exposed to hazards you can't possibly appreciate. Hazards that sometimes bring it and them to an abrupt end."

"Like what?"

"Such as theft by greedy multinationals and their governments. Sabotage by your CIA, if the subject falls within what they consider their rightful scope of interest—which is frankly enormous. Blackmail, extortion, even murder when powerful influences feel themselves threatened."

"You're being dramatic, Professor."

"And you, Mr. Morgan, are being naïve."

"Are you saying that you're working on something that will really piss people off?"

"I'm saying that biotechnology itself pisses some people off, as you so vulgarly put it. That it excites all of the emotions that can lead to dangerous excess: fear, envy... avarice. And that I am not willing to betray the confidence that others have placed in me and expose them to those dangers simply because some door-crasher asks me to."

"Is there a particular someone you're afraid of?"

"How can you Americans be so ignorant?" Hassad slapped a pile of papers balanced on the corner of his desk. "Not two years ago, in the basement of this very building an eminent scientist and countryman of mine was assassinated. Afterwards, not only were his research materials and notebooks missing, but also one of his graduate assistants. A female Israeli! Now who do you think was behind that, Mr. Morgan?"

Tom was tempted to suggest the scientist's wife, but checked himself.

"Mossad!" the professor hissed. "No doubt with the connivance of your government."

"Your pal must have been working on something pretty exciting," said Tom.

"We'll never know." Hassad stepped from behind his desk, allowing his palm to trail over a small paper parcel that had been partly covered by a stack of files on the edge of the desk. Tom noted the row of brightly colored stamps as the package disappeared into the pocket of the professor's jacket.

"And now comes some provincial American policeman who blithely demands that I betray the identities and research of similarly vulnerable colleagues. No doubt he'll threaten me if I don't comply. No thank you, Mr.

Morgan. I will not."

Tom's reply was precise and his voice modulated. "And if there's a connection between your dead colleague and the man whose photo I just showed you?"

Hassad dismissed the suggestion with an impatient wave of his hand. "You're fishing." He moved toward the door. "Now if you will excuse me, Mr. Morgan, I must prepare a lecture." It was a dismissal.

"One last question, then. Humor me."

Hassad sighed. "If I must."

"When were you last in the United States?"

Hassad hesitated. His answer, when it came, was a curt and peevish, "This morning."

"For what purpose?"

"A personal matter."

Tom counted silently to ten, then twenty.

"To see my dentist," Hassad spat.

CHAPTER 19

om grabbed a handful of departmental brochures on his way out of the building, and then strolled over to *l'Parc Lafontaine* hoping to bring order to the jumbled impressions of the morning: an address for a company named Ulabs that turned out to be grocery store with no customers; its owner, a university professor named Hassad, who did nothing when a surprise visitor claiming to be the NeuroGene owner turned out to be an impostor, and who claimed not to recognize Billy Pearce's photo, but appeared to know that the man in it was dead.

The normal response of a healthy mind, Tom knew, is to provide an answer to a direct question. It may be a lie, or even nonsense, but a clear direct question will almost always prompt an answer. He had resuscitated many a dying deposition by repeatedly triggering that mental reflex, when someone less persistent would have dropped a handful of dirt and called it a day.

Who is Hassad?

Someone who knew Billy Pearce, but doesn't want to admit it. Who sends stuff to a tiny Coldwater biotechnology company, but doesn't want to say what. Who spent enough time in England to pick up an accent, but at an age too advanced to get it pitch-perfect.

What about the package he palmed?

Incoming, not outgoing. Those weren't Canadian stamps.

And what about Father Gauss' not so subtle hint: *"It may be that I know quite a bit about Billy Pearce that our Sheriff doesn't. But there's little I can tell... ?"* Gauss wasn't going to violate a confidence. But if he had information that could help solve a murder, didn't another ethical obligation came into play?

Questions continued to pop into Tom's head almost at random. *What could Billy have been carrying that might have got him killed? How can anyone characterize a Wall Street deal maker as low energy? What happens to my high-powered career if I don't get back to New York soon to save it?*

Lost in thought, Tom almost missed the familiar profile moving fast along the sidewalk beside the park. Throwing bills at a push cart vendor selling college logo-ed sportswear, Tom grabbed a UQAM cap and broke into a jog to catch up. If Hassad looked around, maybe his tail would appear as just another fish in the school, so to speak.

Striding briskly through the spider web of streets and alleys east of the park, the quarry never paused or looked back. Minutes of twists and turns later, he entered the same grocery store that Tom had visited earlier. Sounds of a whacking great argument poured from the store. Then the disputants came onto the street, with the grocer who claimed not to know a Professor Hassad screaming loud and long at him before abruptly breaking off and dashing down an alley. Hassad took off in the opposite direction. Tom followed.

South across *l'rue Rêne-Levesque* and down a series of unmarked streets that ancient memory told Tom were near the outskirts of Chinatown. Turns and more turns, then a brief glimpse of Hassad disappearing into a storefront mosque. Tom sensed that he was back in the neighborhood of the grocery store, but he couldn't be sure. *Rabbits run in circles, Tommy, when they sense the hunter.* The idlers outside the mosque stared at the man wearing a student's sports cap. One of them glared and then disappeared inside. Tom stuffed the cap in his pocket, but the idlers continued to stare. He backed away and looked for a street sign that would identify the location of the rabbit hole. Joe would want to know.

* * *

The rental car remained unbooted where Tom had left it. The philosophy tome on the front seat was undisturbed as well, though Tom had forgotten to lock the passenger side door. Father Gauss' parting gift might fall into the category of 'read later when you feel like it', and have nothing to do with the current dramas of their respective lives. But instinct and experience told Tom that was unlikely. He took the priest's letter from the book and reread it, thinking it might help. It didn't. But then he noticed the digits scrawled on the back. He reached into his pocket for the paper with the numbers he'd copied in the internet café earlier that morning. The seven digit sequences all began with the same three-digits.

Father Gauss was in Montreal.

Tom switched on his cell phone for the first time in days and dialed the number scribbled on the back of Gauss' letter. A woman answered.

"*Couvent de San Gabriel.*"

"*Père Gauss, s'il vous plait,*" he said.

"*Attendez.*"

There was a click on the line, a long wait, and then a familiar voice on an answering machine. "Hi. Leave a message."

"Hi Father. It's Tom Morgan. What are you doing in a convent? I'm in Montreal this afternoon. If you can get to LaFontaine Park, I'll be sitting there for the next few hours, under a tree with my nose in Spinoza. If you can't make it, call my cell."

* * *

For the next few hours, Tom sat with Spinoza and waited for Father Gauss to call or Dr. Hassad to pass the park again. The afternoon waned. As the air began to chill, Tom remembered the other mission that Joe had given him, "if he was feeling ambitious:" to look up the fellow who had dropped his business card at Billy's funeral.

The address on the card that Joe had stapled to a copy of a Montreal drivers license, was on the south side of *l'Village*, along the *rue Sherbrooke*, past *l'Musée Juste Pour Rire*. Tom circled the block before parking in front of a garish storefront where he felt even more conspicuous than he had in the neighborhood surrounding Dr. Hassad's mosque. The sign in pink bubble script read *Furry Paws*, and beneath it, in scarlet and black another announced *Going Out Of Business*. The O's were embellished with eyelashes and teardrops.

A disturbingly life-like mannequin posed in the storefront window, majestic in thigh-high, pink plastic boots and matching bumper-sticker sized shorts. A thin metal chain spanned her open vest, attached to anatomical piercings that made Tom wince. He stared mesmerized and slightly queasy.

"Interested in body jewelry?" A youth in day-glow spiked hair and black everything else stepped out of the store and greeted him.

"Is there another kind?"

The boy willed the touché grin of an experienced salesman. "Everything you see is 50% off." Tom cut the chit chat short, and handed the salesman a photocopy of a Montreal driver's license. "Is he in today?"

The salesman's deference morphed into a smirk. "Gérard! There is a tax man here to see you!" He shouted through the open door and twirled to enter. Street lamps hummed to life.

The interior set up of *Furry Paws* was similar to that of any other variety store of Tom's experience: wide rows of brightly packaged merchandise, eye-catching displays of this week's promotional items and security cameras strategically placed to intimidate the larcenous. Only the merchandise itself was uncomfortably unfamiliar: leather this, battery operated that, pointed metal devices whose intended effect he did not wish to contemplate—and all of it celebrated, illustrated and discounted in both English and French. The young man behind the counter gave him an elevator look and asked, "May I accommodate you?"

"I'd like to chat with you about Billy Pearce. If you've got a minute."

"Who?" He pronounced it "oo" in a sharp Quebecois accent.

Tom slid the *Furry Paws* business card across the counter. "Somebody dropped this at his funeral."

"Monsieur Bonnefesse does not work here anymore. The recession, you know."

Tom passed the photocopied driver's license across the counter. "Same name on this license as on that card," he noted. "Both with your picture, Monsieur Bonnefesse."

The counterman shrugged. "What do you wish?"

"Like I said, to chat with you about Billy Pearce."

"Yes?"

"He was murdered. I was hoping his friends might have some thoughts on who might have done it."

"And you are who?"

"A friend of the family."

"Not a policeman?"

"Just a friend."

The top of the young man's head barely reached Tom's collar-bone. He found himself looking down onto close cropped, multi-colored hair, plucked eyebrows and doe-y brown eyes, and tried not to stare. It was not until the boy turned his head, as if in thought, that Tom noted the faint wrinkles and patches of parchment skin that suggested he was older than he first appeared.

"Do you like the Starbuck?"

"I'm addicted."

"Come." The boy/man led Tom down a narrow street, coming alive now that darkness had fallen. The establishments that lined it—places with names like *Freak Haus* and *Piercing Palace*—gave Tom the feeling that he had stepped onto the set of a sailors-on-leave-and-looking-for-a good-time movie. He did not realize that he'd been squeezing his breath, until Bonnefesse pointed to the Starbucks sign at the end of the street and he heard himself exhale.

Inside and seated in a corner away from the windows, Tom started to introduce himself. But Bonnefesse interrupted. "I saw you with that handsome policeman at the funeral. You look like him, but not so big. You are the sister's old boyfriend, no?"

"That's right."

"Billy hated your stomach."

"I'm told he hated everybody."

"True. He was not fond of the sister, also."

"Still, she'd like to know who killed him… and why."

"Yes? I did not think that she cared so much for Billy. Only for his house."

"Did he say that?"

"Billy was a talker, you know? For a long time he spoke only about his big house and how his sister wanted to steal it from him. It becomes boring."

"Did you believe him?"

"It makes no difference."

"Then what about who might have killed him? Or why? Any thoughts?"

Bonnefesse snorted. "If I knew that, I would tell your police."

"Or who wasn't his friend? Who had Billy pissed-off so badly that they might have wanted to kill him?"

Bonnefesse sighed. "Many people."

Tom felt himself floundering. *Joe was right. He's the pro, he should be doing this. I'm just butchering it. This guy brought me here to say something, but he's not going to say it unless I ask the right question or give the secret handshake or whatever it is he's waiting for that I'm not doing.*

He tried again. "Did Billy ever mention a priest by the name of Gauss?"

"Often. He was trying to make trouble for him, I think."

"How?"

"Oh, saying that the priest did things. That sort of thing."

"Was he telling the truth?"

"I have no idea. Billy could be such a liar."

"Did he ever mention a Frankie Heller?"

Bonnefesse hesitated and then shrugged. "The name means nothing."

"Mike Sharp?"

Bonnefesse shook his head.

"Dave Willow?"

"The sister's *patron*? Yes. They had something together, I think. A long time ago."

142

Tom felt his spine straighten.

"Billy tried to make trouble for him too," Bonnefesse added.

"How?"

"Not trouble, I think. Pranks. Phone calls. Billy could get very excited."

"Did he ever mention a Dr. Hassad or a U-Labs?"

Bonnefesse hesitated. Tom watched his eyes move up and to the right. "I don't think so."

"Did he hang out with ... for want of a better word, foreigners?"

"Quebecois?"

"People from parts of the world where Americans are unpopular."

"That is everywhere, no?" Bonnefesse shook his head sadly, his voice almost weary. "Billy told me once of a friend he had when he was a boy. A foreigner, as you say. The friend was older than Billy, and really just after the sister. When Billy understood he was just *le barbe*, he was very hurt. 'The beard', is that English?"

"Sort of."

"Billy distrusted dark people after that. It limited his social life, I told him frankly."

Tom took a deep breath. He felt like he was thumbing a skinny phone book with no idea what to do once he got past the Z's. "How about Joe Morgan?"

"Ba, ba, ba, boom!" Bonnefesse did a drum roll on the top of the wooden table. Tom held onto his latte. "Le Super Trooper!!"

"Right. Did Billy try to make trouble for him, too?"

"Never! Billy thought he was very handsome."

Tom lifted the paper cup to his lips. The liquid was cold. In the absence of an inspiring alternative, he decided to opt for candor. "You're going to have to help me here, Gérard. I don't know if you know anything useful. But is this name dropping giving you any ideas?"

Bonnefesse spread his hands.

"Let me ask you this, then. If I said there was a reason why you brought me here... why you simply didn't tell me you knew nothing and end our conversation there in your shop. What would you say?"

"That I thought you might be interesting?"

"A reason related to Billy. I'm guessing here. But I'm asking you to guess, too. What do you know about Billy, that you really want to tell somebody? That you think somebody should know. Tell me."

Bonnefesse looked away and then nodded. "He was happy."

"Happy?"

"Yes. In the last few months Billy was very happy. I had never seen him such. Almost as if he were in love."

"Go on."

"I was jealous."

"Did you ask him about it?"

"Of course!"

"And what did he say?"

"Lies, I think."

"What did he say, exactly?"

"He said that he was going to make a lot of money, soon. And that he was going to make everyone who was ever hurtful to him suffer badly."

"When did he say this?"

"A month passing."

"Did he give details?"

"No. But he was truly excited. I was happy for him. I thought maybe he had made peace with the sister."

"That might have gotten him money. But what about the revenge part?"

"Just talk, I think. Or maybe he was going to make sport with the priest again."

"Father Gauss?"

"Yes, I think. Billy called him the Father Gas. He said he had pictures, but I didn't believe him. He would have showed them to me."

"So you think this was about Billy and his sister? Or maybe Father Gauss?"

"No. Now that I tell you this, I can see it was something else. But I don't know what."

Tom could feel his focus begin to fragment as it did lately whenever the subject turned however obliquely to Susan.

"You are thinking of something?" asked Bonnefesse.

"About happiness. It's a recurring theme lately."

"I don't think now that Billy found it. Excitement yes. But the happiness is not so loud."

"What do you mean?"

Bonnefesse bubbled his cheeks and raised his brows in a Gallic mime. "Happiness is quiet, you know? Friends. A little shop that fills a need. Enough money, but not too much."

Tom made a mental note to add the sex shop owner's idea of happiness to his thickening recipe book. "Maybe if I can find what Billy was so excited about, it might lead to his killer."

Bonnefesse's expression was distant, but his voice was serious. "Be careful, Monsieur. Whoever killed Billy is a vicious person. No one should die like that. Not even a little prick like Billy."

* * *

It was time to head home. Tom retrieved the rental car, suppressing an impulse to thank the window mannequin for guarding it so vigilantly, and began to weave through streets sclerotic with Friday night traffic. Near the *Champs-de-Mars* he pulled next to a fire hydrant and tried Gauss' number again.

"Couvent de San Gabriel."

"Père Gauss, s'il vous plaît."

"Attendez."

There was a click on the line, a long wait, and then a voice in English demanded briskly, "May I help you?"

"Hi. This is Tom Morgan. Father Gauss asked me to call."

Silence.

"Hello?"

More silence. Then, "How do you have this number?"

"Father Gauss gave it to me."

More silence. He had the impression that he was listening to a hand palming the mouth of the receiver. Then, "I don't understand how that could be."

"The machine in the room I was switched to earlier today has Father Gauss' voice on it. The body that goes with it should be there somewhere."

More silence. Then a dial tone.

CHAPTER 20

C *ouvent de San Gabriel*—Betty Ford North to those in the Chancery who had occasion to call upon its services—had a reputation for austerity and discretion. But the order of nuns that ran it sometimes neglected to follow Chancery guidance on the treatment of cases sent there. Monsignor Marchetti had been dispatched to make clear what was required in the matter of Father Gauss.

Marchetti felt cold in the spare, under-heated space that was the facility's administrative office. Sixty was still a few years away, but days and places like this seemed to age both body and soul. Sœur Dion might have been as young as forty or half as old again. Marchetti couldn't tell. The nuns of San Gabriel clung to the traditional black habit, making estimates of age, and sometimes gender, difficult. He tried not to overestimate her level of experience with men like Gauss.

"He's like an old union boss," Marchetti explained, "or a tenured teacher who can't easily be fired. The sin of disobedience is hard for such men to resist."

The nun looked at Marchetti with neutral expression. "Is that what you wish me to address with Père Gauss? Disobedience?"

"No. I need you to determine whether our brother in Christ is guilty of more serious sin."

Sœur Dion folded her hands on top of her bare metal desk. "I have read the dossier. It is disturbing. But the record of Père Gauss' session with your attorney reveals a man who acquits himself well. Does it not?"

"That's part of the problem, Sister. Your patient has a quick mind and a sharp tongue. But this isn't a debate in one of his seminary philosophy classes. If Father Gauss has broken vows other than humility and obedience, His Eminence is determined to take action. His legal advisers say that would be difficult based only the letters and other materials you've seen. None of Gauss' accusers have come forward in person, much less testified under oath."

Sœur Dion opened her folded hands. "How do you wish me to proceed?"

I want you to wring his head like a sponge and bring me what's in there.

Marchetti recalled the Bishop's warning that if he appeared to favor a specific outcome, the Sisters of San Gabriel were sure to provide the opposite. He paused to formulate an appropriately diplomatic instruction. A soft knock on the door came while he was struggling to find one.

"*Entrez!*"

A tall, black robed nun entered and exchanged brief words with Sœur Dion. Marchetti understood only one of them, but that was enough. *Gauss.*

"Trouble already?"

Sœur Dion dismissed her colleague and shut the door. "You asked to be informed if anyone tried to contact Père Gauss while he is with us. A Monsieur Morgan has called twice in the last few minutes."

"The policeman?"

"Sœur Gabriel did not convey an occupation."

"How did he get this number?"

"From Père Gauss, it would appear."

"Was he told that Father Gauss is not here?"

"A lie?" Sœur Dion's voice was firm.

"To protect your patient's privacy."

"The caller mentioned hearing Père Gauss's voice on the telephone answering machine in his room when his earlier call was transferred there."

"You've given Father Gauss a telephone?" Marchetti struggled to keep his voice from skipping octaves.

Sœur Dion lifted her chin. "This is a retreat house, Monsignor. It is not a prison. All of our rooms have phones… unless we have been instructed otherwise."

"Please remove it. Father Gauss is here for prayer and reflection. He should not be distracted by calls or visitors."

"As you wish, Monsignor."

Marchetti tried to keep the impatience out of his voice. "Have you made progress?"

"No."

"Have you gone through the file with him?"

"Père Gauss has declined."

"The man is in no position to decline!" Marchetti heard his voice grow louder, and he throttled it back. "Does he understand that?"

Sœur Dion spread pale, long-fingered hands. "Père Gauss informed me that he had already gone through the file with the diocese's lawyer. He said that he does not feel the need to repeat the exercise with a 'shrink.'"

"I see." Marchetti began to pace. "Did he say anything about the latest letter? I'd at least like to hear what he has to say about that before the lawyers see it."

"The one from the boy who drowned?"

"Hardly a boy, but yes. Did he have a reaction?"

"Nothing overt. I showed it to him during our session this morning. He read it and then asked to go to chapel. He's been there most of the day."

"His Eminence is particularly interested in Father Gauss's reaction to that letter. It would be helpful if you could get him to share his thoughts, Sister."

"I will try, Monsignor." She looked calmly at the bishop's representative. "Does His Eminence wish to know… everything?"

Marchetti was firm. "He desires that I do." The Bishop's parting instruction had been clear. *"Find out the truth, Monsignor. Then consider the needs of the Church."*

* * *

Tom had intended to brief Joe on his visit to the U-lab address that turned out to be a storefront grocery that did no business, as well as his meetings with Hassad and the mourner at Billy's funeral. But he found Joe in no shape to absorb a briefing. The young candy striper asked Tom to steady the metal basin while she went to find a doctor. "There's blood," she added, inclining her head toward the contents of the pan.

After a few sanguinary heaves, Joe collapsed into the pillows, gulping air. "What did you find?" he croaked.

"It can wait."

Joe's face was ashen and his eyes glazed and unfocused. "All right. But I want to find that priest of yours next."

And my lawyer wants me to get my ass back to New York to save it. "You think Father Gauss had something to do with this?"

"They're hiding him," Joe wheezed. "And he likes to take boys for boat rides."

"What do you mean 'hiding' him?"

Joe waved toward the pile of papers beside his bed. "I got through to a Monsignor Marchetti after you left. He seems to be the gatekeeper for Gauss's bishop. The party line is that your friend Gauss is 'on retreat.'"

An unfortunate choice of words. "Did he say where?"

"He wouldn't," Joe wheezed. "When I pressed, he coughed up the number of a lawyer named Dolan."

"It sounds like Monsignor Marchetti was expecting your call. Or somebody's."

Joe attempted to shrug, but his shoulders remained flat on the pillow. "If I have to, I'll get a warrant. But I'm betting you can find your buddy quicker."

"Maybe," said Tom. "He left me his phone number. I've left him a few messages. I think he's at St. Gabriel's."

"That clinic the nuns run on the other side of the lake?"

"The number he gave me is one of theirs. The voicemail tape is him. That doesn't mean he's there now, but I suppose I could have a look."

"They're not going to let you in the front door, Tommy."

"Do you know another way?"

"Not that you could use. Do you think Gauss left you his number because he wanted to get something off his chest?"

"It's always been the other way around."

"Might be different this time."

The candy striper returned with a brace of doctors and nurses. Tom stepped into the hall to give them room. On his way out, and while Joe was heaving in the opposite direction, Tom lifted a file from the pile beside the bed. Outside, he leaned against the wall and read what his brother had earlier not wanted him to see.

According to the autopsy report, Billy was a mess. The deceased had hepatitis B and C, two different kinds of sexually transmitted disease, 375 LDL cholesterol and a blood alcohol level of .18. But none of that killed him. The cause of death was listed as drowning. When the doctors came out of Joe's room, Tom asked if they were any closer to knowing what was wrong with Joe or how long he was going to be laid up.

Sayed walked him down the hall. "It's not food poisoning," he said, "or other bacterial contamination. With those, the symptoms peak a few hours after ingestion and then start to decline. Your brother's still vomiting and it's been almost forty hours."

"So what is it?"

"We don't know yet. But it's acting like a toxin, where the symptoms don't diminish as long as the toxin is present. The aspiration suggests ingestion. But cutaneous is possible, given his multiple head and forearm lesions."

"You mean he swallowed something or got it in a cut?"

"Perhaps both. We'll know better when the lab work comes back."

"When will that be?"

"Tomorrow at the earliest. If you leave a phone number at the nurses' station, someone will call you."

* * *

Tom felt his fingertips skim across the steering wheel like an oracle on an Ouija Board. The truck began to move with no apparent need for direction or explanation, down Lake Boulevard past Our Lady of The Lake church, and up the tree lined drive to the cobbled semi-circle in front of the Pearce mansion.

He had not consciously intended to come here. But he was not surprised that he had. If he was going to keep helping Joe, then testing the conjectures of Billy's Canadian friend was the logical next step. At the top of the circular drive, he sat for a moment listening to the sounds of approaching night: chirping crickets, the flutter of an occasional bat, clicks and groans from the cooling engine and the rustle of trees and bushes in the breeze off the lake. *But that's not why you're here, is it?* It was a simple question, but there was no simple answer.

Minutes passed while he sat and brooded. Then a light flickered above the front door and Susan stepped into its glare, shading her eyes with a hand. "Joe?"

Tom stepped out of his brother's truck and into the light. "No. It's the handsome, lawfully prosperous Morgan brother." *Profile subject to change.*

She folded her arms over her chest, frowning at her long-ago lover. Serial emotion flickered uncensored across her face: surprise, suspicion, attraction, indecision. When she spoke, it was almost a whisper.

"Why are you here?"

I don't know. Though his mouth conjured other words, "I have something to show you."

Susan led him through the house to a wicker-themed sun porch overlooking the lake. The last time Tom had been in that room, Susan's mother had walked in on her daughter and boyfriend entwined on top of a bamboo love seat. Tom grimaced at the memory of leaping guiltily to his feet, smashing heads with Susan and promptly suffering a massive, unstoppable nosebleed. He had not been in this room since.

An ancient stereo scratched a stringy Pier Gynt Suite. A jacket-less book lay face down on the glass topped table beside the couch. Susan chose the wheat-backed chair nearest the French doors and sat with her arms crossed.

Nothing had been said. No eye contact made. But the connection and discomfort was .intense He slid one of the Quebec University brochures across the tabletop. "There's a picture on the inside back cover." His voice trembled.

She glanced at the photo and then put it down.

"Do you recognize anyone in the picture?"

"No."

"Not the gentleman on the left?"

She picked up the brochure and looked at it again. "Dr. Hassad?"

"Do you know him?"

"No. That's just what it says beneath the picture."

"There was a man sitting behind you at your brother's funeral."

Susan lifted her chin and sighted the tip of her nose on the center of Tom's forehead. "Suliman Twafik," she said slowly.

"Not the man in the photo?"

Susan studied it again. "I know I shouldn't say this... but sometimes they do all look alike. I mean the beard and everything. But Suliman is tall and this guy looks short... though he's sitting down."

"And who is Suliman Twafik?"

"A face from the past. Our fathers worked together when Dad was with ARAMCO. Suliman lived with us for a while as a foreign exchange student when we first moved here. He's a couple of years older than me."

"Do you keep in touch?"

"No. He was close to Billy, though. They played GI Joe together."

"How did he find out about the funeral?"

"He said the story about Billy's death made the wire services and got picked up by his local newspaper. There's only one funeral home in Coldwater. It would have been easy enough to get the number and information on the church services."

"Did he say what he's been doing all these years?"

She turned her head toward the window. "Teacher, somewhere. He never went home, I guess. I didn't pay much attention. It was a rough day for me."

Tom tried to watch her eyes, but she wouldn't make contact. "I spoke with a friend of Billy's who said that Billy was unusually happy the month before he died. That Billy claimed he was going to make a lot of money soon and settle a lot of old scores."

Susan looked up. "He didn't seem happy to me."

"Any idea where he thought he was going to get his hands on a pile of cash?"

She hesitated. "Not really. Unless I agreed to sell this place, which he knew I wouldn't."

"His friend says Billy was pretty upset about that, too."

"Yes, I know. And If I thought helping Billy get his hands on a chunk of money would turn his life around, I'd have done it in a heartbeat. But it doesn't work that way, does it? Billy's problem wasn't money, it was his life. He didn't have one... or the confidence or discipline to build one. Any money he got his hands on, he would have blown. Then he'd have come back to me for more."

Tom stood.

"Is that it!? Is that all you came here for?"

"I've got a few more errands to run for my brother." Her face tensed. He turned at the door. "Look, what would you say if I told you that I saw your friend Suliman, or maybe the guy in that photo, up at Frankie Heller's the night of your brother's funeral?"

Her voice went from peeved to petrified in a nanosecond. "I'd tell you to leave Frankie Heller alone. He's dangerous."

* * *

Tom left Susan in the sun room and made his way to the front of the house. Outside, a silver two-door Lexus idled at the throat of the circular driveway, its driver gripping the steering wheel with knuckles white from strain. Tom's mind was on state prosecutors and Susan's warning about Frankie Heller, and he didn't see the Lexus until he was almost grille to grille with it. The driver stared straight ahead and made no move to lift his hands from the wheel or move his car from where it blocked Tom's exit. Tom recognized the NeuroGene owner, Dave Willow.

Tom hopped out of the truck and moved toward the side of the idling car.

"You okay, Willow?" The man behind the wheel turned his head so slowly it might have been under water. "Are you okay?" Tom repeated. Cool air wafted from the lake, bringing with it the smell of booze.

"You're bothering her," said Willow, his words petulant and slurred.

Tom suddenly remembered Susan's allusion to a brief grad school marriage, and Sharp's to a long ago relationship between his partner and his research assistant. Tom stepped away from the car, eyes probing the blotched face and bloodshot eyes. *No way.*

Willow opened the car door and stumbled out. "She doesn't want you around," he blurted.

Tom didn't bother to look at the face of the man coming toward him. Instead he looked at the hands and pockets... empty and flat, respectively. It was a little catechism that the original Sheriff Morgan had drilled into his boys, though he was sure that Joe had made the most use of it over the years. "I was just coming to see you," said Tom.

Willow stopped. Whatever he had expected in response to his Dutch courage challenge, it wasn't that.

"You scammed your partner, didn't you? Though I'm sure he still thinks it was the other way around. It depends on who hid the better card, I suppose. NeuroGene is worth more than he realized, or a lot less than you thought. Have you figured out which it is yet?"

Willow said nothing. Which was as good as holding up a sign.

"Did you have something brewing in the lab that Sharp was too dull to notice – pardon the pun? Something that's going to make you and your new investor a lot of money? Is that what you're celebrating tonight?"

"You're not the detective in the family." The voice was slurred and the cadence deliberate. "You're just the boring over-achiever."

"I've spoken with your pal, Dr. Hassad."

Willow said nothing, but his face rippled.

"Sharp thinks he's the only one who dealt with Hassad. But the professor told me that he dealt with you, too." He wondered if Willow was in any condition to appreciate the significance of Hassad's confirmation. "You keep some of the things he sends over, don't you? And you sent him things too, for safe keeping. Things you didn't want Sharp to know about."

Willow stood silent.

"How many companies have you started, Willow? A dozen? I'll bet you've got it down to a formula by now. Run it on a shoestring until your partners give up and sell out to you cheap. If you've got something tucked away with your pal Hassad, you bring it out then. If not, you bring in new investors and start the scam all over again. You're not in the research business, Willow. You're in the investor fleecing business."

Somewhere in the stand of pines at the far end of the lawn, an owl hooted twice and broke into flight. The NeuroGene owner swayed grandly but said nothing.

Tom laughed. "You shouldn't drink, Willow. It slows your thinking. Right now you're desperate to say something clever. But you're afraid to open your mouth." He watched the color return to NeuroGene owner's face. He checked the man's hands and pockets again.

"All you were to her was a stud," Willow blurted. "She told me so."

"Does she know about you and Hassad?" Tom asked quietly. "Or about Hassad and Billy?"

"Stud!" blubbered Willow, as if it were an insult and not the Morgan brothers' favorite four-letter word.

"Go in there and make your peace," said Tom. "If she'll let you. I'll be at your office tomorrow when you're sober. We can skip the fairy tale about Billy breaking into your mail room. He couldn't have gotten in without a security card. Someone gave him one, either you or Sharp, so he could do his deliveries and pick-ups after hours. We're going to talk about who and what, and whether that's what got him killed."

CHAPTER 21

Tom turned off the engine, doused the headlights and allowed the truck to roll over the crest of the hill. A full moon winked behind a broken bank of clouds revealing a shallow ditch where the shoulder of the road should have been. He held the truck to the center of the road while the question he'd been unable to answer in Susan's driveway repeated itself now against the back beat of his staccato heart. *Why am I here? To prove something? Or to help Joe?*

The truck dipped a sharp thirty degrees as he turned off the road into the driveway of Heller's Junkyard. Yellow light oozed from under a pair of roll-up garage doors. The clang of metal on metal echoed behind it. Susan claimed to have heard Frankie Heller screaming at Billy that he was too stupid to live. Hours later, that prediction apparently came true. So *you're going to go down there to strike up a conversation about funny coincidences? Is that the plan?* Tom opened the glove compartment, felt inside and remembered that Joe had returned his cop toys to the patrol car. He remembered, too, his brother's rhetorical question about whether any local ever brought his car to Heller's garage for repairs and why the answer was no. But from the sound of it, one was being disemboweled down there right now.

Sliding from behind the wheel, Tom stepped quietly away from the truck.

He tried to minimize the crunch of shoes on the gravel and to ignore the angry inner voice that hissed, *"Stupid, stupid, stupid!"* in a shrill crescendo that accompanied each hesitant step. *"Little brother's not going to save your ass this time!"* As he reached the garage, the Susan-like voice was a full-throttle scream, *"You're going to get yourself killed, Tommy Morgan!"*

Marching his kettledrum heart to the back of the garage, Tom took a position beside a door that opened onto the junkyard. The top of the door was quarter pane glass. Through it he could see Frankie Heller standing beneath a hydraulic lift doing something with a blowtorch to the floor of an old Ford Fairlane.

Frankie had gotten big, like his father. Though he was no taller than he had been in high school, maybe five foot nine, he'd acquired a substantial girth since then. Tom estimated him to be at least two hundred forty pounds. His hair was dark and greasy still, though it had gotten long, which struck Tom as ironic, since Frankie used to enjoy beating the crap out of boys with long hair.

A rolling metal tool chest with a Styrofoam cup on top and a pack of Marlboros beside it obscured the view. But from what Tom could see, Frankie Heller had been living hard these past years, a poster boy for multiple medical implosions a decade down the road. But he looked just as mean as Tom remembered, and a whole lot larger now.

As Tom eased closer to the window, a strip of fluorescent light from inside the garage brushed the side of his face.

"ARHG! ARHG! ARHG! ARHG! ARHG! ARHG!"

A bucket-mouthed mastiff crashed against the glass and two lethal paws hammered the door beneath it. Tom fell backwards, scrambled to his feet and ran into the junkyard. He made it as far as the first row of wrecked cars before the garage door burst open and the howl of moist, hot pursuit surged after him. He leaped to the hood of the nearest junker and from there to its roof, inches ahead of snapping jaws, fanged, slavering and maniacal.

The massive canine reared on its hind limbs, pressed paws the size of toasters on top of the doorjamb and opened his snarling maw to within a hot breath of Tom's ankles. Frankie Heller's voice followed at a more leisurely pace. Wafting through the darkness, it was almost musical. "What we got here tonight, boy?" The snarling canine rose another inch, lips pulled back from dripping, yellowed teeth. Tom heard a sharp click and then a powerful flashlight blasted a tunnel of light through the darkness. He pressed a forearm above his eyes and tried to peer below the glare.

"Ho! Ho! Ho!" The sound of his old adversary's voice, its self-satisfied intonation and malevolent intention, made Tom want to throw up. "You done good, boy!"

There was nothing for Tom to do but wait and try not to pee. The cone of light fell from his eyes to just below his belt, where it began a slow, steady circle.

Frankie laughed. "That's where Soldier goes for, don't you boy?" The slavering Mastiff answered in a low, Pavlovian growl. "You're in a shit-load of trouble, Tommy Morgan. A shit-load of trouble."

"Get that stupid dog out of here." His voice trembled and his hands shook.

"Hear that Soldier? Why don't we just pull this sorry trespasser off there and see who's stupid? Whatdaya say?"

The dog growled low and long.

"I think Soldier here's wantin' a nice juicy taste of your privates." Heller addressed the dog, softly, "Just be patient, boy."

Tom's knees and hamstrings began to vibrate. He tried to control them, but the smooth, sheet-metal roof of his car-top perch cantered sharply to one side, moist with evening dew.

"Now why don't you just start to explain yourself," Heller commanded.

Tom thought that might be a good idea, but could think of nothing helpful to say. After a long enough pause, Frankie grunted, "Have it your way." He dropped the light to Tom's foot and murmured something to the dog. Instantly, the animal sprang forward, snapped a row of teeth around Tom's ankle and wrenched him off the car roof and onto the ground. Tom landed hard and lay stunned and panting.

"Release!" The dog stepped back and looked Tom in the eye, daring him to move. "Here's the deal," said Frankie, almost conversationally, "I shine this light on some soft, juicy part. Say 'sic. ' Then Soldier there takes a hold

159

of it. I don't call him off right away, he yanks it a bit. I still don't call him off, he rips out a chunk."

Tom tried to sit. The giant canine leaped forward and roared in his face, backing him down. "You getting the idea, yet?" Frankie asked.

Tom lay with his face toward the stars, his chest heaving and his torso basting in dog drool.

"Now let's start again. What are you doing here?"

"I have a message for you," Tom gasped. "From Dr. Hassad."

"Heel!" The Mastiff took a reluctant step backward and Tom propped himself on an elbow. "That's far enough," said Frankie. "Say that again?"

"I have a message for you," he repeated, this time with a bit more breath. "From Dr. Hassad."

"I don't know a Dr. Hassad," said Frankie, cautiously. "What's the message?"

"It's a question. Can you replace the delivery boy?"

Frankie shone the light directly on Tom's face and then began to circle it. "I don't know what you're talking about, Tommy Morgan. And my gut tells me you don't know what you're talking about, either."

"Think about it," Tom answered, gulping air. "What else would I be doing here?"

Frankie circled the torchlight across the top of Tom's thigh. "That's sort of the question, isn't it?"

A sound escaped from the back of the dog's throat like an opening of a blast furnace.

"Be patient, Soldier," soothed Heller. "I think he's full of it, too. But we got to be sure now, don't we?" The furnace noise subsided but did not disappear. "Hush!"

As Frankie stroked his stubbled face, a pair of headlights cleared the hill above the garage and slid fast down the gravel drive into the junkyard. The car came to a halt about twenty yards away from the men and dog, its high beams freezing them like deer on a roadside. Only the dog did not put a forearm to his eyes.

Tom heard the squeal of un-oiled door hinge and the crunch of steps on gravel. He could only guess what lay beyond the glare; and he muttered a prayer that it was Joe, risen from his sick bed to save his brother's ass one more time.

"Looks like you got here at a good time," said Frankie in the direction of the new arrival. Then an explosion split the air behind the headlights and Frankie's torso jerked backward as if yanked by a rope. Blood splashed across his sweat-stained beater shirt and wicked outward in a fast spreading arc. The dog whirled, first toward Frankie and then toward the glare of headlight. Another explosion concussed Tom's ears, followed by *a* yelp, and then a third explosion.

Tom leaped from the ground and dodged behind a row of wrecked cars. *CRACK! Ping!* Shots ricocheted from car to car, the sound of metal on metal like some giant pinball machine. Tom ran between rows of junked cars, around and behind them, through ones with missing doors and under a pair that were propped together on end like a tepee. He tried to circle behind the lights, banging time and again into sharp, unseen protrusions. But the clap of gunfire and ping of punctured metal kept herding him in unhelpful directions. It seemed the shooter preferred to keep him in silhouette.

Diving into a wrecked Lincoln Town Car filled with cobwebs and mouse droppings, Tom lay on sodden upholstery trying to catch his breath, and felt something slither from beneath the seat and disappear beneath the one in front. His bladder rippled. Through the broken windshield, he watched a cone of light work its way from side to side along the row of junked cars. He slid through the door-less side of the wreck and crawled away from the light.

He tried to remember the layout of the junkyard from his visit with Joe a few days earlier. A chain link fence surrounded the yard, open at the front by the garage and somewhere in the rear a gate that the shooter's car had driven through. Heller must have left it open, expecting company.

The spotlight reached the end of the row and went out. For a moment, Tom saw only moonlight and heard only crickets. He moved cautiously through wet weeds, broken glass and assorted metal debris, trying not to crash or curse out loud.

Then the headlights started to move, turning slowly away from the garage and stopping in the narrow row between the first two lines of junk cars. The spotlight came on again and began to wand between the rows of wrecks, moving methodically from side to side and car to car.

Tom crawled toward the fence. After a few minutes the headlights moved again, lighting up the alley between the next rows of cars with the spotlight moving back and forth between them like a metronome. He reached the fence and began to crawl along its perimeter, feeling as if he were in one of those WWII submarine movies where the destroyer lays out a grid and slowly closes in on the helpless submarine crew trapped on the bottom. Bits of broken glass and plastic junk punctured his knees and palms. He tried to remember the last time he had a tetanus shot, and then grimaced at the foolish optimism behind the thought. Part of him must think he was going to survive the next few minutes.

The headlights moved again. From the angle of the fence he could tell that the car must be near the final row. He had no idea how far he might be from the gate, or if it was open. Up ahead, facing the yard, he could see the silhouette of an owl sitting motionless on top of the fence. Another hunter out for its evening prey. The flat-faced head swiveled slowly in its socket and focused an appraising eye in Tom's direction. The headlights moved again, a row away now.

Then a loud metal squeal made Tom's neck go rigid. The spotlight passed through the door of an old yellow school bus, where from inside burst a sound like a million tiny flags snapping in a hard wind.

THUT! THUT! THUT! THUT! THUT! THUT! THUT!

The owl swooped from the chain link fence and dove toward the light. Suddenly, the air was thick with small, mouse-like creatures zooming in dense, dark clouds. Tom crouched low and sprinted through the cloud of frenzied bats, found the gate and disappeared into the darkness.

CHAPTER 22

Cold, aching and hurt, Tom hid in the woods until he saw headlights pull away from the junkyard and disappear over the hill beyond it. When he tried to stand, his hamburger-ed knees refused to bend and punished him for trying. Stumbling onto the dirt road and goose-stepping up the hill to his brother's truck, he held his clawed hands to his chest like a battered Frankenstein. He wondered later why he had not anticipated what came next.

From inside Joe's truck came a high-pitched bleat of horror. The door flew open and the sound from inside rose in scale and volume. "Tom! Tom! Tom! What happened?"

"Ignored your advice," he croaked, stumbling against the truck's chest-high fender. Susan's fingertips hovered near his chest as though uncertain where to press that wouldn't hurt.

"Who did this to you?"

"Frankie Heller." The words came out in gasps. "A dog the size of a Shetland pony, someone I didn't get a look at and a few acres of shrapnel and broken glass."

Susan pried his hands from his chest. Her face drained of color when she saw what was left of his palms. "They're raw!" Her voice skidded octaves unable to find footing. "We have to get you to a hospital."

"Need to think, first." Susan put her hand beneath his arms and helped him into the truck. "Where's your car?"

She started the truck and gestured to where its headlights washed over a late model BMW nose down in a ditch. "I turned off my lights so no one would see me and I ended up down there."

Tom rested his head on the back of the seat and tried not to feel all of the places that hurt. He wheezed out a question, "What made you come here?" But her whispered answer made it no farther than the windshield, and he was too weary to ask twice.

They rode in silence along the familiar route that led to the tree lined drive and the house above the lake. She drove the truck across the terraced lawn and down to the boathouse, then lifted Tom's arm over her shoulder and helped him climb the wooden steps to the loft. There, she eased him onto the bed and began the sanguinary task of removing his shredded clothes. He could have used a bit in his teeth for that part. Poised over impacted wounds with a pint of alcohol and an already bloody cloth, she warned, "This is going to hurt." But he was past the point of caring.

As MadDog used to say, "If you can't listen, you've got to feel." usually with a belt in his hand.

When Susan finished cleaning and bandaging, she draped Tom in a thin, nautical-themed sheet and then, almost as an afterthought, closed the distance between their faces and slowly joined them at the lips. Hands and knees immobilized in gauze, he had to call on ancient memory to fill in the parts that might otherwise have come next.

A long minute later she drew back, tucking her legs beneath her. "I don't know why I did that."

"I do."

She leaned her head to the side and waited.

"You wanted to. So you suppressed all the reasons why you shouldn't."

"You've added wisdom to looks. How seductive."

He laughed and lifted the contrary evidence of his bandaged hands. "What we want trumps what we know better every time."

She leaned over Tom's naked torso and pressed her lips to the top of his head. He kept his eyes straight ahead.

"Did you find what you were looking for out there?" she murmured.

"Pieces."

"Worth nearly getting killed for?"

Someone thought they were worth killing for.

"What did you find out?" He raised his shoulders. She reached for the bottle of alcohol. "Don't make me use this again."

Keep it vague and see where this mummy kissing goes? Or answer the question and stick a fork in the hope of it going anywhere? After a moment of indecision, he forced a lungful of breath past cracked lips and balanced a bandaged hand at her waist. "I think I know who killed Billy. And maybe why."

Susan stiffened and pulled away.

"I think your friend Suliman and Dr. Hassad are the same person. That he used Billy to smuggle stuff from his Canadian lab into the U. S. and used NeuroGene to distribute it."

"Frankie Heller told you this?"

"Dave Willow's partner told Joe and me about the distribution part. Hassad confirmed it. I saw him this morning in his office in Montreal. He's the same guy who was sitting across from you at Billy's funeral--the one you know as Suliman. I showed Billy's photo to him and he claimed not to know the man in it. But Willow identified the same photo as the man who broke into the NeuroGene mail room and his former partner Mike Sharp identified him as the guy who delivered Hassad's packages."

"What packages?"

"Sharp and Hassad say it was research samples: vials, petri dishes and the like. When I asked Willow to guess what might be in them, he said that with a bio-research company as cover, he didn't even want to think of the possibilities. That part I believe."

"And what part don't you?"

"Sharp says the package service was an arrangement between him and Hassad and that Willow knew nothing about it. Hassad says he dealt with them both."

Susan shook her head. "I don't know, Tom. I can't imagine Dave Willow involved with anything not completely above board, or anyone trusting

Billy with *anything* important. He'd screw it up. Or rip them off."

"Willow's no angel, Susan. At least not in business. And he wasn't Mr. Niceguy when I ran into him in your driveway a few hours ago."

She looked away. "I didn't invite him in."

A gust of cool air billowed the curtains at the edge of the sliding glass door. It was a moment before Tom regained his train of thought. "Billy was just the mailman, Susan. My guess is that he got started doing occasional dope deliveries for Frankie Heller. When Hassad/Suliman became involved with NeuroGene, he probably looked up his old GI Joe pal and recruited him. Billy was already in the illegal package business. It probably wasn't too difficult to get him to carry an extra one now and then. My guess is Frankie didn't know about Billy's sideline with Hassad... at least not at first. He was probably mad as hell when he found out. Especially if Billy was carrying both Frankie's and Hassad's stuff at the same time, or in any of the cars Billy took in and out of Frankie's junkyard."

"That could have been what I heard them arguing about."

"I don't have all the pieces yet. But I think Frankie may have seen Billy's sideline as something that exposed the bread and butter business he had going through his garage, and that when he couldn't get Billy to stop, he got pissed and killed him. Or Hassad found out the same thing and had the same problem. His little vial-in-pocket operation could have gone undetected forever, but not if it got connected to a regular commercial dope run. In any event. Hassad learned the game was busted when I showed up today and started asking questions. I think he may have come across the border tonight to clean up his tracks."

"What do you mean?"

Tom looked at her closely. "What did you see at the junkyard after you climbed out of the ditch?"

"Nothing."

He tried to catch her eye, but she turned her head and spoke to the wall. "I passed a car before I got there." Her voice was a whisper. "I thought at first it might be you. Then, like I said, I turned off the headlights and tried to coast down the gravel drive and instead slid into that ditch. A few minutes

166

later, you came shuffling out of the woods looking like Lon Chaney's ghost."

"Did you notice anything about the car that passed you, or anyone in it?"

She looked up and away. "Dark sedan. I didn't see the driver. Are you sure about all this, Tom? About any of it?"

He looked at her eyes. "Frankie's dead, Susan. Whoever was in that car killed him. My guess is Hassad/Suliman."

"Guess? You mean you're making this up?"

He held out his bandaged hands. "I'm not making these up. Or Frankie being dead. The person in that car you passed killed him and tried to kill me. The only guess is who it was. Hassad fits."

Her voice was quiet, almost a prayer. "What are you going to do?"

"Tell Super Trooper. Someone who knows what he's doing needs to take it from here. Joe or someone else."

Her hand reached for Tom's thigh. "Are you sure that's the right thing to do, Tom?"

His heart leapt and his throat contracted. "I'm way out over my skis, Susan. Confronting Hassad without a plan for what he might do next was amateurish. So was walking into Frankie Heller's junkyard. Another mistake like that..." He looked at her pale hand on his paler thigh. "*And we don't get to finish this.*" The throb in his ears was deafening.

"But what about NeuroGene and the people who work there?" It wasn't a question, it was a plea. "I can't stay here either, if what you say about my brother is true and gets out."

"There's a killer on the loose, Susan."

"And my parents? Am I the only one who doesn't believe that cockamamie story that they crashed and drowned trying to race a forty-foot boat through Wilson Cove in the dark? *My* father?"

"What are you saying?"

"I'm saying that maybe Frankie and my brother were <u>both</u> killers. And that whatever happened to them, good riddance."

From somewhere across the water came a murmur of voices: early morning fishermen... late night lovers? "It's not that easy, Susan. Whoever killed Frankie isn't finished. I barely got away. Do you think he'll leave it at that?"

Susan pulled her hand away. Tom felt suddenly cold. "NeuroGene is doing important science, Tom. We're close to some real breakthroughs. The company won't survive a scandal like this. If you call your testosterone-fueled brother, all that meaningful work and the people who do it are finished. What purpose will that serve?"

Tom looked toward the light that was beginning to whiten the boathouse windows. He and Susan were talking past each other now, no longer connected. It was a familiar feeling. "There's a cell phone in the glove compartment of the truck." His voice flagged with exhaustion.

"Don't Tom. No good will come of it."

"I know that, Susan. But worse will come if I don't." When she didn't respond, he prompted, "Would you bring the phone, please?"

* * *

Tom needed Susan's help to dial the hospital, and when she reluctantly gave it, he let the phone ring until the sound eventually roused a night nurse. "I'm sorry," he said, to the woman who finally answered, "I know it's late, but I need to talk to my brother, Sheriff Morgan. He's in room 318."

"He was, dear," said the nurse. "He's gone now."

"You released him? He's better?"

"I don't believe so, dear. It says here on his chart 'left against medical advice."

"When did he go?"

"It must have been before 11:00 pm. That's when I come on. There's a note here asking any relative who might call to contact a Dr. Dyer. "He's not one of ours," she added yawning and then gave Tom the number.

He handed the phone to Susan and recited the number. She dialed it and put the phone back in his hand. The voice that came on sounded as tired as Tom felt. "Dyer."

"Tom Morgan. You left a message at the hospital for any relative of a patient who checked out a few hours ago."

168

"Thank god. Are you the brother?"

"That's right. Who are you?"

"Bill Dyer. A toxologist with the Agency for Toxic Substances and Disease Registry. We're part of the Center for Disease Control."

"Is Joe with you?"

"I wish he were. I was hoping that you could help us find him."

Whatever reserves Tom had started with that morning were long gone, and this was a draft on an empty well. "Have you tried his office, his home or our mother's apartment?"

"Repeatedly. Frankly I'm astonished your brother made it to the parking lot, given how sick he is."

"He could still be there then."

"We checked the area thoroughly. Wherever he is, your brother's a sick man. He needs to get back to the hospital fast."

"He can't have gone far," said Tom. "He could hardly lift his head off the pillow when I left him this morning."

"He wasn't much better when he bolted around 10:00 pm, according to the nurse on duty. But she couldn't get him to stay or anyone to stop him from leaving."

"Do you know what's wrong with him? The doctors were waiting on some tests when I left."

There was a moment of silence on the end of the line.

"Spit it out, Doc. If the CDC is involved, I'm guessing it can't be good. Just tell me."

Dyer cleared his throat and then spoke as if from a script. "Subject tested positive for exposure to a Class 3 bio-toxin."

Shit.

"And your government would really like to know where and how he was exposed."

Tom took a deep breath. "One of the doctors said he thought it might be something Joe ate or got in a cut."

"Judging from his symptoms, it's both. That, and the fact that he's not dead. If he'd inhaled it, he would be."

169

"A Class three ...?"

"Bio-toxin. Abrin."

"Never heard of it. Should I?"

"Think anthrax and multiply it by a factor of ten."

Shit, again. Tom felt his body flush with adrenaline and respond with only deeper fatigue.

"Did your brother ever mention the word abrin or refer to it in any way?"

"No." Tom struggled to steady his voice. "How bad is he?"

"We don't have a lot of data on human toxicity. But when it's inhaled, abrin is deadly even in microscopic amounts. Your brother's exposure must have been gastric or cutaneous. It's treatable, but only if we get him back to a hospital fast."

"I'll find him."

"Please. We need him as much as he needs us. He's our link to the contagion."

"How did the CDC get onto this?"

"We were contacted by the lab that examined some samples from an autopsy done at your local hospital last week. I was sent here to follow-up. When I learned that the policeman who had handled the body and inventoried the dead man's residence was in the ICU with unexplained vomiting and fever, I did a field test. It registered positive for abrin exposure."

Tom's breath pounded the phone's mouthpiece.

"Mr. Morgan, we need to find the source of your brother's contamination before other people become exposed."

Tom forced himself to breathe. "Was this autopsy you looked into done on a man named Pearce?" He kept his voice slow and deliberate.

"Yes, did you know him? Can you tell us anything about him?"

"A lot. As soon as I find my brother."

* * *

While Tom was speaking with the CDC doctor, Susan paced the uncarpeted floor. When he finished, he told her the part he assumed she had not overheard. "A-brin!" He stressed each syllable hard. "Does that mean anything to you?"

She shook her head.

"The CDC guy said to think 'anthrax' and multiply it by ten."

"Oh, Tom!"

"Tell me NeuroGene is not fooling around with stuff like anthrax."

"We're not." She met his eye, but did not stop pacing.

"Sit down." His voice was hard.

She continued to pace.

"You recognized the man in that college brochure, didn't you? And you saw something at Frankie's that you're not telling me." Tom spit out the words until they were almost a shout. "I need to know what you're holding back, Susan."

Her face turned toward the light that was beginning to spread over the glassy lake. "I told you everything I know."

Emotions careened like bumper cars in his chest. "I'm tired, Susan. I'm hurting and I have to find Joe. You can tell me now, or you can go to hell... or jail, or both."

Her face remained a mask.

He looked around for something to replace the sheet that was all that covered him now. Then he shuffled to Billy's closet and pushed through half a dozen hangars of clothes two sizes too small. In the end he kept the sheet wrapped around his waist, sparing his abraded limbs the challenge of squeezing back into the soiled and shredded clothes that lay in a heap by the bed. He could feel Susan's eyes on his back.

Unbending legs carried him to the stairs. Bandaged hands shared the weight of his torso with the boathouse wall and helped him maneuver the steps. At the bottom, clear water rippled at the back of the boat slip and shafts of morning sunlight made prism bars across the lakeside opening. Pausing at the foot of the steps to ease the throbbing in his knees, he took a long last look at the locale which seemed now to be little more than center ring in a circus that should have left town long ago.

Dr. Pearce's Chris Craft hung in canvas straps over the water, mist curling beneath its hull and pale light glinting off its varnished mahogany side. Nests of barn swallows lined the beam above it. Rippling sunlight played along the spine of a cedar canoe that lay overturned nearby against the boathouse wall. Beneath it, a large black crow pecked greedily at a stick-like something covered with blood. The bird looked at Tom and pushed its prize farther under the boat. Tom hobbled over to the canoe and lowered himself gently toward the sound of buzzing flies. The crow squawked angrily and held its ground.

"Get!" he yelled.

The crow squawked twice and flew off. Tom swept his bandaged hand beneath the boat and returned with the severed leg of a large, white-feathered bird.

CHAPTER 23

Bonnie helped Tom into a change of clothes, asking a few listless questions about his bloody bandages and his story of getting into a scrap with a dog. She had her own troubles. Joe hadn't come home. She knew where he was, but he'd made her promise not to tell the CDC toxologist who'd been calling every hour since last night. Joe said that the CDC always exaggerates and that he couldn't stay in the hospital any longer with a killer on the loose. Not if he wanted to keep his job. "What am I supposed to say when Mary calls?" Bonnie demanded. "Her son may be dying, but he won't leave the office? I'm angry, Tom. No, I'm frightened. And I can't keep doing this. I won't keep doing it."

Tom held out a bandaged hand. "Where is he?"

"The station. Where else?"

A half hour and a fist full of Tylenol later, Tom found Joe propped behind his desk in the basement of Town Hall. MadDog's stuffed fish and game heads still decorated the wall behind the desk and the big iron ring of jail cell keys still hung on the ten penny nail on the wall. Nothing seemed to have changed since he and Joe had played marbles on the cement floor and peeked in at the Saturday night drunks while their dad caught up on paper work. The only addition was a rack of electronics in what used to be the mop closet. Tom assumed that was how Joe stayed connected to the state trooper barracks in DuBois. The only thing missing was the bottle of Jim Beam that used to sit on the shelf above the water cooler.

"What the hell happened to you?" Joe's voice was an old man's wheeze and his face stretched lines of pain from chin to hairline.

"Frankie Heller."

"Still can't handle him by yourself, huh?"

"He's dead."

Joe eased his head into the cradle of his hands.

"I didn't kill him, Joe. But I was there when someone did. I thought at first it might be you. But whoever it was started shooting at me, too." He paused.

"What?"

"It wasn't you, right?"

"Don't be funny. Sit. Spill."

"You need to call this number first." Tom threw a scrap of paper on the cluttered desk. "He's a toxologist with the Agency for Toxic Substances and Disease. He says you've been poisoned."

"Feels like it."

"And he's threatening to call out the National Guard to find you if you don't get back to the hospital pronto."

Joe lifted his head from his hands. "Agency for what? State or Fed?"

"Does it matter? Something in Billy's autopsy report scared the shit out of him. The report you didn't want me to read."

Joe grunted. "I told you why."

"This guy seems to know what you have and what to do about it. He was pretty convincing that you'd better do it quick, or he'll be looking at your autopsy report next. From what I can see, he may not be exaggerating."

Joe wheezed. "Can't, Tommy. Lieutenant Grogan of the State Trooper Border Security Task Force called a few minutes ago. *Ordered* me not to leave, if you can believe that. Little prick."

"Sorry for your troubles, brother. But this is more serious than the state troopers poaching your turf. The Toxic Substances doc says, 'think anthrax only worse. ""

"Bullshit. I'd be dead."

"If you breathed it. You only ate it, he says, and maybe got it in those cuts."

Joe dropped his head into his hands again. "How am I supposed to stay holed up in a hospital with Paulie Grogan's nose up my ass, dead bodies piling up all over town and no friggin' idea of how they got that way?"

"Don't be stupid, Joe. Go back to the hospital and let them do what they have to. You're not going to solve anything if you croak."

Joe moved his head in obvious pain. "All right. But tell me first how Frankie got dead and where you put the body."

Tom didn't laugh. "Then you go back to the hospital."

"Fine. As soon as Grogan and his new best friends get through with me." Joe stared at Tom's bandaged hands and lacerated scalp. "Looks like both of us could use a pretty nurse. Frankie do that?"

"Indirectly. We'll leave that for last."

Tom recounted his trip to Montreal, Hassad's explanation of the Neuro-Gene connection and his claim not to recognize Billy's photograph while referring to the man in the photo in the past tense, his uneventful visit with Billy's friend Bonnefesse and his eventful one with the now deceased Frankie Heller. Then he started to connect the dots.

"Start with means," said Joe.

"All right. Somebody's got to have a boat and get Billy into it. You remember when we visited Heller's junkyard the first day I was here—the day the Dooley twins dragged Billy's body out of the lake? Do you remember what was sitting in front of the garage?

"A boat on a trailer."

"That's right. Fishing season's been over for weeks, but the boat's not inside yet or pulled around back or anything. It's not even covered. It's just sitting there like it's going out or just come back."

"Go on."

"Billy wasn't big. But someone still had to get him into a boat. If he went willingly, then anyone could have done it. But if not, Frankie could have handled Billy easily."

"Motive?"

"I think Billy ran errands for Frankie... harvest deliveries and such. Susan heard them arguing about something, so there was some sort of connection. I don't think they were just buddies. But Billy branched out and started carrying stuff for this Hassad character, too. Maybe he combined trips—used Frankie's cars. Maybe he left something behind one day. In any event, Frankie must have found out. He would have seen Billy's sideline as a risk to his business. Or maybe it wasn't even that logical. Maybe he and Billy just got into it. Frankie's got a temper, and Billy had a knack for pissing people off. Maybe he just lost it."

"Needs work. What about opportunity?"

"According to Susan, Billy was as sick as a dog the night he was killed. She says he was holed up in the boathouse. Frankie could have tied his boat alongside, talked or dragged Billy into the boat and then gotten rid of him out on the lake. Only he never got out of Wilson Cove because he heard you coming in the patrol boat when you thought you were after some poachers. He had to dump Billy fast and get out of there before you put a spotlight on him."

Joe lifted his head and smiled weakly. "It's a theory. You got a bit of the old man in you after all."

The compliment didn't make Tom happy. "It would be nice if it happened that way. Clean anyway."

"But?"

"There're some pieces that don't fit, Joe." Fatigue lay across Tom's shoulders like a weighted net, but his voice was firm.

"Lots of them, brother. Which ones jump out at you?"

"A dog that doesn't bark, a boat that makes it through Wilson Cove running without lights and a bird leg."

"I'm listening." His voice firmed, too.

Tom held up his bandaged hands. "I got maybe two inches into Frankie Heller's junkyard last night before Cerberus took a chunk out of my shorts. But you went down there and had a forty-five minute powwow with Frankie while I sat in your truck maybe fifty yards away. And I didn't hear one bark."

"Dogs like me."

"You were out in Wilson Cove in the patrol boat. But whoever dumped Billy's body got out of there ahead of you running without lights." He paused for breath. "When I used to know Wilson Cove like my way to the bathroom, I put a whacking great hole in Dr. Pearce's Chris Craft one night running without lights. Only I was only going about two miles an hour. Maybe someone who knows Wilson Cove better than I did could make a midnight run through that rock garden without lights and without hitting anything. But not at speed. Not running from a police boat."

"Keep going."

"A couple of days ago, I walked in on Susan when she wasn't expecting me. She's got this pet cockatoo that doesn't like people getting near her. Before she could call it off, it carved a couple of chunks out of my scalp and the top of my arms where I put them over my head. Billy had one of those birds, too. They go bat-shit on anyone who even comes close to their owner." Tom took a plastic bag from his pocket and threw it on his brother's desk. Inside was the severed bird's foot he'd found in the Pearce boathouse. "I'm pretty sure the one that was attached to this attacked whoever tried to get Billy out of the boathouse the night he was killed. Only whoever it was fought it off with something that sliced off its leg."

Joe looked silently at his brother.

"I figure there's probably enough stuff under these claws to figure out who that was."

Joe said nothing for a long moment while he stared thoughtfully at his brother. "Got a suspect?"

It was Tom's turn to pause. When he spoke, his voice was weary, but firm. "When you picked me up from the airport the morning after Billy was killed, you told me those cuts on your head and arms came from some thorn bushes around a dope patch you'd been pulling up."

"That's right."

"But they look an awful lot like the ones I got from Susan's bird…" He displayed the cuts on his forearms and gestured at his wounded scalp. "I don't think anyone could have made it across Wilson Cove running without lights. But a police boat out chasing poachers could be running full-out, all lit up and nobody would give it a second thought."

"Motive?"

"Super Trooper. This is your turf and Billy Pearce was a reckless low-life, doing something you had to stop. But quietly and in your own way."

"Like what?"

"I don't know yet."

"Why wouldn't I just arrest him?"

"I don't know that either."

"But you have a theory."

Tom nodded. "You inherited Dad's job. Maybe you inherited his sources of income as well. I don't know. I never wanted to ask."

"What sources?"

Tom glared at his brother. "Your little cabin in the woods is a castle, Joe. Your truck cost more than I paid for law school. You live large, just like he did. And the numbers don't square with the salary of a small town cop."

Brother glared at brother.

"So you think I knew something about Billy, but I couldn't arrest him because I was taking money from him and Frankie?"

"It can add up like that."

* * *

Tom tried to steer with one bandaged hand and dial with the other, thankful that no ditch awaited his graceless swerve to the shoulder of the road. Waiting for his breath to slow, he loosened the gauze on his hands and then tried the number again.

"Doctor Dyer."

"Tom Morgan. I gave my brother your number. Has he called yet?"

"No. Where is he?"

"In his office in the basement of Town Hall. He said the state troopers are on their way and want him to stay there. He'll go back to the hospital as soon as they're through with him."

"I'll send someone to make sure he does."

"That would be prudent."

"I still need your information on that fellow whose autopsy I read."

"Give me an hour. Where can I meet you?"

"I have a team gathering to examine the deceased's last residence. Do you know where that is?"

"I'll meet you there."

Tom cradled the phone between ear and shoulder while he opened the book on the car seat and took out the folded letter. Then he dialed the number scribbled on the back.

"Couvent St. Gabriel."

"Père Gauss, s'il vous plait."

The click was instantaneous and followed by a dial tone. *That was rude, Sister.* He squeezed the steering wheel. *I've got a serious problem in ethics here, Father. Père Gauss could really help a poor sinner, if he'd get out from behind sister's skirts.*

Tom pulled the car back onto the road and drove slowly toward a place he did not wish to go.

* * *

Mary tried to rise from the couch but had to settle for extending one arm and clutching her chest with the other. "What happened to you?"

"Frankie Heller's dog."

"Tommy, Tommy. I thought your brother had that family under control."

"He does now." Tom tried to keep his voice steady and his throat open.

"What happened?" Tom's eyes began to fog. Pain, fatigue and suppressed emotion were taking their collective toll. "Is it your brother?"

He nodded.

"Oh dear." Mary eased her weight onto the overstuffed, over-doilied couch. "The hospital told me he checked out. Some doctor has been calling here every hour."

"He's pretty sick, Mom. But that's the least of his problems." Mary's face turned from worried to wary. He hesitated. *How do I tell our mother that her son may be complicit in a killing?*

"What is it, Tommy?"

He shook his head and tried to breathe steadily. Then he began the way he knew best: a lawyer, laying the foundation of a case.

"Dad left you pretty well off." He could see Mary puzzle at the change of subject and the nervy timbre in his voice.

"He was a good provider. A bit wild, but no dummy."

"Do you remember the money the funeral home found in his coat?"

She bit her lip.

"You said then that you didn't think it was anything unusual. That Dad just didn't trust banks. I let it go. There was no point getting into it then."

She remained silent.

"But I need to talk to you about it now. Joe's in trouble and I want to help him, if I can. But if you can't go there, or don't know what I'm talking about, then I'll drop it. You have to let me know."

He waited for her to examine the corner he'd walked her into and the door he'd left open, and then make her choice.

She made it quickly. "I was a policeman's wife for twenty-five years, Tommy. There's not much I haven't seen or heard."

"Then you know where that money came from."

"I have a good idea, yes."

"The Hellers, the Dooleys, the Cashins, all of them."

"I don't know that. I know that it didn't fall from the sky, if that's what you're asking, and that your father didn't save it out of his paycheck."

"That'll do for now. And you know that Joe lives large too, just like Dad did. Larger than his paycheck anyway."

"He's a young man, Tommy. Some of them buy toys."

"And if he's paying cash?"

"I don't know that. And neither do you."

"But you know what I'm talking about?"

"Yes, I do. And I think you're on very shaky ground, young man."

"Frankie Heller is dead, Mom. So is Billy Pearce. They got dead on account of some trouble with the two-bit dope business that Hellers have been running, and Morgan sheriffs ignoring, for as long as anybody around here can remember."

"You said that your brother may be in trouble," she said firmly.

"That's right. The state police are here looking into Billy's death, with Paulie Grogan leading the pack. They're going to find out that Joe was in the Pearce boathouse when Billy left on his last ride and that Billy didn't go willingly."

Mary closed her eyes and pulled in a lungful of air. "Go on."

He recounted as much of the story as he was confident he had pieced together. His voice firmed as he laid out the items of evidence as if they were exhibits in a courtroom: the NeuroGene/U-Labs connection, his encounter with Susan Pearce's cockatoo, the dog that didn't bark at Joe but nearly shredded his mother's other son, the navigational hazards of Wilson Cove at night, the severed cockatoo's foot and the fresh gouges on Joe's head and arms that appeared hours after Billy's killing and that were identical to the ones Susan's bird inflicted on Tom a few days later.

Through it all, his mother sat silent and avoided her son's gaze. When he had finished, she asked, "Have you told this theory to your brother?"

"About an hour ago."

"And what did he say?"

"Nothing."

"And you want me...?"

"To tell me that Joe picked you up from the hospital the afternoon Billy was killed and stayed with you until the next morning, that he spent the entire evening moving you into his cabin, setting you up with a snack cart, CD's and remote TV and that he didn't leave until he came to pick me up at the airport."

"And if I can't do that?" Mary's voice was soft, but not alarmed.

"Then tell me how we survive as a family if we both know baby brother is a killer and we try to keep it as just another family secret."

His mother took her time to answer. While he waited for her to utter the unspeakable, his ears found the sounds of the things that made the tiny apartment work: the hum of the baseboard heater, the whir of the refrigerator motor, the ticking of the clock above the combination stove/oven.

"Oh, Tommy," she sighed.

His response was immediate and merciless. "Billy Pearce was alive when someone stuffed him in that bag. Alive when they dumped it in Wilson Cove. They drowned him."

"So your brother told me." His mother's voice was steady but cautious.

He looked at her and waited.

"And it seems to me that there's some things he's been telling me, that for some reason he's chosen not to tell you."

"I'm listening."

"Tommy…"

"Mom, what I know says Joe is involved in Billy Pearce's murder. I have to decide soon what to do about that. If you know something different, tell me before I might have to tell somebody outside the family what I won't be able to un-tell once it's out."

Mary released a lungful of trapped breath. "Very well. That makes sense I guess. Sit," she commanded.

He took a half step back, propped his back against the floral patterned wallpaper, folded his arms and looked down.

"Your brother was at the Pearce's house the night Billy was killed. That's true. He's been a regular visitor there these past few months." Mary paused to let the significance of that confidence sink in.

"What do you mean?"

"I mean temptation comes with the job, Tommy. And your brother…well, someone like Miss Pearce would only have to lift an eyebrow, wouldn't she?"

Or a shirt.

"Go on."

"Your brother stopped there last Saturday before the start of his shift. Miss Pearce wasn't home, but the brother was. Sick as a dog, according to Joe, and coughing blood. But the brother wouldn't let Joe take him to the hospital. In fact, he ran him off. Joe phoned Miss Pearce from his patrol car and advised her to get home and get her brother to a doctor.

"When his shift was over, he went back there. The house was empty... or at least dark. No one came to the door. Joey said that he walked around the house to see if there were any lights upstairs and while he was in the back he heard a boat pull away from the boathouse. He went down to look. There was no one inside except that fool bird that bit him. He didn't say if it had both feet. The Chris Craft was gone and so was Billy.

"Your brother says he tore over to the marina and raced out to Wilson Cove in the patrol boat to see if he could catch whatever might still be there. He found the Pearce boat right away and Miss Pearce on board. Alone."

"Running lights?"

"Dark as sin. The story Miss Pearce told your brother was that she came home when he called, but that her brother seemed to be better and wouldn't hear about any doctor or hospital. She told Joe that she went down to the boathouse later with some food, and found her brother gone and the place a wreck. She said she could hear the sound of a boat heading out into the cove, running dark. So she took the Chris Craft and went after it. She said she didn't find it, but thought that whoever it was, was still in the cove somewhere playing possum. So she turned off the boat lights and waited. That's when your brother showed up in the patrol boat and put the spotlight on her—not on that other boat she says was hiding out there, with Billy still on it... or not."

Tom paced the tiny room weighing the images in his mind. "Do you believe that story?"

"Of course not. And neither did your brother."

"I mean his story, Mom."

CHAPTER 24

Tom handed his driver's license to the broad shouldered young man with a military haircut whose Chevy Suburban blocked the entrance to the Pearce driveway. "I'm Tom Morgan. A CDC doctor named Dyer asked me to join him down at the boathouse." The young man made a call on the vehicle's two-way radio then waved Tom in.

A stubby white trailer sat parked at the edge of a granite seawall, umbilically connected to the Pearce boathouse by a thick, orange power cable. Two men in stenciled windbreakers fiddled with a pair of satellite dishes on the trailer roof. Tom ducked beneath the strip of yellow tape and found the CDC toxologist inside the boathouse watching a periscope of black snorkel make slow figure eights in the shallow end of the empty boat slip. "You must be Tom Morgan," he said. "I'm Doctor Dyer. My people picked up your brother about a half hour ago."

"Is he going to be all right?"

Dyer frowned. "Since he's not dead already, he's got a good chance. Thankfully, he had the foresight to ask your local hospital to send our agency the medical reports on the fellow who used to live in this boathouse. My colleague recognized a compound in the deceased's blood as something used by tanners to kill cows in the country he grew up in. It's called abrin.

Your brother is getting the standard course of treatment for ricin exposure, which is the closest compound that we have a protocol for. The next step is to find out where and how he got exposed."

"I've got some ideas on that."

The doctor gestured toward a stone bench above the seawall. "Let's sit where I can take notes."

Tom struggled to organize his thoughts and suppress everything else fighting for space inside a brain that did not have enough juice left to power the processor that was supposed to handle it all: murder, aborted romance, poisoning, impending financial ruin. His head hadn't touched a pillow in thirty hours. "You're going to want to talk to a man named Dave Willow," he heard himself say. "He owns a bio-research company called NeuroGene out on Route 6. Also his former partner, Mike Sharp, and a Dr. Hassad who teaches at the University of Quebec at Montreal." Tom gave the addresses as best he could remember. "Bring some muscle when you approach Dr. Hassad, if he's still around." He explained Hassad's connection with NeuroGene, his facilitator role in the informal, cross-border dissemination of biological materials and Billy Pearce's presumed role as an occasional courier.

"This Pearce fellow didn't work at NeuroGene?"

"No. The NeuroGene owner claims he found Pearce in the company mail room late at night about two weeks ago. He says Pearce refused to explain what he was doing. My guess is he was there to send something out with the rest of the NeuroGene deliveries, or he was picking something up."

As Dyer scribbled notes, a bandy-legged man wearing a diver's wet suit waddled up from the boathouse holding a clear Plexiglas box with a pair of rubber gloves fit into one side of it. "Found this next to one of the pilings," he huffed. "There's a bunch of cement blocks down there. This was under one of them."

"How deep is the water where you found it?" asked Dyer.

"Waist high, maybe."

"That would be about right. Box it up and get it off to the lab."

"About right for what?" asked Tom.

"For taking something used to kill a single cow and turning it into something designed to kill thousands."

"Cows?"

"People." Dyer explained, "One of the reasons there isn't a lot of data on abrin toxicity is that the compound isn't toxic in its natural state, which is inside the shell of the rosary pea. The pea is ornamental, and it's often used in cheap jewelry. The toxic part is inside the shell, and its lethal use to date has been limited to killing cows, one at a time. But if the toxin in the rosary pea can be aerosolized, it could be a mass killer. The manufacturing challenge is that abrin, like anthrax or ricin, is nearly impossible to work with safely outside of a lab environment. It has to be mixed with some sort of carrying agent, and in the process the person doing the mixing and packaging has to be careful not to inhale, ingest or let any of it come in contact with an open cut."

"And that box solves the problem?"

"If it's what I think it is, Pearce probably received the ingredients in sealed containers, placed them in the box, immersed the box in water and opened the containers under water inside the box, using the rubber gloves fitted into the side. That way nothing could escape into the air for him to breathe during the mixing and repackaging process. Low-tech, but effective."

"So how did my brother get exposed?"

"Perhaps Mr. Pearce didn't fully appreciate the danger of what he was working with. Maybe once or twice he decided to skip the cold swim and do his work inside. He wasn't a trained scientist, I take it."

"He barely made it out of high school."

"If he didn't follow the procedure and use that underwater mixing contraption, and if he did some of his mixing up there in that boathouse loft, then anyone who has been in there since then could have become infected by any residue that remained there. Your brother told me that he investigated the premises shortly after Pearce's body was recovered."

"There've been a few people up there since then."

Dyer eyed Tom's bandaged head and hands. "You?"

"Last night, or early this morning. I'm not sure of the exact time."

"Anyone else?"

"Pearce's sister."

"The woman who owns this property?"

"Who also works in the NeuroGene lab."

"I see. Wait here." Dyer walked over to the trailer and spoke to one of the men standing outside. When Dyer returned, Tom asked, "So you're saying Pearce could have done all this mixing and packaging down in the boathouse, either under water in that box, or if he got lazy and didn't follow the procedure, up in the loft?"

"That's right. And from the autopsy report, it's obvious he did get lazy."

"Okay. But he didn't die from abrin. He drowned."

"So the autopsy said. But he was a very sick man when he did. Your brother told my colleague who escorted him to the hospital that he saw Pearce just a few hours before he died. The visible symptoms your brother described are consistent with abrin toxicity."

"Did you find anything that might help identify who killed him?"

"'Who,' is not why I'm here."

Tom stiffened. Maybe it wasn't Dyer's job or nature to care who killed Billy Pearce. But Billy's Montreal pal was right. No one should die the way Billy did.

"Look, I know that sounds harsh. But person or persons unknown have almost certainly been using this location to assemble lethal compounds for the purpose of committing mass murder. I'm here to find the source of their raw material and seize it." He folded his notepad. "By the way, a message came through for you up at the command post a few minutes ago. Your brother wants you to call him at the hospital. He says it's urgent."

* * *

Tom walked up to the main house, avoiding the two men in stenciled windbreakers guarding the front door. Retrieving a brass house key from a hiding spot that had apparently not changed in a decade, he let himself into the house by the side entrance near the kitchen. Away from prying eyes and ears, he called Joe.

"Right after you left," Joe rasped. "Called. Wants... to talk to you ... about a Gérard Le Pak... , a. k. a. Gérard Bonnefesse." The words came in groups of three and four, followed by shallow intakes of breath. "Claims... he's an *officier de paix*... from the *'Montreal... Commissariat,'*" adding unnecessarily that they meant 'police inspector' and 'police department,' respectively.

Tom felt a wave of cold seep from his chest and spread through his limbs. "That's the friend of Billy's you sent me to see. The one who owned the sex shop and who claimed Billy had found happiness."

"Found his maker," Joe wheezed. "He's dead. One of your cards in his pocket."

Tom pulled the receiver from his ear, but his brother's gravelly voice snapped it back like a rubber band. "Grogan and his posse ... left here a few minutes ago... looking for you. If you can tell him... how I killed... Bonnefesse... from my hospital bed... he'll be... grateful, I'm sure."

Tom started to speak, but Joe kept talking. "Call this *'officier... de paix'*... first before you do... anything else. I don't need... the Dudley Do-Rights... down here on top... of everything else."

Tom slumped on the stairs that led from the pantry to the third floor bedrooms, and sat there trying to collect his thoughts. Joe sounded like hell. Worse than even a few hours ago. But he had been gone from the hospital since yesterday evening. Doing what? And from then until he ensconced himself in his office in Town Hall a few hours ago, no one had seen him. That was more than enough time for a round trip to Montreal. Though he didn't seem to be in any shape to make that kind of trip, or if he did, to do anything strenuous once he got there. And why would he kill Bonnefesse? Frankie, sure. But what motive could Joe have for killing the little Canadian sex shop owner? The unexplained threads through the Coldwater Sheriff had become a web. But unless the story he told to Mary was true, which seemed doubtful, then he'd been lying about almost everything.

Without knowing why, or what he intended to do when he got there, Tom started up the stairs toward the family sleeping quarters. A dozen plus years ago, Susan's bedroom had been at the end of the doglegged corridor that ran the length of the upper floor. Her parents' and Billy's rooms had been in the south wing on the opposite end of the house. Tom was surprised and pleased that he could still navigate the steep passageway without turning on a light or stepping on a creaky board.

Moving quietly along the uncarpeted hall, lined on one side with built-in bookshelves and on the other with six pane, waist-to-ceiling windows, he looked outside and spotted a pair of state troopers pacing the gravel circle. If either of them had looked up, they would have seen him.

The short spur at the end of the hall and the door at its end opened onto the familiar, daisy yellow bedroom with a crow's nest view of the lake. Three occupants of the White House had come and gone since Tom had last been in this room. He stood for a moment wondering if he might have acted differently on his last visit, if he had known it was going to be so long before he returned.

The room had changed, of course. Gone were the rock star and *Women in Science* posters, replaced by delicate watercolors and spare ink drawings. But the ambiance remained the same: piles of books and music disks lay everywhere around the overstuffed chair by the dormer window. The sagging four-poster bed gave a familiar wood and metal squeal when he sat on its edge. He picked up the volumes piled on the wicker nightstand: Kipling, Nabokov, a biology text titled <u>Mean Genes</u> and behind them a small pen and ink drawing—almost certainly in Susan's own hand—of an altar-like rock surrounded by trees and grass.

Tom stared long and hard at the drawing, then lifted it to his face. A strip of blanket peeked from behind the rock and several immature plants fronted it. A stiff, brimmed Smokey the Bear hat anchored the blanket. Tom's heart accelerated and his breath shortened. *You son-of-a bitch, brother.*

After a hurried inventory of the room—looking for what he didn't know, he pocketed the drawing and hustled down to the library.

Dr. Pearce had been meticulous in his organization of that part of the family book collection that most interested him. Fiction, being largely his wife's preserve, was scattered among various shelves in the sun room, main sitting room and in the upstairs hallways. Non-fiction, scientific and reference works were gathered in the library and music rooms and organized there by subject and author.

Tom sat with the <u>Peterson Field Guide</u> and the <u>Newcomb Guide to Wildflowers</u>, flipping pages and comparing what he saw there to what Susan had recorded in her drawing. Only when he heard the sound of tires crushing gravel, did he remember Joe's warning that Paulie Grogan's troopers were looking for him.

Taking the drawing and reference books, he hustled back to the pantry. Footsteps crunched gravel on the other side of the wall as he passed through the music room, followed by silence as whoever it was stepped off of the path and came to peer through the window. From the game room, he watched a jacketed torso move sideways along the row of windows toward the cypress hedge.

Hurrying down the hall, he arrived back at the pantry just in time to turn the bolt on the outer door. Then retreating to the recess of the covered staircase, he watched as a pair of uniformed trousers rounded the hedge and came down the path. Backing deeper into the stairway, he listened to the sound of a handle being turned and a door shaken in its frame. Sensing but not seeing the figure appear at the window over the steel sink, he moved higher still. The figure tried the window, too. But it was cranked tight.

A torso-shaped shadow moved across the pantry floor and then disappeared in the direction of the shoreline. When it didn't return, Tom stepped from the covered staircase and approached the window. The man had made his way down the lawn to the boathouse and stopped there to speak with someone fiddling with the satellite dishes on top of the trailer. Tom looked closely at a profile he had not seen in a dozen years, and then not often. But he was pretty sure it was Joe's former deputy. When Grogan left the trailer and disappeared into the boathouse, Tom returned the house key to its hiding place and then slipped away to look for a half-remembered rock in the woods above Coldwater Lake.

* * *

Forests may be timeless, but they are not changeless. Small trees grow big, big trees die and fall. Grass clearings become populated by shrubs and saplings that block out the sun, kill off the grass and return the clearing to woodlot. Where Tom stopped at the end of an overgrown dirt track, nothing looked the same as he remembered it. *How long had it been? Twenty years?*

Two listing pillars still marked what had been almost a century ago the entrance to the Barrows estate. The main house that stood at the top of the hill facing west toward the lake had burned to the ground in a mysterious fire shortly after the 1929 Crash. He and Joe had discovered the ruins while still in grade school and had claimed it for themselves and their friends by right of conquest.

The hill was smaller than he remembered. It took less than an hour to climb, not the half day it once had. But the geography was the same. The hill still rose high above town and lake. The distant school fields lay where they always had. Only they seemed closer now.

Joe had said that he ran into Susan while he was out taking inventory of the new spring plantings on Watermelon Hill. Maybe he did. Maybe he changed the locale of the story for good reason. But the rock in Susan's drawing was here, not there—on the opposite side of town from Joe's story and too close to civilization for illicit, commercial horticulture.

There was no mistaking the rampart of the make-believe fort where he and Joe had held off invaders with sticks and stones through endless summer afternoons... until the day Joe laid open an invader's head with a well-aimed rock and they were forbidden to play there again. For a few years they obeyed. But in time, each had apparently made the same discovery—that a soft blanket on warm grass behind a concealing stone, with a panoramic view of the town and lake, was an ideal spot for a post-game picnic and hormone-fueled frolic.

He located the old fort without difficulty. The plants in the drawing were there in front of the long rock, their slightly increased height giving approximate date to the drawing and what it implied. He opened the Newcomb Guide and compared the plants in front of the rock to the ones in the marked pages. With the digital camera he'd liberated from the glove compartment of Joe's truck, he took a dozen shots. Then gathering books, drawing, camera and thoughts, he drove fast and grim to Coldwater Hospital.

CHAPTER 25

Mary sat in the plastic visitor's chair by the side of Joe's hospital bed. A single metal crutch lay on the floor by her side. "Your brother's not well," she warned. "No more of this Billy Pearce business."

Joe looked away and said nothing.

"There's a guy at the end of the hall talking into his wristwatch," said Tom. "He's here to see Joe about 'this Billy Pearce business,' too. Little brother would be smart to try out his story here, and get it straight before he has to sell it to the pros."

Joe struggled against the grip of the pillows. He pulled in shallow breaths and blew out words on the exhale. "Mom. Tommy and I... need to talk. Maybe you could go... to the cafeteria. Get something to eat."

Mary gestured at the crutch on the floor. "And how am I supposed to do that?"

Joe sank back into the pillows and half-closed his eyes. "I suppose you'd better go ahead, brother."

Tom handed Joe the *Newcomb Guide to Wild Flowers* opened to a Post It noted page. He gestured at the laptop on the table beside the hospital bed. "Mind if I borrow that?"

Joe nodded.

Removing a cable from a side pocket of the camera case, Tom connected the digital camera to the laptop and screened a close-up image of a large, green plant. "If you look at the screen and at the picture in that book, I think you'll agree that they're pictures of the same plant."

Joe shrugged.

Tom pointed to the text below the photo. "Read the description."

"*Matricaria parthenoides... Also known as Feverfew... Many branched... with finely furrowed stems... Daisy-like flowers... borne in tight flat clusters. ' Okay?"*

"Flip to the next Post-It." Tom ordered.

"*Sceletium...tortuosum. Also known...as Kanna. '"*

Tom screened another close-up. "Read the description and compare the illustration in the book to the plant in this photo."

Joe did as he was told, pausing every few words to catch his breath. "Pretty scrawny specimen," he wheezed.

"Turn to the last page."

"*Hypericium. '"* Joe went through the drill one more time and after finishing snapped the book shut. "Okay... I give up. What's this...supposed to mean?"

"All three plants produce serotonin uptake inhibitors. The stuff you said Susan claimed to be working on at NeuroGene... and the stuff in those plants you pulled up and had analyzed in that lab report you gave me to read on our way to see Willow's partner in New York."

Joe pressed his lips together and nodded slowly. "Okay. I remember."

"They're not native to this area. And they don't grow together naturally."

Joe's eyes narrowed. "Where'd you find them?"

Tom screened a landscape photo of the group of plants spread out in front of a large rock. When Joe remained silent, Tom prodded. "Remember Bobby Ambler?"

Joe turned his face to the window.

Mary looked from one son to the other. "That was the little boy you two hooligans attacked with rocks! His poor mother was hysterical. The father threatened to sue us."

"That's right." Tom turned to his brother. "I found them in front of our old fort, Joe."

Joe fixed his gaze on something beyond the window. "What made you go there?"

Tom handed his mother the pen and ink drawing that he had taken from Susan Pearce's bedroom. "Can you hand this to my brother, please?"

Puzzled, Mary looked at the drawing and then warily passed it to her younger son.

"Where'd you get this?"

"Susan Pearce's bedroom."

"Oh dear," said Mary.

Joe shook his head, appearing more frustrated than guilty. Tom took back the drawing. "You told me you ran into Susan out planting on Watermelon Hill."

"That's right."

"This drawing is in her hand. The rock in it's on the other side of town from Watermelon Hill, and that's your hat on the corner of the blanket sticking out from behind the rock."

"What did you expect me to tell you?"

"The truth."

"Tommy!" pleaded his mother.

"Joe's whisper was a feeble growl. "You're a... masochist. So I... showed a girl... a good time?"

"Joey!" Mary bleated.

Tom pointed to the rock formation at the center of the drawing. "So that's our old fort, isn't it?"

"I said yes."

"And that little garden in front of the rock would be Susan's?"

"Go on."

"Wouldn't it?"

"I said... go on."

"It's not yours, is it?"

Joe shook his head.

"And given where it is and what's in it, it's not likely to be anyone else's is it?"

"Tommy, quit acting like a lawyer and make your point," Mary snapped.

Tom gestured at the drawing and the landscape image still screening on the laptop. "There's another plant in front of the others, taller and wider." He took the Taylor's Master Guide to Gardening and handed it to his mother. "Take a look at the tabbed page, Mom, and tell me if the plant on the screen here is the same as the one in the book."

Though there was little doubt the plants were identical, Mary would only allow, "I suppose they could be."

"And would you read the description, please?"

"'*Abrus precatorius*,'" she recited obediently. "'*Also known as Rosary pea.* '" She looked up from the page. "The church used to sell Christmas decorations using something called Rosary Pea. After the leaves fell off you could string the peas together to make a rosary."

"Same plant," said Tom. "Did they warn the moms to keep the beads away from the kids?"

"Now that you mention it, yes. They said it could make them sick."

"Actually, it could kill them. The rosary pea contains a toxin called abrin. If a kid swallowed one he'd probably be okay, since the pea has a hard shell. But if he chewed it and any of the inside came out, he could die."

"Oh, dear."

"Susan doesn't… have kids," said Joe. "And I don't… see her… as the rosary type."

"I don't think Billy was chewing rosaries either," said Tom. "But according to his autopsy report, he had abrin in his blood when he died. A lot of it."

"Snoop," said Joe.

Mary closed the book, her face a pastiche of sadness, confusion and worry. Tom retrieved the book and handed it to Joe. "Read," he ordered.

In a sarcastic, singsong whisper, Joe recited: "*woody vine… with auxiliary cluster… of pink… or lavender… flowers. Warn children… that the seeds… though attractive… are poisonous.*" He dropped the book on the bed cover.

"And isn't that the plant in the photo?" asked Tom. "And in the drawing?"

"What if… it is… brother? Billy drowned."

"So did Rasputin. But before that, he'd been fed enough arsenic to kill a bear, shot in the face at point blank range, bludgeoned, bound and shoved through a hole in an iced-over river. But when they found his body, the ropes were broken and his lungs were filled with water. He drowned, too."

"You saying... I killed Billy?"

"Rosary pea was on the lab list you gave me in the car on the way to New York. It's the overlap between the plants you say you took off of Watermelon Hill and this group here. That, and that all the others are serotonin uptake inhibitors."

"Tommy!" whined Mrs. Morgan. "What are you saying?"

"Joe knows, Mom. A dog that doesn't bark. A boat that makes it through Wilson Cove running without lights, a severed bird leg and now this witch's garden on the sunny side of our old fort."

"Joey?" Mary pleaded.

"If you've got a story that'll string this all together," said Tom, "you might as well practice it here on family before you have to sell it to Dick Tracy outside."

"I ought... to beat... the crap out... of you," Joe whispered.

"I know you mean that lovingly. In the meantime, try the truth."

Joe glanced helplessly from Tom to his mother and then sank back into the bed, defeated.

"Joey?" his mother whispered.

Joe turned his head toward his brother, his face a mask of exhausted defeat and his words sputtered with labored breath. "Mom told you... I saw Billy... a few hours... before he was killed. That I called... Susan to get... him to a hospital. That I found... them both gone... when I went back... after my shift."

Mary looked away.

"She told me that story."

"When I went... into the boathouse... to look for them... that bird... attacked me. It was already... missing a foot. Whatever they find... under that claw... won't be... from me. The Chris Craft... was gone... too. I could hear... a boat... out in Wilson Cove... but I couldn't see it. It took me... five minutes... to get down to... the marina... and out... in the police boat. Maybe another five... sweeping the cove... with a spotlight... before I picked... up a boat... drifting dark."

"Anyone on board?"

"Not that I... could see. It took me a while... to get there. Even with... the halogen spot... you've got to... be careful of rocks... in that place. When I got close... I heard a thud... and then... a few seconds later... a splash. It was a big... wooden cruiser... like the Pearce's... so I yelled. But no one answered."

"Jesus, Mary and Joseph!" whispered Mary.

"There was no one... on deck... when I pulled... alongside, and when I checked... the cabin... was empty."

Tom's and his mother's stares triangulated on Joe's moist, chalky face.

"Then I heard... another splash... off the stern. And I went to see.. . what it was. There were more... splashes... so I yelled... and shined a light... on the water. Then out of the dark... and up to the side... of the boat... swims you know who. 'Hi... ,' she says. Perky... as you please."

Mary groaned.

Tom locked eyes with his brother. "Let me guess. She's got on this modest, one-piece swimsuit?"

"Not a stitch."

Mary's face went from ghostly to livid in a nanosecond. Had she been strapped to the same machines as her son, the electronics would have imploded. "And so you forgot what you were there for, didn't you? That you were a police officer investigating a murder!"

Joe shook his head. "I didn't know... I was investigating... a murder. No one knew there'd been one... until the Dooley twins... fished Billy... out of the lake... the next day."

Tom continued to stare at his brother. "Did you ask her what she was doing out there? And did she know that Billy was gone?"

"Eventually."

"What did she say... *eventually?*"

Joe released a lung full of air. "She said Billy... was fine... when she got home... but gone when... she went down... to the boathouse later. That she'd heard... a boat driving... away and tried... to follow it. But she lost it."

"Did you ask about the bird?"

"Or the mess the place was in?" asked Mary.

"Not right away."

Mary groaned.

Tom shook his head. "This is what you police types call a *modus operandi*, isn't it? Girl distracts over-sexed cop by taking off her clothes? She's got you figured out pretty good little brother."

Joe's voice regained a measure of strength and volume. "I'm going... to beat... the crap... out of you... when I... get out of here."

Tom hooted. "You know what that first splash was, don't you?"

Joe closed his eyes and lifted his face toward the ceiling.

Mary looked at Tom like he'd abruptly changed the subject and that it didn't promise to be good.

"Billy. In a weighted sleeping bag. Still alive."

"Oh, no!" Mary's hands leapt to her mouth. Joe surrendered a long, reedy groan.

"You're going to need a damned good lawyer, little brother."

"Don't know any."

* * *

A phone rang in a nearby patient's room. A rasping voice audible through the wall began to recite symptoms to an unseen listener. The pulse at Tom's neck throbbed. The smell of hospital disinfectant seeped into his nostrils. Down the hall, a sobbing child called for its mother.

"I don't understand," said Mary, breaking the silence. "*She* killed her brother?"

Tom nodded. "It looks that way. Or rather, she sped up something that was already underway. My guess is that when Joe called her about getting Billy to the hospital, she went home and found Billy near dead anyway. I think Frankie Heller was there first, and that's why the boathouse looked a wreck and that's how that bird got its leg whacked off. But Frankie just beat the stuffing out of Billy. He didn't kill him."

"Then how *did* he die?"

"He drowned," Joe moaned.

"Frankie must have left in a hurry when he heard Susan come home. She knew Billy was sick, and the abrin bit says she knew what from. Father Gauss said that he'd heard Billy was trying to get Susan to sell the family estate and that he was making her life miserable because she wouldn't agree. Billy's Canadian pal confirmed that. My guess is Billy flaunted what he was doing for Frankie and Dr. Hassad. And that doing it right out of the boathouse under his sister's nose was part of his campaign to get her out. The abrin must have been a recent addition, and he must have contaminated himself almost immediately."

"What makes... you think?" Joe's voice was barely a whisper.

"Because if he hadn't, once Susan had found out that he'd graduated from pot to poison, she would have turned him in. Brother or no brother. She's a scientist, not a terrorist."

"But if he was already dying, why give him the poison from that Rosary Pea?" asked Mary.

"To speed things up. And to do it in a way consistent with accidental exposure. She must have reasoned that even if the abrin were detected, there would be evidence that Billy had quite a bit of it about and that it would be attributed to the same source. A source that certainly wasn't going to come around and dispute the connection. It was good, quick thinking."

"That seems to be Miss Pearce's specialty," Mary observed.

The brothers' eyes stuttered past each other like wrong-way magnets.

"So why... did she need... to speed it up?" asked Joe. "If he's... already dying?"

Tom glanced at his mother. She was staring off into the middle distance, isolated, but still listening. His answer was unsparing. "Because Super Trooper was coming to the rescue and the striptease gig might not work with Billy throwing up blood all over the place."

"Tommy!"

"Think about it." Tom spoke directly to his brother now. "This low life, scum-bucket had just about finished killing off his sorry self. And whatever misery he'd been heaping on Susan and whatever threat he posed to her work and reputation was within hours of coming to an end. Not to mention the bigger threat of this toxin and the people who paid Billy to mix it up in batches. But Super Trooper is on his way and there's no time to stop him."

Joe said nothing.

"When you called her, did you happen to say something manly, like that if she didn't get Billy to the hospital by the time your shift was over, you'd come and drag him there yourself?"

Joe wouldn't look at him.

"Did you?" Tom demanded.

Joe bowed his head.

"So she poisoned him?" asked Mary, wanting it spelled out plainly.

"From what the CDC doctor told me," said Tom, "she would only have had to crush one of those beans in a cup of liquid. Maybe she crushed a handful to finish him off fast. He was at death's door anyway, it was just a matter of hours. When it looked like the potion had worked, she must have zipped him up in that sleeping bag. Maybe he was using it as a bed cover or something and was already lying on it. It gets pretty cold at night on the water, and there was only a sheet on the bed when I went there yesterday. Then she dragged the bag with Billy in it down the steps and into the boat."

When Tom finished speaking, the family Morgan fell into an exhausted silence. Each stared off in a different direction like strangers in a crowded elevator. Mary was the first to snap out of it. "That's quite a story, Tommy. But isn't it what they call circumstantial? You can't prove any of it. Can you?"

Joe answered for his brother, his voice a feeble gasp. "I think... we'll find pieces... of Frankie Heller... under those bird claws. I took... a lot of stuff... from Billy's room... right after we found... his body. Maybe we'll get... some abrin... out of a mug... or something. We'll get more... of Billy... from the boat. It couldn't have... been easy... dragging him... over the side... in and out. We'll get fibers... from the bag... at least."

Tom paced in the space between bed and door. "The first story Susan tells after she gets hit with this is going to be the best chance of getting anything near the truth. You've got to tell your pal Grogan to bring her in before she has a chance to polish some fairy tale."

Joe struggled to speak. "I know I'm compromised, Tommy. But I can't…"

"It's not just Susan, Joe. What about Hassad and what he was up to with Billy? Who's going to stop him before he skips town? You? Me?"

CHAPTER 26

om pulled up beside Susan's dented BMW sat at the far end of the NeuroGene parking lot, and there had another of those 'what am I doing here?' moments, conscious that he was having a lot of them lately, with Susan Pearce as the common catalyst. This time the answer came easily. He had come for the truth.

Willow leaned unsteadily on the edge the reception desk, flanked by a young man in an un-pressed white shirt, clear plastic pocket protector and about three inches and a hundred pounds on Tom. "Leave," said Willow.

Tom addressed the hulking youth at Willow's side. "He pay you to get hurt, too?"

The young man turned to the receptionist. "Amanda, call the police now."

"Go ahead. It'll make his day."

While the receptionist called the Coldwater police station, the door behind her desk opened, and a mixed group of business suits and lab coats came through it. Tom sidestepped the group and entered the corridor behind them.

Hustling down hallways, room-to-room, focused and fast, he paused at a metal door where a thick glass porthole framed a long white lab coat and a mane of honey hair draped like a lampshade over a polished microscope. Coherent thought dissolved until he remembered that he was looking at a probable killer who may have poisoned and then drowned her own brother.

The Apostle Paul had warned that 'he who increases knowledge increases pain.' Tom opened the door, hoping that Paul was wrong.

Susan looked up. "I knew you'd come back."

Words can be pain too, when they come too late.

"There's a posse of state troopers at your house, Susan. Did you know that?"

"Yes, they showed up early this morning."

Something that looked like a picnic cooler sat on the floor next to Susan's feet. He watched her remove a slide from the polished metal cylinder and add it to the stack of others inside the cooler. She was packing.

"How long, do you think, before they find out that you killed your brother? And that you fooled mine into helping you get away with it?"

"What!" She looked genuinely shocked and surprised. "How could you think that?"

"I found your little garden, Susan. Your brother's autopsy found some of it, too. Inside him."

She laid a slide back on the lab table. "That's not possible."

"Is that your story?"

Susan leaned on a corner of the lab table and lowered herself onto the stool beside it. Then raised her eyes to look at her long ago lover. "I didn't kill Billy."

Tom recited the contrary evidence. "Joe found Billy down at the boathouse sick as a dog. He called you here and told you that Billy needed to be in the hospital. He said that if you couldn't get him to go, he'd come and drag him there himself. Billy was dying, but you didn't want him going to the hospital and getting saved. You wanted him dead."

Susan met his cold stare with one of her own. "That's right. But I didn't kill him."

"So you made him some tea or soup or something, from one of those Rosary pea plants. Then you dragged him down to the boat and took him out into the lake."

"No."

"Joe came by as you pulled away. He heard you and followed in the police boat. It took a while for him to get through Wilson Cove. And before he got close enough to come on board, he heard a splash. That was you dumping Billy overboard. Alive."

"You've got it wrong."

Tom laughed. "Which part?"

"The part that isn't there." Susan's voice recovered a measure of volume and animation. "The Frankie Heller part."

Surprise and suspicion swirled in equal measure through Tom's sleep-deprived brain. "You've got one chance to get this right, Susan. Tell me some fairy tale now and improve it later... and I'll see you fry."

"You've gotten cold." Her voice was a whisper.

"What I know says I'm talking to a killer. Show me I'm wrong and maybe I'll thaw."

Susan stepped away from the lab table. "Alright. Billy and Frankie were arguing about something all week. Billy was getting scared... and sick, too. I think he finally told Frankie about Suliman and what he was doing for him. I think Frankie saw immediately what Billy didn't. That Suliman came from a bigger pond than the one that floated Frankie and his little cannabis business. And Frankie was smart enough to be scared of the bigger fish.

"And you're right. When your brother stopped by that night, Billy was in bad shape. I'm pretty sure he was dying. Joe called me at work and told me to get Billy to the hospital. But by the time I got home, Frankie was back again, and he and Billy were down at the boathouse going at it like they were in a bar fight: screaming, breaking things. I wasn't going to go anywhere near there. When the noise stopped and I heard a boat engine start up and pull away, I went down to check.

"The boathouse looked like a bomb had gone off. Billy and Frankie were gone. Billy's bird was screaming. I could see it was injured, but it wouldn't let me come near. Then I heard your brother drive up. I didn't want to see him, or anyone else, right then. I needed time to think. So I took Daddy's boat and headed out into the cove."

Tom's voice was hard. "Where was Frankie's car?"

Susan hesitated. "I don't know. He must have come in his own boat. From

205

the sound of it, that's how he and Billy left."

"Why didn't you want to see Joe?"

"Think about it!" she hissed. "My brother had gotten himself and God knows who else exposed to some lethal neuro-toxin! He'd been running drugs from Canada with Frankie Heller, and now they're at each other's throats. He's dying. But for the moment, he and Frankie have gone off someplace and maybe, just maybe, they won't be back."

Tom pressed. "When Joe came out in the police boat and found you in the middle of the cove, why didn't you tell him then?"

"I didn't know then that Billy had been killed. I just knew he'd gone off someplace with Frankie. And that maybe he'd die there."

"And what about the abrin?" Tom's voice was throttled by calm. "How did a bit of rosary pea from a garden you planted out in the woods, in a spot my brother showed to you, wind up in Billy's corpse?"

"I don't know."

"You're lying."

She recoiled as if slapped, then she drifted toward the window. It was a long half-minute before she spoke. Tom was ready to call Joe and have him send the state troopers.

"I'm a scientist," she said at last. "But I read the newspapers like everyone else. When I read about those terrorists in London being caught with something called ricin, I looked it up and found that the plant it came from was from the same family as the rosary pea plant I was using to keep the deer away from my research plots, and that their toxins were similar. So when I harvested the plants, I took some of the rosary pea too, to look at in the lab. Scientific curiosity, that's all."

"How did it get into Billy?"

"I don't know."

"Guess. Because if you can't explain that part, the rest isn't going to make any difference to anybody."

For the first time, Susan looked unsure of herself. She paced in front of the windows overlooking the strip of woods between the office building and the road. "Let me think out loud. Because I honestly don't know."

He waited.

"When I first brought everything back to the house," she said, "I left the peas on the kitchen window sill to dry. Then I forgot about them for a while. When I noticed them again, I realized that I was going to need a mortar and pestle to crush them into something I could work with. I didn't have one in the lab at the moment. But I'd seen a small head shop version down in the boathouse in Billy's bathroom. So one night while he was out, I went down to borrow it. Only he came back there while I was there using it. I guess he got the wrong idea about what I was doing, because he picked that moment to tell me about what he was doing with Frankie and hinting about what he was up to with Suliman. We got into an argument. I told him I wanted him to move out. He laughed and said he'd take it up with Frankie—that maybe he could arrange another boat accident. It was a naked threat. I got out of there fast.

"I'm guessing now that I forgot to wash the mortar and pestle before I left, and that there would have been a residue of powdered rosary pea in it. Actually, considering what had just happened, I'm certain I didn't remember to wash it. Then Billy must have used it sometime after that for mixing one of his happy powders."

She stopped pacing and sat down at the lab table. "Anyway, that's my guess of how the abrin might have gotten into him. But as I told you, I don't really know."

Tom waited for his own reaction, and found he had none. He was on overload. Numb. He didn't know what to think.

"It couldn't have been a lethal dose," she added. "It would have been just the residue. And besides, he drowned, didn't he?"

"Why didn't you tell this to Joe when the Dooley twins hauled Billy out of the lake?"

"I was going to. But then all of a sudden your brother started avoiding me and ducking my calls. If you'll remember, I was up at his cabin the very next morning looking for him. That's when I met you. But Joe was running away from me all of a sudden. And by the time he wasn't, I had decided it was better to let it slide."

"Why?"

"I can't believe a Morgan is asking that."

Tom closed his eyes while a wave of fatigue swept through his body. "I'm in no mood for guessing games, Susan."

"Fine. I'll spell it out. Did you or your brother tell anyone about the thousands of dollars in cash that Morini's Funeral Home found in your father's coat?"

A small, choking noise spit from the back of Tom's throat.

"Did you really think Morini was going to keep a secret like that? In a town like this?"

A surge of adrenaline set his heart pound against his ribs.

"What good would have come of my washing the Pearce family linen after Billy died? I like Coldwater, Tom. I love my work. I want to stay here and enjoy a peaceful, productive life. Even if it helped put Frankie Heller in jail for a while, do I really need to worry about someone like him getting out in a few years and coming after me? Or sending one of his friends to do it? Do I deserve that?"

He had no answer, and Susan didn't wait for one.

"I do not! I kept my family's secret for the same reason that you and your brother kept yours."

Tom tried to form a coherent thought. If true, this latest version of Billy's death was Hellenic tragedy. Everything that Susan had hoped to keep private was going to become public no matter what she said or did. There was no way to stop it. And if untrue, it was brilliant. Those who might deny the story were dead. And those who might disprove it were compromised.

He looked at her hard. "If they find fibers from Billy's sleeping bag or anything like that on your father's boat, then this story's going to turn around and bite you."

"They won't."

But he could hear the hesitation in her voice. Or maybe she just saw the men in stenciled windbreakers through the lab door window, about to break in.

CHAPTER 27

Tom had a pretty good idea of where they had taken him. The rumbling eighteen-wheelers behind the curtained, ground floor window were one clue. The smell of deep fried fat that clung to the clothes of the public servants who took turns questioning him was another. The tub/shower had a curtain but not a door. The toiletries included shampoo but not conditioner. He assumed he was in one of those rent-a-beds along the strip of fast food palaces and used car lots on the main drag heading out of Coldwater. It wasn't the Hilton.

The corner door opened without a knock and three thick bodies crowded in. One took the straight-backed chair beneath the curtained window, one a corner of the twin bed against the wall and the other stood. The one on his feet introduced himself as Mr. Johnsen. "With an 'e'," as if Tom might need that information later. "With the Federal Emergency Management Agency." He identified the others as National Bioforensic Analysis Center and something called BARDA. He did not volunteer names. A fourth person came in during the brief introduction, attached a laptop to the television and left.

"We've decided you should see this first," said Johnsen. "Then we can chat."

The time stamp at the bottom of the screen read that day's date, but Tom could not quite make out the time. The screen showed a man at a podium and behind him a large map of the northeast United States and eastern

Canada, with Coldwater at the center. Johnsen turned up the volume.

"As you can see," said the man on the screen, "there are eleven outdoor stadiums located within a two-hundred-mile radius of the first contamination." He aimed a laser pointer at the map projected on the wall behind him. "Each holds between twenty to sixty thousand people. All but two are on the U. S. side of the border. Absent extreme weather, two-thirds of those stadiums will be filled on either day of each weekend between now and the end of November." He pressed the controller in his hand and the border map was replaced by a photo of the Plexiglas box that the diver had recovered from the water beneath the Pearce boathouse. He explained where it was found, its probable function and that the boathouse's last occupant had tested positive for something called 'abrin.' "For those of you not familiar with the compound abrin, and I assume that's virtually all of you, it is a close chemical cousin to that other terrorist toy, ricin, only about seventy-five times more potent."

He clicked the slide changer again, and an image appeared of an open automobile trunk with a box the size of a footlocker wedged inside. The next slide showed the underside of the same car with a Frisbee-sized hole cut through the floor of the trunk and the bottom of the box inside it. The final slide was a crude diagram of a wire cable passing through a box and the back seat of a car, ending in a loop next to the driver's seat. The opposite end of the cable was attached to a plastic disk that covered the hole in the bottom of the box and trunk. "Like an old-fashioned bathtub plug and chain," he explained.

"We found two cars modified with this homemade device in a junkyard less than three miles from where we found the apparatus in slide number two. One was on a hydraulic lift inside a commercial garage and the other was parked in an adjacent junkyard with full tank of gas and an ignition key under the driver's seat. We don't know how many of these vehicles may have been cobbled together there or whether any have been made in other locations. But it's ingenious, low-tech, easy to make and simple to use."

Someone spoke from outside the range of the video monitor. The speaker cupped a hand to his ear and then leaned toward the microphone. "I'm just coming to that." He opened a three-ring binder and consulted a tabbed section before resuming.

"Our wonderful planet is full of deadly compounds. That one may be seventy-five times more potent than another is hardly significant, if both are one hundred percent lethal and kill their victims one at a time. But what slide two and three are telling us is that someone has developed a way to deliver the toxin abrin in aerosol form, thus enabling murder by the thousands.

"We don't have data on abrin in aerosol form. Until now, we didn't know that it existed outside the lab, much less ready to be manufactured and delivered in mass quantities. But that's what these slides seem to be telling us.

"Based on the delivery mechanisms we found at this site, the Biomedical Advanced Research and Development Authority has made modifications to the anthrax contamination model created by Dr. Inglesby at the Johns Hopkins Center for Civilian Biodefense and which is still the most up to date scenario we have for aerosol bio-attack. The revised projected outcome is subject to a number of variables and is probably conservative."

He turned to another tab in the note book and began to read:

"In Inglesby's scenario, a car modified like the one in slide number four cruises by a sports stadium while a game is in progress. The driver pulls the plug at the bottom of the trunk using the cable device shown in the last slide. Several kilos of powered toxin spill from the bottom of the vehicle, spread over the highway and then start to blow across the cars in the nearby parking lot, into the stadium and through the surrounding neighborhoods. The model predicts that, depending on prevailing winds, one out of five people who attended the game will inhale a number of molecules of toxin sufficient to cause illness or death. From that point forward, the day-to-day progress of the contamination is as follows:"

The reader's crisp voice was momentarily muffled by the undertone of Tom's disbelief. *What have you done, Susan?*

"Hospital personnel are overwhelmed and confused, some fearing for their own safety. Those who can find them, begin to wear anti-contamination suits, photos of which are widely displayed on the news. Tests conducted by the National Bioforensic Analysis Center on blood samples taken from the first to die confirm the presence of abrin."

"People who have not yet been infected begin to flee the city. Massive traffic congestion and widespread panic result... The mortuaries are full. Funeral homes close. The accumulation of dead bodies threatens to cause additional health crisis. State health officials order the dead to be cremated, setting off violent protests by several religious groups..."

By the end of Day Eight, eight thousand people are symptomatic and over two thousand have died.'"

The man behind the podium looked up. There was no conversation, no rustling of papers, no movement or stirring of any kind. He flipped a final page in his notebook.

"'Six Months Later,' he read, "the stadium is abandoned. Businesses in the surrounding neighborhood have left. Commercial and tourist travel to the city has all but disappeared. Of the fifty thousand people in and around the stadium on the afternoon of the attack, ten thousand became symptomatic and twenty-five hundred died... Economic losses as a result of the attack are estimated to be in the billions.'"

He closed his notebook and addressed a silent room. "The Inglesby scenario I've just read is based on a single attack from a single vehicle. Multiple simultaneous attacks at different locations and serial attacks over time are not only possible, they are to be expected. We don't know if a weaponized version of abrin is as effective as the toxins and spores we know more about, like anthrax—whether it's half as effective or one hundred times as effective. Assuming that it is effective—and judging from slide two and three, some people seem ready to put it out there for a test—the purpose of this gathering is to identify intervention points in the revised Inglesby Scenario where timely and coordinated efforts of the agencies represented in this room might minimize fatalities or achieve other positive results."

Johnsen turned off the television. "We can skip the rest. There aren't enough medical supplies and personnel to cover all of the possible sites ahead of time and the federal government isn't going to warn and protect one city and not another. Frankly, we just have to make sure that a catastrophe like the one you just heard doesn't happen."

Tom looked at the three strained faces. "I get it. But why am I here?"

The bearded man, who Johnsen had identified as from the National Bioforensic Analysis Center, answered. "We have a tape of this fellow Hassad coming over the Champlain Bridge last night. He used the name Aza and a green card to go with it. He hasn't been spotted going back. Our Canadian friends tell us that he hasn't left from any of their airports and we know that he hasn't left from any of ours. So our best guess is that he's still hanging around. We assume for a reason. Something to protect. Something to finish. Maybe both."

The man sitting on the bed with his back against the wall interrupted. He was the one Johnsen had identified as BARDA, and he looked like an ex-boxer whose only defeat had been to acne. "We had that guy you say you didn't kill—Heller—under observation for over a year, hoping that he'd lead us up the food chain. Our Canadian friends had the other end covered. But their guy got dead last night." He read from a blue spiral notebook. "Bonnefesse. The last they had from him is that this Hassad passed something to Heller just a week ago—a couple of trunks of something, not the usual collection of bottles and baggies."

Tom tried not to react to the information about the gay sex shop owner. He spread his bandaged hands, palms up, but did not repeat his question.

"A Miss Susan Pearce will be out on bail by tomorrow. There's no evidence against her that we're willing to share at this point and it's better if she thinks there isn't any. What we want, is for you to stay close to her and let us know if and when this Dr. Hassad shows up."

"You must have twenty guys at her house already," Tom protested.

"On the outside," Johnsen agreed. "But we're told that you may be able to get... closer?"

They don't miss much. Still... Susan might have accidentally poisoned her brother or even looked the other way while Frankie Heller took Billy on a one way boat ride. But Tom couldn't believe she was involved in mass murder. "Look," he said. "I don't think that there's a recent connection between Miss Pearce and whatever this guy's name is now. With the brother, yes. But not her."

The little man on the hardback chair took a folder from his briefcase and handed it to Tom. "NeuroGene is a Nevada corporation. It takes a bit of work to pierce the corporate veil out there. But you can see from the top document that the corporation is majority owned by a Canadian holding company. A few months ago, the same company purchased a small island on Coldwater Lake. A local real estate firm handled the transfer, using a general power of attorney. There's a Federal Express receipt there for the closing documents, signed by an S. Pearce."

Tom looked at the signature. Small, neat, precise. Like her. It was genuine. He pressed the back of a bandaged knuckle into his eye socket. His head ached. His hands throbbed. The wounds on his scalp and knees felt like piecrust. How long had it been since he slept?

"There is *definitely* a recent connection," said Johnsen.

"But isn't it dangerous for her if Hassad shows up? Assuming he killed Frankie Heller and Bonnefesse. If you're right about a recent connection and he's already dusting his trail, then he'll go after her too, right? Even if she just thought she was helping an old friend with a real estate transaction?"

No one in the room took up the suggestion.

"You're using her as bait," he pressed. "Does she know that?"

"She might, if she'd talk to us," said Johnsen. "But she's lawyer-ed up already—which as far as I'm concerned speaks for itself."

"*You* could tell her," said the nameless man sitting on the edge of the bed. "Help us, and we might consider helping you with some of your other troubles."

They don't miss anything.

When Tom didn't respond, the man turned to Johnsen. "Did we decide yet what to do about that Barney Fife who thinks he runs things around here? The one with the monster truck that costs more than my house. Have we decided whether he's taken money from the rag-head, too, or just the locals?" He looked at Tom. "It's that kind of town, I hear. That kind of family."

214

Tom ignored the pugnacious stare, but the man wasn't finished. "If a brother were helpful, maybe we wouldn't have to waste time digging into any of that. Or let that state trooper, Grogan, do it. He seems to have a real hard on for your brother."

"We do have more important things to do," added Johnsen, "and precious little time to do them."

CHAPTER 28

G auss sat alone on a stone bench outside the St. Gabriel chapel, his hands folded in meditation. A small fountain bubbled nearby making sounds like a running toilet, though not loudly enough to cover the sound of footsteps echoing on cloister stone. He looked up. Bishop's Mczynski's gopher, Monsignor Marchetti, came to a halt and dropped an unsealed envelope into Gauss' lap. "His Eminence has received another letter."

"I would have thought he might be over the thrill of these by now."

"And photographs."

"Ah." Gauss opened the envelope and retrieved a color print. The lighter-skinned of the two sunbathers wore shorts and a silver crucifix and sat upright facing the water. The darker one lay face down on a lounge chair and wore nothing.

"And the letter?"

"You have some explaining to do, Father."

"Do I?"

"These are serious charges, Father. And this is damning evidence."

"Evidence of what, Monsignor?"

"Is this a friend of yours?"

"An acquaintance."

"What sort of acquaintance?"

"An intellectual acquaintance, for want of a better word."

"I'm not interested in his IQ, Father. I want to know what the two of you were doing together in your birthday suits."

Gauss glanced at the photo. "Actually, only one of us is in his birthday suit, Monsignor. I seem to be wearing the same pair of swim trunks that I've had since the seminary. Can't afford new ones on the pittance His Eminence pays his vineyard labor."

"That man is stark naked, Father! And that's you sitting next to him. Or do you deny that?"

"Oh, no. That's me alright." He put the photo back in the envelope and returned it to the Bishop's man. "Some of our summer residents like to swim in the nude, Monsignor. The European ones, anyway. Locals tend to keep their clothes on, as you can see. But we're not so arrogant as to tell people how to dress in their own homes."

"Please answer my question," Marchetti demanded. "What's your relationship with this man?"

"He's the owner of an island on Coldwater Lake across from Our Lady of the Lake Church. The one with the Frank Lloyd Wright house on it. His name is Hassad."

"Go on."

"Dr. Hassad, bought the island last winter and put guard dogs on it. When I took the church row boat past there this spring after the ice out, the dogs lept into the water and practically chewed the boat to bits. Dr. Hassad saw it happening and called them off. Then he invited me for lunch so they could 'get my smell', as he put it, so they would leave me alone the next time I rowed past the island. He's an interesting man. Claims to be from Afghanistan, though I don't think that's true, since he'd never heard of Ahmed Zahir. But it turns out we both like Merchant Ivory films."

"I don't understand," said Marchetti.

"You would if you lived in a town where fishing rods outnumber library cards."

"Arrogance!" Marchetti blustered.

217

"Is that what this mystery letter accuses me of? Arrogance?"

"It accuses you of being this man's lover!" Marchetti snapped a fingernail against the envelope.

Gauss sighed. "I suppose that makes sense. Pearce might even have thought it true this time."

"How…? Are you admitting…?"

Gauss regarded his inquisitor from beneath raised eyebrows. "Don't you do any homework before you take on these assignments?"

"Are you?" demanded Marchetti.

"What?"

"A homosexual."

Gauss sighed again. "I'm a celibate, Monsignor. And if you'd bothered to read the files you gave to Sister Inquisitor, you'd know that Billy Pearce began writing this kind of drivel as soon as I put the kibosh on his first attempted romance with one of my altar boys. Hasn't it occurred to anyone in the Chancery that all this so-called evidence may just be Pearce penning under different names?"

"I didn't say who wrote the letter," Marchetti protested.

"You didn't have to." Gauss lifted a pair of bony shoulders. "Have you ever been to Stockholm, Monsignor?"

"I don't see…"

Gauss talked over him. "I stopped there on my way back from the Vatican a few years ago. The friend I was there to see got tied up and suggested that I go to the park across the street to kill an hour. There I was sitting on a park bench, soaking up what passes for sunlight in those parts, and here and there on the grass and on the other benches I see these young office girls sunbathing—with their shirts off! It was quite a sight."

Marchetti's face turned scarlet, but Gauss continued. "When I met my friend later, he laughed and asked how I enjoyed my lunch. 'Sometimes we get people visiting our little city for the first time who go to lunch and never make it back.'"

Marchetti folded his arms and rocked on his heels. "And the point of this scurrilous story?"

"That if somebody had taken my picture that afternoon in Stockholm, sitting on a park bench enjoying my holiday and sent it to the parish newspaper along with a nasty letter, what would that prove? Except that I didn't go native there either."

"So you're denying the authenticity of this photograph and letter?"

"No, the photograph is real. It just doesn't mean what you think it does. If Billy Pearce was on Pocket Island when that picture was taken, then I didn't see him. But I wouldn't be surprised if he was a regular. I understand Dr. Hassad's mix of house guests is somewhat eclectic. As for the letter…, I haven't seen it. But we're talking about someone found trussed in a sleeping bag fished from the bottom of Coldwater Lake… not some cherub-cheeked seminarian. Someone whose parents died in a boating 'accident' that even his friends find unlikely."

"What are you saying?" Marchetti demanded.

"That you're taking at face value what common sense ought to tell you not to."

"Arrogance." The Bishop's emissary turned the envelope over in his hands and frowned. "Your answers leave His Eminence little room for permitting you to resume Holy Office."

"They don't leave him anything, as far as I can see."

"Just you in a pornographic photo taken by a murdered homosexual."

"And a letter the bishop doesn't want me to see?"

Marchetti glared at the priest and, with equal irritation, the running fountain. He no longer attempted to hide the anger in his voice. "I've spoken with your housekeeper."

"What now?"

"She says that you knew this Billy Pearce better than you've let on."

"Does she?"

"She listens in on your phone conversations, Father. And on your 'counseling' sessions. She also reads your email."

"I'll have to have her say a penance when I return."

"You're not returning anywhere, Father."

"Really?"

"This housekeeper says that Pearce called you the evening before he was found murdered."

Gauss clasped his fingers behind his head.

"That she heard you yelling into the phone and using foul language."

Gauss closed his eyes.

"That you left the rectory in a hurry and didn't come back before she'd left for the evening. But that when she returned in the morning there was a pair of wet trousers and a wet tee shirt in the laundry."

"Coldwater's own Miss Marple."

"And she wants to know what to say to that persistent sheriff who's been to the rectory twice now and who was on the phone with me this morning demanding that we produce you for questioning."

"I didn't ask to be hustled away in the night, Monsignor."

"We'll have to produce you sooner or later."

"I'm sure you will."

"And our attorneys advise that it would be better if you talk with Sister Dion first."

"I have. But we seem to have run out of new material."

"And that you undergo a general examination of conscience."

"With you?"

"There are legal as well as spiritual advantages."

"I'd rather have my tooth drilled."

* * *

At Dr. Dwyer's direction, the Coldwater Hospital put Joe through a vigorous gastric decontamination followed by several rounds of magnesium citrate cathartics. After two days of torture, there was nothing left to come out and nothing inside that wasn't raw. The hospital doctors said he was ready to go home.

Mary came with her geriatric boy toy, Herbert to bring her son home. Joe thought she looked like hell. There was a weariness about her that had not arrived with her fall or in the days afterwards. She had lost weight. Her eyes were rheumy. When he kissed her cheek, it felt chilly and clammy. He reached his hand to her forehead.

"I'm not sick, Joey," she snapped, pushing it away. "I'm worried sick. There's a difference."

He didn't need to ask about what.

"It's a good thing you're getting out of here. Because your brother's about to do something stupid, and you need to stop him."

As the originator of several large and recent stupidities, Joe withheld condemnation. But she pressed. "You need to talk to him."

"About what?"

"Don't be thick. About the Pearce girl."

"You're a pyromaniac, Mom."

She waved a hand in dismissal. "Your brother doesn't know whether he's coming, going or been there with that girl. That's going to get *him* and *you* into serious trouble."

Joe could think of nothing he might say or do to respond to his mother's directions. He wasn't even sure he understood them. He said so.

"Your confused older brother seems to think he's a Pearce. That family didn't adopt him, they used him. It's time he understood that."

"I'm not following you, mom."

"Didn't you and your father ever talk?"

"About the Pearces?"

"About what they were doing with your brother."

"The only thing Dad ever said to me about Susan Pearce was that there was nothing wrong with Tommy's eyesight."

Mary snorted. "For a man who didn't speak much, your father could pack a lot in a few words." She turned to Herbert. "Be a dear and get me a lemonade from the cafeteria. I need to take my pills."

"There's some water in that pitcher, Mom."

"I need lemonade," she said firmly.

Herbert nodded. "Sure thing, Mary. Mind if I stop and chat with that pretty candy striper while I'm at it?"

"Knock yourself out." When he had gone, she resumed, "There's something

I need to tell you. Then you need to talk to your brother."

"Something you don't want Herbert to hear?"

"Family business." She took a breath. "The Pearces' didn't care for your brother. But they were happy to use him. The mother especially. The rich don't like to be reminded of how they got that way, and Tommy was a walking road map: cop's kid who doesn't know which fork to use, but as smart as any of them, and a go-getter with it."

He leaned back into the pillows. His mother was launched.

"Mrs. Pearce was from the South… some part where they don't have Catholics. Having your brother mooning around her daughter—right after that foreign exchange student… it made the poor woman take to her bed with the vapors." She paused. "Your father never told you any of this?"

Joe shook his head.

"Just before Tommy showed up, the family had the son of some foreign diplomat living with them for the school year. He went to Coldwater High at first, but some of the boys there gave him a rough time. Pushed him around. Shaved a swastika on his head. That sort of thing. He refused to go back to school, and he just hung around the house. I'm sure the Pearces didn't know what to do with him."

"I heard something about that," said Joe, "at a parole bash for one of the Hellers at the VFW. Maybe some of it was b.s.—my cousin's a bigger bad ass than yours—and they were all drunk as skunks. But it was more than a haircut they were bragging about."

She gave her son 'The Look'. "Since when did Hellers start inviting Morgans to their parole parties?"

"It was a long time ago, Mom. When I was bouncing at the VFW. I remember it, though. Pretty rough stuff."

"I'm told the young man was quite handsome. A little older than Susan. Well mannered… well-traveled… rich. You can imagine the rest for yourself. Your father stumbled across them a couple of times out on Pocket Island."

Joe felt himself smiling for the first time in days.

"The parents sent the boy home, of course. He pitched a fit before they got him out—threatened to slit their throats. His father had to send some toughs from their embassy to collect him and ship him off to one of their religious schools. Dr. Pearce was going to send Susan away to boarding school. But she threw a fit, too, and the mother was scared she would hurt herself. Then along came your brother."

Joe felt the release of long held breath. "Wow! How do you know all this?"

"Mrs. Ryan. She told anyone who'd listen after the Pearces let her go. She kept house for them, don't you remember? She told me she heard the mother telling the father, 'Better a Catholic than a…. Well… as I said… Mrs. Pearce was from Georgia, or someplace. She used the 'n' word."

"That's a juicy piece of ancient gossip, Mom. But what's it got to do with me talking to Tommy about Susan Pearce?"

"I should think that would be obvious."

He shrugged. "Not to me."

She spelled it out. "She went back to him."

"To the foreign exchange student?"

"That's right. The one you sent your brother to talk to. In Montreal."

"Dr. Hassad?"

"Whatever his name is. Mrs. Ryan recognized him when he stopped at the Quick Mart on his way to the funeral."

Joe released another cloud of astonished breath. "And you think he and Susan are involved again?"

"I think they never stopped."

"What?"

"Opposites attract, Joey. It's the only explanation for most pairings."

He felt his mouth open and head wag.

"Oh she's had other lovers, of course. She's a big girl and all that." Joe felt her eyes search for his. "But my guess is that dark foreigner has had her heart all along. That she's always done anything he's asked and always will."

"Wow!" was all he could say.

"Exactly. And the sooner your brother realizes that, the better. It's not something he'll be grateful to be hearing from you, I know. But it's not something he'll believe at all from his mother."

Joe sat up straight in bed. "Why didn't Dad say something to Tommy? Or to me? I would have talked some sense into him. Why would he let his son get sucked into something like that?"

"It suited his purpose."

"What purpose?"

"Your father felt that your brother wasn't cut out for the family line of work. He was wrong about that. But until Miss Pearce came along, he was worried that your brother was too smart to be allowed to hang around it much longer. 'An experienced piece of timely distraction,' was how he put it. The romance solved both families' problems."

"That's cold, Mom."

"And what would you have done? How long did it take your brother to figure out that herb garden business… or your moonlight frolic over Billy Pearce's dead body?"

"Okay. So he's a bright boy."

"So are you. Your brother just spent too much time with that priest when he was young, that's all. He's an innocent, still. And that's what'll get him and you hurt."

Joe raised his eyes and chin toward the ceiling. "Do you think it's possible that Susan has been in contact with this Dr. Hassad all along? All those jobs in university labs and bio research companies?"

"I imagine that someone in his line would find those associations useful. But the romance had to be genuine, or Susan would have sensed it and moved on long ago. A girl like that doesn't lack for attention."

He felt that one too and winced. Partly to cover, he asked, "I wonder if there was also a connection between Hassad and Billy? Or was Billy just driving Frankie's cars for pocket change when Susan came back to town and brought him into a bigger game?"

"Mmmm," said Mary, without enthusiasm. "It's past the time to be worrying about who did what to Billy Pearce. It's your brother needs minding now. Or you'll both end up in the soup."

But he had to finish the thought. "And if Billy didn't have a connection to Hassad, then bright boy's theories of who did what to whom and why, are full of…."

"Holes," snapped Mary. "Which is why you're going to talk to him before he falls into one and drags our family down with him!"

CHAPTER 29

When the Feds let Tom go, he returned to Joe's empty cabin, collapsed into bed and drifted through twilight vignettes staring Susan Pearce, Frankie Heller, the New York Attorney General and a red headed French lawyer he was certain he had never met but would certainly like to. In the more coherent snippets, he found himself noting that when one's life fell apart, there was not necessarily a visible bottom. Or would there be a final warning just before the god-awful splat?

He might have laid there forever wallowing in the imponderable, had not two hundred decibels of *AH-OOGA!!* blasted him back to consciousness. Rolling from the mattress to the split-log floor, his first thought among the dust motes and carpet hairs was that Joe's gun was not outside in the truck. He held his breath and remained still. An innocent visitor—even one of the stenciled windbreaker boys—would soon be shouting apologies and knocking on the sliding glass doors.

AH-OOGA!!

Or maybe they had, and he had not heard them.

He crawled to where he could peer through the gap between the peeled log wall and the heavy slat curtains. Outside, oblivious to halogen light and klaxon horn, two visitors stood tearing rows of plants from the wooden boxes on top of the waist-high railings. One snorted blasts of frosty air through dripping nostrils. The other stepped noisily along the row of wilted plants. One had antlers, both had hooves.

Releasing a blast of compressed breath, he pulled the louvered curtains from the window and peering cautiously outside. The visitors did not look up. The first snow of the year was falling.

He punched the security code into the wall pad and slid the glass doors open. The klaxons stopped and halogen lights dimmed. Stepping onto the snow-covered deck he inhaled deeply. The two intruders eyed him petulantly before bounding onto the lawn, their heart-shaped hooves pressing a scattering of Valentines into the new snow.

After the horn and light show, the sound of compacting snow was almost, but not quite, inaudible. He turned his head. The sound was heavy, not delicate… Big Foot, not Bambi. As the crunch came nearer, he squinted through a curtain of snowflakes. A figure in a hooded parka strode through it, one snow-flaked fist gripping a silver cell phone and the other a large black handgun.

"Thank you, Mr. Morgan," said the voice inside the hood. "I was beginning to get chilled out here."

* * *

Hassad backed Tom into the cabin, drew the curtains and sat him on the couch next to the table phone. He had no small talk.

"Listen carefully," he ordered. "I want you to call Miss Pearce and arrange for her to meet you on Pocket Island. Communicate the rendezvous in a way that will not be understood by anyone who might be listening."

Tom didn't move.

Hassad pointed the gun at Tom's chest. "Don't make me persuade you."

"What if she's not home?" The sound of his voice seemed unnaturally high and hollow.

"Then you are of no use to me."

"What about after the call?" It came out almost a whisper.

"I need a boat to take me to Pocket Island and to help with certain tasks

227

once I get there. Understand that I have no reason to keep you alive if you refuse."

Tom picked up the phone. Though he had known the number by heart since he was a teenager, he fat-fingered it twice and had to hang up and start over again. Hassad held the gun impatiently at the level of Tom's chest. The sound of the phone's ringing reminded him of a dentist's drill.

"Pick up, Susan," Tom murmured.

"Pray that she answers, Mr. Morgan."

The ringing stopped, followed by an audible click.

'Hi. You've reached 628-4952. No one is able to come to the phone right now....'

"Susan, it's me."

'... but if you'll leave your name, number.... '

"Susan! Pick up!"

'... and a brief message, someone will get back to you as soon as possible.'

"Susan! I have to talk to you. Now!"

Click.

Hassad raised the gun to Tom's forehead. "Bad luck for you, Mr. Morgan."

Tom lifted his hand and lowered his voice to an intimate whisper. "Hey, sweetie, it's me. Can't sleep. Just me and the sheep. Remember our Rubaiyat readings? Wish you could join us there now. Lady might have a ride if you need one."

He waited. Hassad motioned him to replace the phone. "Explain," he ordered.

The answer came in breathless gulps. "'Lady' is Our Lady of The Lake church. There's a rowboat at the church dock. And a runabout in the boathouse. Susan used to borrow them sometimes to sneak out to Pocket Island at night. There'll be watchers at her house. She'll need another way to get to the island."

"And the other reference?" Hassad demanded.

"'Sheep? ' That's you. Line in a nursery rhyme. She'll get it."

"How clever." He sounded more peeved than impressed. "But if Miss Pearce doesn't play that message within the hour, it's of no use to me. Or to you."

228

"She's already heard it."

"Explain."

"I could hear her," he lied. "She picked up the phone as soon as the message tape ended. She just didn't say anything. Maybe there was someone there."

Hassad pointed the gun at Tom's face. Tom watched Hassad's eyes. Each held tight to the whirligig of his own suspicions.

* * *

From the passenger seat, Joe watched Bonnie's headlights making bas-relief of the tire tracks that patterned the long, snow-covered driveway. At first he assumed the tracks had been left by Tom, and he braced himself for what had to come next. But he abandoned the idea when he saw that the tracks ended beneath a rusty, blue sedan parked out of sight of the cabin. The car was a stranger. Tommy of the hamburger hands and knees would not have parked so far away.

"Bonnie, stop." Joe reached into the glove compartment and retrieved a pair of binoculars, training them on the front of the cabin. There were footprints in the snow leading around back. "It's probably nothing. But I want you to take the kids to Mary's and wait for my call."

"Joe, please call for help."

"I will." He did not look at her face.

When the car disappeared down the driveway, Joe climbed into the woods above the cabin, feeling as jelly-limbed as he had after the first weekend he'd spent in bed with a girl. The temperature had dropped sharply since they'd left the hospital. Snow fell heavily and the wind gathered strength. Part way up the hill, he leaned against a dry patch of tree trunk and trained the binoculars on the landscape below. Maybe Tom was inside with a visitor. But there were no lights. *And where is my truck?*

Joe turned the glasses on the security pad beside the front door. A small green light would be lit if the system were armed—a red one if it had been tripped. He could not see a light. But then he remembered then that he had shown Tom how to turn the system off, but not how to re-arm it.

Crossing the face of the hill, he had a clear line of sight to the back of the cabin. The wind from the lake carried his small noises into the woods above him. Falling snow muffled the rest. He steadied the glasses on a chest-high branch and examined the back of the cabin. The curtains behind the sliding glass doors were drawn and the room behind them was dark. A group of does browsed the yew hedge near the deck, grabbing an easy last meal before the snow covered everything. Nothing else moved. No lights showed.

He retraced his steps until he was opposite the windowless north side of the cabin. Deer browsed the bushes nearest the deck and snorted when he broke the tree line. A pair of motion activated cameras under the eaves followed him as he approached. White tails lifted and hooves stomped, but they did not retreat.

Boot tracks in the snow against the cabin had only a light dusting of flakes in the tread. The tracks led to the deck and from there to the sliding glass doors. The security pad next to the door was dark. Beside it, warm air leaked into the great outdoors. He reached to his waistband for a handgun that wasn't there because they made him send it home from the hospital. Curtains rustled a warning. He slid the glass door open and entered the room.

Three thousand square feet of open space lay in front of him, surrounded by a perimeter of peeled log wall. Not by accident, there was no place to hide. Joe stood with his back to the wall, motionless and alert. If someone was here, he would soon know. If it was his security-disarming, door-left-ajar, wet-behind-the-ears brother, the sanctimonious brainiac would be moving out in the morning. This wasn't a drill he cared to put his family through more than once.

Minutes passed in quiet the opposite of tranquil. Falling snow muffled the ordinary sounds of outdoor evening and amplified the tics and hums of the living house: appliance clocks, ventilation fans, contracting timbers and soft, regular billows of the listener's breath. He looked at his watch. He'd known professionals who could keep still for hours. But anyone else would have made a sound by now. Moving quietly along the interior walls and up the split log stairs to the loft took only seconds. The cabin was empty.

A trail of wet led from the deck to the couch opposite the fireplace. A puddle fronted the wing back chair beside it. Booting the computer, Joe logged onto the security system where digital flickering showed the date and time the alarms were triggered and when they were shut off. He downloaded images from the security cameras and screened them twice.

Tommy was one brave comedian.

The images from the outdoor cameras showed him stepping onto the deck, hands in his front trouser pockets, turning to face the camera and then slowly pulling his pockets inside out. A tall figure in a hooded parka pressed a gun to Tommy's face. Tommy arched his back, moved his hands to his rear pockets and calmly pulled them out as well. The camera followed him and the hooded figure across the deck and down the steps until they disappeared around the edge of the cabin. A few frames later there was a flash of black monster truck racing down the driveway. Before he was out of range, Tommy had managed to turn out the pockets of his jacket as well.

"I got it the first time, brother. Pockets. Pocket Island." He had to admire Tommy's perseverance. And his courage.

Grabbing a 12 gauge from the gun locker, Joe ran to the patrol car and fish-tailed down the driveway and the mountain to Skippers Marina. On the way he thought briefly about his promise to Bonnie to call for help. There was enough of it around now. But the more people you add, the more ways there were for things to go badly. And each one of them ended with Tommy dead.

Joe followed the double line of tire tracks across Skippers' unplowed parking lot to where they ended beneath his truck abandoned at the edge of the seawall. The patrol car headlights held the truck and the two-foot swells that lifted the empty wooden docks beyond it, like a scene in a winter snow globe.

He'd left the Coldwater patrol boat tied to the inside of the T at the end of the dock where it would be protected from waves and easier to get in and out of the marina. But the police slip was as empty now as the rest of the marina, and the islands beyond Wilson Cove had already disappeared behind a thick curtain of windblown snow.

* * *

Gusts of northwest wind pressed clouds of swirling snowflakes into horizontal sheets. White capped swells pushed the bow of the Coldwater patrol boat twenty degrees above the horizon and then dropped it stern-first into the trough that followed. Visibility was fifty feet. Tom did not try to keep the boat inside the channel. A low speed collision in the surrounding rock garden wouldn't put a hole through the hull. But a propeller might sheer off, and that would be just fine. Disabling, but not hypothermic.

Avoiding the visible rocks, he maneuvered the boat through places where they waited just below the surface. The hull scraped some and the skeg caught more. But the boat remained stubbornly intact and the engine undamaged. When the hull ground over a particularly lengthy patch of submerged rock, Hassad lifted his gun and aimed it at Tom's chest. "What do you think you are doing?"

"Steering," Tom answered, waving a hand at the curtain of falling snow. "There's channel stakes somewhere, but I don't see them. Do you?"

Hassad moved closer and pressed the gun to the back of Tom's head. "Maybe this will improve your vision. If we hit anything more, it goes off."

Tom lifted the skeg until the prop rode just below the water's surface and they hit nothing else. Once outside the cove, he checked the compass mounted above the wheel. Hassad clung to the overhead and kept his gun at the back of Tom's head. "How long will it take to get to the island?"

"Fifteen minutes, maybe twenty. If we don't miss it."

Hassad's eyes widened and the end of his pistol found Tom's neck. "Make sure that we don't."

Tom removed a hand from the wheel and waved it at the curtain of snow that surrounded them. "Then you let me know if I miss a turn."

Pocket Island wasn't large, maybe a half mile long and a quarter wide. It would be easy to miss in weather like this, except for the windbreak effect of the bluff that rose seventy feet above the waterline. When wind and wave began to subside, cut off by the bulk of the not yet visible island, Tom eased back on the throttle. "We're close. I'll look for a place to bring us in."

"No," said Hassad. "I want you to take us to the cove on the other side of the island"

"That's not going to be easy. There'll be some nasty water outside this lee. Worse than what we just came through. The church boat Susan's coming in isn't big enough to make it to the other side in this weather. I don't know that we're big enough."

Hassad shoved the barrel of his pistol hard against Tom's head. "Do as I say."

Tom swung the wheel to port and followed the compass south. Pieces of island drifted in and out of view fifty yards to the starboard. As they neared the end of the island, six foot waves began to crash against the bow.

"This is going to get worse in a minute. We can still pull in here."

Hassad shook his head.

Tom pressed the throttle and eased the boat out of the lee. Wind and water seized the thirty-foot craft and spun it like a top. Hassad shouted. But Tom's entire attention was on trying to keep the boat from keeling over while it completed a series of counter-clockwise pirouettes. When the waves split the bow, he held the boat against a wall of water that swept from the west like a phalanx of barbarian horsemen. "Hang on!" he shouted. "I'm opening it up. We'll swamp if I don't bust through this!"

Three yards of bow rose halfway to vertical and the rest slid into the trough. Two tons of boat pitched like a toy in a bathtub. Hassad's mouth contorted and the sound that came out of it blew like a cork from a bottle. "Go!"

Tom slammed the throttle. Hassad lurched into the well of the cuddy, somehow retaining a grip on his gun. The thirty-foot craft rode the hills of water like a rocking horse. Twice it spun in gut emptying circles. Each time Tom fought to hold the wheel and bring the bow to face the oncoming waves. Hassad crouched in the well of the cuddy, his gun tracing zig zags in the direction of Tom's torso.

Twenty white knuckle minutes later, Tom spun the wheel to starboard and pushed the throttle toward the deck. A half-pipe of water corkscrewed over the transom and hurled the boat sideways through the mouth of Pocket

Cove.

They were in.

CHAPTER 30

Two snow-wet Dobermans drifted silently from the woods and stood over Tom as he secured the bow and stern lines to the seawall at the back of the cove. The dogs looked at Hassad and nowhere else. He shouted something to them in a language that Tom did not understand, and the dogs leapt to the deck, baring large, slavering teeth.

"They can swim," said Hassad. He pressed his gun to the back of Tom's head and marched him toward a switchback of stone steps that led to the top of the bluff. From there, a beaten path led to a glass and concrete structure perched on a rocky precipice overlooking the water.

Several winters in a row, a teenage Joe Morgan and friends had broken into the bluff top house that was Pocket Island's only structure and its only winter occupant other than the colossal beech and pine trees that surrounded the island to the water's edge. Tom had never been inside. But from his brother's long-ago description he assumed that the interior was similar to the Falling Water House that its famous architect had built a decade earlier. Joe had described built-in, patterned concrete everything, spectacular views, unbreakable furniture and a cleverly hidden liquor cabinet.

But Hassad did not turn on a light when they got inside. All Tom could see was a large open space broken by a freestanding fireplace and surrounded by floor-to-ceiling glass. Hassad put a hand on the back of Tom's head and shoved him toward a darkened stairwell. "Move!" he hissed.

A spider web at the top of the stairway caught Tom's face. He raised a hand to brush it away, and Hassad brought his pistol down on top of Tom's head. "Hands down!" Tom tumbled the length of the steps. Head, hands, shoulder and knees collided with concrete at the bottom. Hassad's outline loomed above.

Clink. Something landed at Tom's feet. "Pick it up," Hassad ordered.

Tom's fingers found a piece of flat, serrated metal the size of his thumb. A door key. He tried to picture it a weapon.

"Turn around, find the keyhole and open the door."

If Hassad was going to kill him, this was an opportune time and place. But the moment provided no choice other than obedience, and no strategy other than watchful waiting.

* * *

Joe strained to see through the veil of snow. Somewhere behind it, a faceless parka held a gun to Tommy's head—if he was still alive. The Coldwater patrol boat was gone. A call to Johnsen would bring another boat, as well as choppers, guns and overwhelming manpower. But a decade of zoo-keeping Coldwater's menagerie of small-time criminals, had taught Joe what punks do when cornered. They panic; and the killers among them kill. It would not take an army to save Tom. But that is what Johnsen would send, and that's how Tommy would get dead. Joe would not call for help.

"Idjit!" A voice began to scream. The voice was angry... almost crazed. "You goddamn moron!" The voice was closing fast, followed by what sounded like a swarm of bees.

"You had to make one more trip!"

"Shut up, Mickey! I'm not the goddamn weatherman."

"We almost drowned!"

As the swarm grew louder, an aluminum jon boat appeared out of the storm. A vibrant humming seeped from a padded wooden box fitted over its outboard engine. The wet, familiar faces in the boat gaped at the figure poised on its toes at the end of the dock.

"Clever muffler, Mickey. Keep the salmon. Leave the boat."

* * *

Hassad turned a dial beside the cellar door. Yellow light revealed a wall of empty wooden racks. Stacks of surplus ammunition boxes covered a rough plank table in the center of the stone floor. Two metal footlockers filled the space beneath it.

"Bring everything to the boat," he ordered. "Carefully."

Tom worked as slowly as he dared... hands numb... knees cracked and bleeding. A knot of throbbing flesh swelled the back of his head where Hassad had clubbed him with the pistol. Other than to keep from freezing inside his soaking clothes, there was no reason for Tom to hurry. As soon as he ran out of jobs, Hassad would surely kill him.

The insides of the metal boxes clinked like wind chimes as he carried them up the stone steps. The two Dobermans rode his heels, snarling at his every twitch. Hassad screamed caution and speed at the same time, and when Tom couldn't budge a pair of footlockers, he shoved him to the floor and tested their weight himself. The professor's nerves were frayed, and Tom wondered how long before they snapped.

Hassad grabbed the canvas strap at one end of the locker and ordered Tom to take the other. Their combined strength was enough to haul the heavy trunk out of the cellar and across the snow to the top of the bluff, though the effort exhausted them both.

Tom tried to visualize how he might unbalance Hassad on the steps leading down to the cove and, with luck, send him tumbling onto the rocks. *A kick to the knee?* He shook his head and tried to clear his mind. *And a bullet to the face, if you miss. Think!* But his mind was as numb as his body, and it took all his energy and focus to hold onto the heavy trunk. He licked a snowflake from his swollen lips and ran his eyes along the steps leading down to the cove and the rocks below. *Why not just shove the trunk into his chest?* He looked up to see Hassad watching him.

"You first," said Hassad, gesturing him forward. Placing his pistol along the top of the trunk, he added: "If you so much as stumble, or even hesitate... I can manage from here on my own."

Tom willed himself to remain alert for weapons and opportunity. But nothing that his exhausted brain proposed had any reasonable chance of success. He could turn the boat broadside to the swells outside the cove and try to capsize it. After that, he could try to swim to shore before he froze to death or drowned. But neither capsizing nor survival seemed likely. And the professor remained vigilant.

Hassad marched Tom back to the house and ordered him to drag a Morris chair to the plate glass window overlooking the lake. From a pocket inside his parka, Hassad took a roll of duct tape and ordered Tom to wrap his ankles to the chair's front legs and his right wrist to its flat wooden arm. Ocher liquid oozed through tattered cloth as Tom forced his crusted knees to bend one more time. Hassad wrapped the final appendage and fortified the others with extra turns of tape. "Now we wait."

Tom didn't ask for what, or who. Hassad couldn't handle a boat in this weather. He'd need someone who knew the lake to take him wherever he needed to go next. When Susan showed up, if she showed up, he'd have one more pilot than he needed.

At the risk of having Hassad use the duct tape on his mouth, Tom began to probe. "If you don't mind me asking, did the NeuroGene owners know what they were handling for you?"

Hassad's answer was curt and dismissive. "I should think you'd have other things on your mind."

Tom tried to smile, but the effort made his temple ache where Hassad had clubbed it with his pistol. "What's in the trunks, then? It felt like cement, but it's not, is it?"

Hassad's eyes widened. "Call it justice, Mr. Morgan."

"As in the 'free exchange of ideas and resources'?"

"Excuse me?"

"The shit you were shoveling in your office."

"You *would* think that," he dismissed.

"I don't think it's grandma's crystal clinking around in those little boxes? What is it? The plague?"

Hassad's face grew hard and his voice irritated. "Dark skin, foreign accent? That must mean something nefarious, mustn't it, *Tom?*" The slip to informal address was pointed, but not friendly.

"The gun and the duct tape don't mean good times... Suliman."

Hassad scowled.

"Justice for what?" Tom demanded. "From who?"

"Surely you know. Surely Susan has told you about me. About us?"

Tom shook his head. The effort made him dizzy.

"I find that hard to believe. She's spoken so much about you."

"It doesn't seem to have done me any good."

"No. And frankly, it's irritating. That and her inflated view of your intelligence."

Shit. "Susan and I were over a long time ago," said Tom. "If you think I'm standing in the way of something now..."

Hassad waved the pistol at his duct tape handiwork. "Hardly."

"Then why did you drag me out here, at gunpoint? For what?"

Hassad eyes locked on his. "Why don't you guess, Tom? I'm told that you're exceptionally good at games. Is that true? Or is Susan confused about that too."

The chill from the concrete floor spread through Tom's torso. *Shit, shit, shit.* He cocked his head as far as his neck would allow. "And what do I get if I win?"

"Another gold star. I'm told they're important to you. Almost the only thing."

Fuck you. Sweat dripped from Tom's temples, though the temperature inside the glass and concrete room was low enough that he could see his breath. *But what was the alternative?*

"Okay, I'm game. Let's see if she's right." He took as long as he could and then began. "First, even if this is personal, which I can't believe, you don't need anything on that boat to get rid of me." He lifted his chin toward the gun in Hassad's hand. "You could have used that at Joe's cabin and saved yourself a dangerous boat ride."

"And that tells you what?" Hassad's tone was mock pedantic. "Show me Susan isn't exaggerating."

"It tells me you're not just pissed at me. And that your hit list is long enough for a boatload of mystery boxes to come in handy."

"Anything else?"

"That there's a chance that the folks on your list will be in the same place at the same time, so you can use whatever's in those boxes on them."

"Perhaps. What else?"

"That you're mad enough to risk your life to have a chance to do it."

"Angry not mad. But otherwise excellent. You're not just a pretty face, after all." Tom's ears flushed at the line Hassad could only have gotten from Susan. But further banter was forestalled by the opening bars of Vivaldi's *Le Quattro Stagione* trilling from Hassad's cell phone. Hassad pressed the keypad and walked to the far corner of the large open space. Tom couldn't overhear words, but the tone was diffident and cautious.

Dobermans began to howl. A door slammed. Tom twisted his limbs beneath the tape without result. Minutes passed. Then a draft of cold air swept across the floor, followed by footsteps. "We should leave soon," a new voice said. "I was out there a long time. Someone may have seen me."

Tom squeezed his eyes and lifted his head. Only his mother's voice could have been more unnerving.

* * *

Hassad raised his arm toward the row of windows. "There's a large police boat tied up at a dock at the bottom of that cliff. Can you drive it?"

"Yes," said Susan.

"Are you sure? It's still snowing."

"It's just a squall. They pass quickly. When the wind dies down, we can go."

"Good." Hassad raised his gun to the back of Tom's head. "You don't have to watch this."

Tom tensed for the sound or sensation, or whatever was going to come next and last. Though instead of the blast of a handgun at close range, or a half-hearted plea on his behalf, what came next was more Vivaldi trilling from Hassad's cell phone.

Footsteps retreated. All Tom could see was snow swirling through trees. All he could hear was Hassad arguing loudly with whoever was on the other end of the phone. He waited for Susan to say something, to offer excuses, or help. But she said nothing... did nothing.

He knew that he did not have time to be angry. Intent on survival and with mind and voice his only tools, Tom began to riff. "Do you remember the Barney and Fred story you told me?"

She didn't answer, but Tom continued as if she had.

"I have another version. I want you to listen carefully." He spoke quickly, almost sarcastically. "Fred leads his group on a hunt for a new home. Night falls, the temperature drops and a drizzle that's been falling all day turns to freezing rain. The little Freddies are wet and hungry. But the group gets lucky and Fred stumbles across a deep, dry cave. Everyone except Barney rushes in.

"Something about the cave gives Barney a bad feeling. He shouts after the others. But only Betty and Bamm-Bamm pay any attention. Barney convinces them to go back out into the rain to look for another shelter.

"Barney doesn't have a word for the instinct that warned him not to go into the cave. But it's what saved him and his family. A pride of Saber Tooth tigers had found the cave first and ate Fat Fred and all the little Freddies for dinner."

Susan was silent. He ploughed ahead and hoped that she was listening, and even more that he was making sense.

"You and I are the great, great grandchildren of _intuitive_ Barney, Susan. Not _Fat_ Freddie. Do you see the difference between that and the story you told me?"

From the next room came the sounds of harsh, guttural arguing. Susan remained mute. Tom could not tell if she had heard his little parable, or if she was listening to Hassad and whomever. He could not tell if she was tuned-in at all.

"Listen to me, Betty," He prompted. "Your instincts have got to be screaming at you now. Listen to them! When does Solomon start asking what you've done for him lately? How soon before his fanatical buddies tell him to kill anybody who knows anything... including the infidel girlfriend?"

"Suliman," said Susan quietly. "His name is Suliman. He loves me."

Tom felt lightheaded, almost breathless, his lungs shrunken and shredded. "Non-overlapping immune systems? High energy?" He hectored his own reflection in the floor to ceiling glass. "Is this the happiness you were preaching to me about? What's your goal here, Susan? Mass murder?"

Her voice was a whisper. "Peace."

"What?"

"You wouldn't understand."

"Susan, the only peace that comes from what's on that boat is Eternal Peace."

"That's not true." Susan's voice trembled, but the tone was defiant. "We have biological weapons in this country, and worse. But we'll never need to use them because it's enough that everyone knows we have them."

Tom felt his heart galloping. "Susan! A trunk full of toxins isn't a national defense. It's the arsenal of a hit squad. I don't know what this Suliman told you, but this isn't about peace. It's about settling old scores here in Coldwater. He was bragging about it, just before you got here."

Hassad's side of the phone call had grown louder and angrier. He was screaming at someone now, and it was clear that that they were screaming back.

"He won't kill you," Susan whispered. "He's a scientist, not a murderer."

"Susan! His finger was squeezing the goddamn trigger when his phone rang!"

"He's not like that. You don't understand."

"No, you don't. Frankie would have beat Billy to a pulp... not poisoned and drowned him." He spoke to the window, to the snow that had stopped falling and the trees that no longer swayed. "That peaceful 'scientist' out

242

there killed your brother."

Susan said nothing.

"Or you did."

* * *

Darkness fell. He could no longer see the lake, only the trees, and above them the stars. There was nothing left to say. He waited for an answer and strained to hear it when it came.

"He broke one of the packages," Susan whispered. "It was an accident."

Tom squeezed his eyes and locked onto her voice.

"Suliman was bringing one of his colleagues – a doctor. But Joe showed up first on his way to work and Billy chased him away. Joe called me from the patrol car and said that if I didn't get Billy to the hospital, he would come back and drag him there himself."

Susan's voice drifted behind his back. He closed his eyes and locked onto it.

"Suliman told me to get Billy to the island and that he'd meet me there. By then, Billy was hallucinating. I got him down to the boat and wrapped him in that sleeping bag."

"With two cement blocks in the bottom?" He almost snorted, but he kept his voice low, whisper for whisper.

"He was delirious," said Susan. "The transom on that boat is only knee-high. I had to make sure he didn't fall overboard."

"But he did."

"I know." Her voice cracked and all but disappeared. "We were almost through the cove when the patrol boat came out from the marina. I turned off the lights so your brother wouldn't see us. He started fanning a spotlight, so I shut off the engine and let the boat drift."

He let the silence swell and then prompted, "Go on."

"As soon as I shut off the engine, Billy went berserk, screaming and flopping all over the place. The patrol boat turned and came straight toward the noise. I had to hold Billy's head over the side to muffle the sound."

"Go on," he whispered.

"That's how he went over."

"What do you mean, 'That's how he went over?'"

"When the patrol boat came alongside, it threw up a wake. We tipped in it. Billy overbalanced and I couldn't hold onto him. He fell over."

It was Tom's turn to be silent, his brain too fried and his body too numb to evaluate this last iteration. Whether it was even partly true didn't really matter. Hassad was going to kill him just as soon as he came back to the room.

"You haven't answered my question." Tom's voice recovered its volume and urgency. "What do you think is going to happen here next? What are your instincts screaming at you right now? Not your heart. Your gut."

No answer.

"Susan! That non-overlapping immune system out there is going to come back in here and slaughter me! Then he's going to do whatever he's got planned for what's on that boat—which I doubt is world peace, if he had to kill me to do it."

Seconds passed. Tom could no longer hear Hassad's voice. Whatever the argument had been, it was over. Footsteps approached the back of his chair. He braced for the blow or the *coup de gras,* or whatever was going to come next... and last.

Pale fingers tore at the tape over his wrists. Gossamer hair swept his chest.

"Hurry," he said.

Susan clawed the tape with her nails and then with her teeth.

"Find a knife."

But as he spoke, Hassad shouted. Footsteps pounded across the floor. Hassad's pistol slammed against the side of Susan's head. He lifted the phone in his other hand and screamed into it what was unmistakably a curse. The arm with the gun straightened in the direction of Susan's fall. Tom could see red welling through wheat, but he could not see Hassad. Susan moved her head from side to side, mouthing, but not speaking. She struggled to her feet beyond Tom's line of vision. Hassad cursed again – at Susan, into the phone, at himself... The blast of his gun, contained and amplified by glass and concrete, was deafening.

Tom had no thoughts or sensations. He did not know if he had been shot... only that he was not yet dead. *Cogito ergo sum.* Footsteps hurried from the room and then returned. A thin cold blade penetrated the tape and skin at his wrist. The hand holding the blade carved backwards and then moved to the other wrist and ankles in quick order. Blood oozed through severed flesh, cloth and bond.

"Move!" Hassad hissed.

Tom pitched to the floor, hands slipping in a pool of blood. Hassad yanked him to his feet. A litany of foreign curses spewed from his throat. On the path leading to the bluff, Tom pitched forward onto his hands and knees. Hassad put a boot to his ribs.

Tom fell again on the steps and on the seawall. The Dobermans barked in frenzy at the smell of blood. Hassad shoved him into the pilot's seat, cast off the lines and braced himself against the cuddy. The dogs jumped into the boat.

Dazed and exhausted, each breathe was an agony. Susan was surely dead and Hassad would just as surely kill him once they got to wherever he wanted Tom to pilot the boat.

"Move!" Hassad shouted. His gun traced a palsied ellipse in front of Tom's face.

The wind had died just as Susan had predicted, and the swells at the mouth of the inlet had fallen to less than a foot. There was no moon or stars. Grey clouds covered the sky to the horizon.

"North," Hassad ordered.

Tom turned the wheel and eased out of the cove.

"Faster!"

Tom opened the throttle. The police cruiser surged and began to skim over the water. Hassad shouted instructions... curses. Tom was no longer listening. His eyes were locked onto the nautical compass.

Hassad pressed the pistol to his cheek. "North!" he screamed.

Tom looked away and let the wheel drift to port. The speedometer read twelve knots and climbing. Hassad screamed again as the boat held steady at north north west. Oblivious to the gun beneath his eye, Tom turned and looked over his shoulder. The impact felt like being struck in the back by a falling tree.

A hundred yards north north west of Pocket Island, the propellers of the twin Sea Witch engines caught the underwater ledge known to local boaters as Sunken Island. The transom of the patrol boat shot clear of the water and fell back with a spine-fusing jolt. Hassad flew the length of the deck and through the door of the cuddy. The Dobermans barked in panic and at each other. The outboard propellers ground the underwater obstruction, screaming metallic agony. Hassad struggled to pull himself upright. When the props regained clear water, Tom leapt over the side.

* * *

His body sank.

Icy water paralyzed limb and thought. He tried to turn his torso toward light, but his limbs would not respond. His body felt like a pillar encased in wraps. He did not try to hold his breath or struggle not to breathe. Those mechanisms were locked and frozen. What senses still functioned told him that he was drifting. Thoughts came at widely spaced intervals.

Hassad shut off the engine and flipped a toggle above the symbol of an anchor on the panel behind the wheel. A splash and the sound of scrapping chain followed. The boat began to swing at the bow and then steadied. The dogs were already in the water.

Tom felt the thud of anchor hitting rock and heard the grind of chain against hull. Seconds into the icy water, his brain had gone someplace else, but he could feel it returning. No light... only wet and cold. He could not see his body.

Then boots scrapped something firm and his legs extended to feel bottom. Opposite would be up and air. Boots found muck, pushed hard, rose inches and then settled again.

Longer than he could have believed or imagined, his head breached the surface. Lungs hauled air and then froze in mid-bellows. Wheezing gasps triggered answering growls. He could not stop choking. He might just as well have rung a dinner bell. The Doberman was on him in seconds.

Pointed teeth skewered his frozen shoulder. Hardened claws raked his torso. A mangled hand found the canine's collar, but the dog's grip was a lock. Tom felt the grind of canine teeth on human bone. Then they began to sink. Holding tight to the dog's collar, he twisted, but otherwise ceased to struggle. His only advantage now was his awareness of mortality and a determined attachment to it. Somewhere along the endless descent, the canine released its grip, but Tom continued to twist.

Toes entered muck. He began to count: one thousand one, one thousand two. He twisted the studded collar hard. The canine raked his claws the length of Tom's torso. Frenzied jaws snapped empty water. Tom held tight, and with all his remaining strength, twisted. One thousand nineteen... one thousand twenty.

Claws and teeth turned away.

One thousand thirty. Tom released the leather strap, felt for bottom and pushed hard.

Up and air was impossibly far this time. He could not lie to his lungs now. They knew the truth. But he told them that they had no choice but to hold or to fill with life ending water. Waving arms and scissoring legs, he tried to banish thought. When air came, it was like an awakening from a long, cold sleep.

Hassad heard the splash and turned the patrol boat spotlight toward the sound. The second Doberman answered with a frenzied bark. Tom filled his lungs and treaded water. When the dog lunged, he surrendered his body and took the canine's studded collar.

* * *

Joe tied the Dooley's jon boat to the trunk of a massive beech tree, its smooth, gray bark scarred with hearts and initials as high as young passion could reach. There was no hope of finding a path through the overgrown woods. He scrambled blind through thickets of laurel and blow-down pine, then followed the ridge at the top of the hill to a stark glass and concrete octagon at the edge of the bluff.

Holding the riot gun in his outstretched hands, he approached the rear of the house. Inside, Susan Pearce lay sprawled beside the hearth of a double fireplace, cold to the touch. Flags of severed duct tape hung from the arms of a wooden chair that faced the row of windows overlooking the lake. There was no sign of Tommy.

Blood-streaked footprints painted a grisly path through the snow leading to the cove. The sound of waves drifted up from below. From somewhere beyond came the menacing bark of an angry dog. Joe dropped to his haunches and cocked an ear to the sound. There were no boat noises or any human sound. But the howl of frenzied predator closing on its prey was clear and close. Joe sprinted back through the pitch black woods to where he had left the Dooley's boat.

* * *

Tom's head breached the surface. Hassad swung the spotlight toward the splash. The struggle with the dogs had carried Tom far astern of the crippled police boat. Sunken Island was somewhere close, but he could not tell where. His left arm was stiff and useless where the dogs had mauled it. He had no feeling below the knees. Little strength remained to swim or even to stay afloat.

A sharp whistle skimmed across the water, followed by a harsh, guttural shout. "You can die without my further help, Mr. Morgan!"

The spotlight on the patrol boat stuttered like a broken metronome. Tom paddled beyond its reach and listened to an anchor winch groan. He leaned into the waves and kicked feebly.

"It shouldn't be much longer," Hassad shouted. The scream of battered outboards overwhelmed the rest of the outburst.

Tom tried to kicked harder and stroke with his one good arm. Hassad's high-pitched taunts struck cold, hollow notes of madness. But it did not make them untrue. It was unlikely Tom could survive long in this frigid water. His teeth were cracked from chattering. He'd lost all feeling in face and limb. But he forced himself to kick with two legs and paddle with his one good arm. If his body quit, so be it. But he would not let his mind give the order, or assent to it.

He kicked again, though he could no longer sense movement, and raked the water with his one good arm. When the image of a resurrected canine flashed across the back of his eyelids, he withdrew his mind. When numbed extremities signaled stalled movement, he brought himself back. Misery crouched on his shredded shoulder and whispered surrender.

A needle-like pain stabbed the back of his leg. He shot a panicked hand to stop it. Knuckles scraped ragged hardness. Fingers touched where hard and soft connected. Numbed brain thawed the answer to what had punctured the back of his leg. Had his frozen face retained the required mobility, he would have laughed. His butt had found Sunken Island in the dark.

The tiny voice that sometimes appears when you're about to do something stupid, hissed at Tom to be thankful, sit still and keep his mouth shut. Instead, he braced himself on the underwater rock, gathered breath and shouted.

"Yo!" His throat was raw and his lungs shredded, but he continued to bellow. "Eat shit and die, asshole!" Tom struggled to his feet and staggered noisily through the shin-deep shallows. The spotlight from the patrol boat leapt toward the sound. As the boat drew nearer, he dropped and rolled to his back, as if he were afloat in deep water. The twin Sea Witch outboards roared and the thirty-foot cruiser leapt through a cone of halogen light. Tom lifted his one good arm and waved. The battered cruiser hydroplaned erratically through the water like a wounded shark. The bow-mounted spotlight bounced above and around its target, losing and then finding it again. Tom could see Hassad's face in the halo of light—cadaverous and grim. He could see his eyes, mad and murderous. The little voice screamed at Tom to be quiet and lie still. He crouched in the shallow water, extended his arm and raised a finger.

The thunder of colliding rock and boat was orgasmic.

Twin six hundred pound outboards knifed their skegs into the edge of Sunken Island. Twelve thousand pounds of forward thrust ripped the engines from the transom and the transom from the boat. The butt-less police cruiser skidded a dozen yards and began to settle at the stern. Within seconds it was underwater.

CHAPTER 31

Tom lay in a Coldwater Hospital bed, wrapped shoulder to shin in tight, white bandage. Clear thin tubes snaked between layers of gauze on either side of his body. One drained from his crotch, another from beneath his arm pit. He could move his head and one of his arms, but everything else was wrapped tight. A fat nurse with a faint mustache helped him with the essentials.

A week of dozing and watching cable television began to heal his body. But his head and soul felt flayed beyond repair. When he thought about Susan, the fingers around his heart closed in a fist. When he thought about his busted career, they moved to his gut. The sessions with Johnsen and his pals were almost a welcome distraction.

The BARDA boys started questioning him even before the painkillers kicked in, and they kept at it until they'd sucked everything he had to give. They wanted to know about Frankie, Billy, Susan and Joe, and each of their histories and interconnections. They asked little about Hassad, realizing early that he knew little. They focused instead on Coldwater's legacy of live and let live cross-border commerce, spending hours on the Heller junkyard depot, and even longer on MadDog Morgan's "scheme" to send his sons north every summer to perfect their "foreign language." Who had Tom stayed with? Who had he met? Who had he slept with? It was obvious his inquisitors hadn't a clue what they were looking for. But he fed them answers until they quit asking. It wasn't like they were going to stop, or that he had any place to go.

Tom asked to see Joe, but Johnsen said he was busy helping them with their inquiries. They let Mary and her friend Herbert come twice, and Bonnie called once with a distraught Luke listening in. The boy needed to hear that his uncle was okay. Tom babbled in Pig Latin, telling Luke that he should take his dad and Mr. Thompson out to try and catch that big salmon.

Between naps, Tom lay thinking about Susan, her theory about happiness, about the Eurocon mess and how he'd better get used to the idea of "starting over again" at nearly forty, and how he needed to get to the mental place where that felt like an opportunity and not an unjust punishment. But what it really felt like was spiritual and financial bankruptcy, with the specter of jail at the end.

He knew he should call Silverstein, but he didn't have the energy. CNN and Headline News were running endless, breathless 'terrorist foiled' stories. But none of them mentioned Susan Pearce, Pocket Island or the Morgan brothers. That pissed him off, but he watched anyway. It was a distraction.

Some octogenarian named Inglesby gave a scary interview about aerosolized anthrax and the frightening implications of what BARDA was rumored to have found in a small boathouse in upstate New York. A spokesperson for the State Police held a press conference and replied to questions, but offered no meaningful answers.

Joe finally showed up at the hospital on day ten. The rings under his eyes would have done justice to a marsupial. "You made a mess out there, brother. Floating dogs. A Demolition Derby with police property...."

"Skip it," Tom growled. "Where've you been?"

"Feds let me out on a day pass."

"Are they getting anything out of Hassad?"

"Last I saw his professorship, he was stranded on Sunken Island, up to his gonads in ice water. Punk was screaming like a baby when I plucked you out and left him there."

"But they have him, don't they? None of the stuff they've been asking me makes any sense if you just left him there."

"After I got you back to the marina, I had Mickey Dooley take Johnsen and his pals out to pluck his professorship out of his ice bath. But I'm not supposed to talk about any of that."

"Since when do you do what you're told?" Tom waved a bandaged hand at the television. "I've been listening to that gibberish for a week. They haven't got a clue."

"Joe shrugged. "The divers got pretty much everything from the patrol boat you sunk. But I hear the lab boys aren't too excited by any of it. Trunks full of pea powder and vials of bupkis. They also found a car in Frankie's garage rigged to spread powder."

"They were excited about that a few days ago."

"That was when they thought they'd stumbled onto a terrorist factory. But Hassad's story is that he was going to have Billy drive one of these powder jalopies around town and settle a few old scores. A half a dozen people, max. Not thousands."

"They're briefing you? I thought you were on their village idiot shit-list."

"Still am. Most of this comes from that Dr. Dyer. He wants to do a paper on my blood. Man Mountain that abrin couldn't kill. I let him leech me twice a week as long as he passes on the agency gossip. Johnsen's been running a few things by me, too. He calls it 'what if' brainstorming. But it's pretty clear he's checking out pieces of Hassad's story. He's also asked me to look into a few things. Who knows, maybe they'll make me an honorary G-man when this is over."

"Do they believe Hassad's story?"

"They've had him for a week. If he's sticking to the same story through what I imagine they must be doing to him, I'd say it's probably true. I'm told he coughed up the cell in Montreal right away. The Mounties pulled in a couple of grad students and two shop keepers."

"The ones in the grocery store I visited? Who didn't know Hassad or U-Labs?"

"Sounds like it. Apparently they all met at this fire and brimstone mosque. One of them is from a place where they use abrin to kill cows. He came up with the car and powder idea. Hassad's story is that, being a chemist, he knew from the beginning it wouldn't work on any large scale. Something about aerosolizing a spore like anthrax being one thing, and doing it to a compound like abrin being another."

"So why go ahead with it?"

"He says he got the idea of using the brotherhood to help him settle some old scores, with no one the wiser if things went wrong. Dyer says they tested the powder in those trunks and found it wouldn't blow more than ten feet out of the homemade dust boxes Frankie made. So that part's true."

"What was his plan for actually using the stuff?"

"I don't know. Johnsen hasn't 'brainstormed' that part yet. But I have this mental image of Hassad coming up behind one of the Cashins on Main Street and jabbing him with an umbrella, while Billy rides by pulling the plug on one of those cars."

"The Cashins?"

"That's who Hassad was after. Bobby, his cousin Vinny and a bunch of low life's who gave him a bad time when he was in school here."

"That doesn't make sense."

"Depends how you feel about getting bent over the hood of a Mustang while Bobby and his cousins take down your pants and have a go at you."

Tom felt sick. "Is that what happened?"

"Yep. You know how the Cashins and that crowd feel about 'furiners.' One of them saw Hassad and Susan together out on Pocket Island and got his pals together to teach the brown boy a lesson."

"I can't believe she never said anything."

"It's not the kind of thing you'd talk about to the new boyfriend. But it's not hard to see why she might help Hassad, if he had a chance to even the score. Or at least why she wouldn't turn him in."

"I don't think he told her his real plan. I think he fed her some line about helping his little country get an equalizer, so they wouldn't get pushed around, and that she bought it."

"Maybe. It's sure not the *end of the world* crap they're running on TV. I don't know if the feds are buying the high school revenge angle. But that's the story Hassad's sticking to."

"And I suppose we're not to share any of this with anyone." Tom gestured again at the muted television.

"Johnsen told me to remind you."

"Or else?" Tom doubted the bunch he'd met in the Coldwater motel room would leave it as a simple reminder.

"He said something about Mom and Al Capone."

"Income tax evasion?"

"There's half a dozen accountants and investigators sniffing around town, Tommy. How much you think they're going to miss? They had the story about the money in Dad's coat on day one. They promised not to share it with Grogan, if I play ball."

"So Johnsen and company keep the cameras and headlines and we keep our mouths shut?"

"What did you expect?"

"I don't know, a parade or something? Peck on the cheek from the President? Don't the heroic Morgan brothers get anything?"

"One gets to keep his job and maybe a new patrol boat, if he keeps being helpful. I don't know how things work in your world, brother. But that's how they work in mine.

* * *

There was one more thing Johnsen wanted Joe to check out.

"That's right, Sister. It's Sheriff Morgan calling Monsignor Marchetti about Father Gauss." Joe clamped the phone between his shoulder and ear and dumped the contents of a manila envelope onto his desk. "I'm sure you've given him my messages, Sister." He picked up a photograph and held it in front of his face. "Here's another one. I've got a pack of reporters outside my office snarling for meat on that terrorist the State Troopers caught making bio-weapons in Coldwater. If the Monsignor wants to keep his pansy priest out of it, he should come to the phone and give me a good reason."

* * *

Tom lay in bed mulling Joe's query. *That's how things work in my world, brother. How do they work in yours?* Stifling the temptation to come up with a snappy punch line, he turned his thoughts to the question of what cops and lawyers had in common. Answers came swiftly: bias to action, power, status, the choice to be a wolf rather than a sheep. Fear of losing that power—or worse, being ousted from the pack.

Keep asking questions.

How do cops and lawyers react to opportunities to get what they want? How do they react to threats to what they have? Answer: the same way everyone else does—pursue the opportunities and neutralize the threats using the tools at hand. He looked at his bandaged appendages. What tools do you have left, Tommy?

When the candy striper came by, he asked her to help him dial the Coldwater Gazette. She placed the phone in his hand while it rang. Thompson answered. "Gazette. Wha-da-ya got for me?"

"A Pulitzer. If you're interested."

"Morgan?" The newspaper owner sounded harried and breathless. "Can I get back to you on Monday? All hell's been breaking loose around here this week. I've got ten extra pages to get to the printer before midnight."

"Fairy tales of terrorists foiled? How about an exclusive on the real story?"

He could hear Thompson's breath. "Look Morgan, you don't strike me as a nut. But, like I said, all hell's breaking loose right now. I haven't got time…"

"Coldwater Hospital, room 203. You want that Pulitzer? Come get it. Otherwise I'm giving it to the Times. They don't need one more. But they'll know how to run a story like this so they get one."

Thompson growled, "This better be for real."

"It is."

"Let me just put this edition to bed, then I'll get over there. 203's the ICU, right? Who've they got there?"

"Me."

* * *

Thompson's eyes were bloodshot from pulling all-nighters all week, and his skin was the color of frozen fish belly. "My god, what happened to you?" he asked.

"Sit," said Tom. "Start taking notes." While the owner, publisher and everything else of the Coldwater Gazette scribbled furiously on a yellow pad, Tom sketched the theme: foreign exchange student brutalized by racist local toughs grows up to attempt revenge on a town that looked the other way. He added details on who, what, when and where and then presented his terms for an exclusive: "The Gazette holds the story until I give you the green light, probably no more than a few days. When you run the story, you leave the Morgan brothers out of it. Let the state police keep the credit, but for solving a revenge crime, not a terrorist one."

"Suppose I run the story right now?" asked Thompson.

"You're a weekly, Jack, and I know where you print. Try to screw me and I'll give it to the Times. They'll break it online and print it in the morning. You'll wind up with bupkis. Play ball with me and you're a lock for a Pulitzer."

"You think of everything don't you?"

"That's why they pay me the big bucks, Jack."

His next call was to Silverstein. Miraculously, he got through to the busy litigator on the first try.

"The elusive Tom Morgan!" boomed the deep, radio-announcer voice, as entrancing to juries as it was irritating to prosecutors and everyone else. "For a man who's in serious need of my kind of help, you're ridiculously hard to get hold of."

"I've been busy on some family business, Moe."

"Life and death?" asked Silverstein, bluntly. "What could be more important than keeping your butt from sharing a cell with Bubba?"

Tom moved the phone a defensive inch away from his ear. "I've got some ideas on that."

"Good. We'll be spending a lot of time together over the next year or so. A fresh perspective can't hurt."

"Actually, I'm not sure we need to meet at all."

There was a moment of silence, then, "Tom, this isn't bullshit. I mean it is…but if we don't put up a first class defense, starting last week, you're going to end up broke and behind bars. Let me be brutally honest."

"Where I don't want to be. Agreed."

"It's up to you, Tom. But you've got to get into the game, or they're just going to steamroller you. They've already started."

"I know. So let me explain how we stop them." Tom moved the phone back to his ear. "Have you got a television in your office?"

"What? Look, this can wait…"

"The terrorist stories from upstate New York," he interrupted. "Have you been watching them?"

"From that Coldwater place? Sure. Tanner mentioned you were up there. But listen…"

"Good. I'm going to give you some information that hasn't been on the news, and then the phone number of a guy named Johnsen from the Federal Emergency Management Agency."

"Never heard of it."

"There's a reason for that. Now hear me out. When I'm done, I want you to call this guy and explain how we can be of assistance to his agency. And how they can help us."

"What's this…?"

"Just listen, Moe."

* * *

A pale, young seminarian ushered Joe into the Chancery's wood paneled conference room where the fugitive priest sat waiting at the end of a polished conference table.

Gauss blew a lungful of smoke toward the full-length portrait of Pope Pius XII that dominated the room. "He didn't know what to do either, when he came face to face with evil. He dithered—and six million people died."

Joe threw a folder onto the table and took a seat across from the priest.

"I didn't come here to talk about a bunch of Keystone rag-heads, Father. I came here for the truth about Billy Pearce." He took a sheaf of papers from a manila envelope and laid them on the table. "The state police have come up with a log of calls to and from Billy Pearce's cell phone in the months before he was murdered. It seems like you and he had a lot to chat about."

Gauss looked thoughtful. "You're friendly with the authorities now? I'd heard you were something of a pariah where they were concerned."

"We're trading favors."

Gauss waited.

"Gay clergy and Islamic terrorists?" Joe elaborated. "Hard to wrap the flag around that one. The powers that be are hoping that this is just a case of recreational fiddling and not some retro-radical priest thing. They've asked me to find out. Discreetly."

Gauss hauled on the cigarette and stared out the Chancery window. "In exchange for what, I wonder?"

"I've got what your Bishop's has. Plus what your housekeeper says she didn't tell the Bishop's gopher, Marchetti. Plus phone records that show you were one of the last people Billy Pearce spoke to before he was murdered. So talk, Father. What was it? Slumming? Or have you been building bio-weapons in the church basement?"

"I wasn't referring to terrorists, Sheriff."

"When?"

Gauss waved the back of his hand at the portrait of the wartime Pope. "The paralyzing effect of evil. I was referring to Billy Pearce."

"I'm listening."

"Good." Gauss stubbed out a cigarette and lit another. "Do you believe in a personal God, Sheriff?"

Joe shrugged.

"The personification of evil?"

"The what?"

"Satan."

"I've seen people do nasty enough without supernatural help."

"Billy Pearce was evil," said Gauss. "Pure evil."

"I kind of doubt that, Father. His rag-head pals, maybe. Pearce was just screwed-up from being odd man out in a family of tight-assed geniuses."

"You're wrong, Sheriff. Dr. Hassad and his colleagues may be religious fanatics. Modern day Crusaders, if you will. That makes them misguided, not evil. But no one misguided Billy Pearce. His actions were entirely self-directed and his ambition was unequivocally evil."

"What ambition was that?"

"To lead young men into temptation and to destroy their souls."

"You want to be more specific?"

Gauss lit a cigarette from the stub in his hand. "Has your brother ever spoken to you of our association?"

"Are you going to tell me he's a Marlboro man, too?" Joe snorted.

"I'm going to tell you that when I first met your brother he was poised on the same path that you seem to have taken. Smart boy. Fundamentally decent, but not particularly moral. Surrounded by the world's temptations and with no inclination other than to go with the flow."

"And you took him in hand…"

"Your brother took himself in hand. I encouraged him… showed him some tools… validated his instinct to be something more than what others expected of him."

"And then he went to Wall Street and made a pile of money. Nice work, Father. He should give you a cut."

"Then he took up with the Pearce family. And all his efforts and mine came undone."

Joe laughed. "I kind of doubt he sees it that way, Father. But what's the connection to Billy's 'leading young men into temptation? ' or to bombs in the church basement?"

"Do you really think I had something to do with Billy Pearce's death?"

"I've got photos, Father—letters, phone records and a gossipy housekeeper all pointing me in that direction. If you can turn me around, you ought to give it a try. I'm giving you a chance."

Gauss stood and walked toward the Chancery window, flicking the stub of his cigarette into the courtyard below. "Miss Pearce led your brother down a familiar, hedonistic path. A spiritual dead end. Empty, but not evil. I'm sure she genuinely cared for him.

"Her brother on the other hand was a predator. He chose young men who had started on the path toward something better and did his best to turn them aside toward self-destruction. He enjoyed it."

Joe clasped his hands behind his head. "What makes you think you know what made Billy tick?"

"There was a boy..."

"I might have guessed."

"Much like your brother. Smart but unfocused. Parents self-absorbed in their own ambitions and not paying much attention to him. I took an interest and tried to help him find his direction. That's what I do, Sheriff. My real vocation, you might say. Billy Pearce became aware of that vocation—probably through one of my failed efforts—and decided to make it his vocation to foil mine. The jealousy of evil in the presence of good, if you will. Sadly, evil won this time. It happens. The boy dropped out of school, got involved in drugs and disappeared. I heard about Pearce's involvement from another of my vocational projects. Also that Pearce seemed to be using me as a sort of talent scout.

"I confronted him. Hence the phone calls. Threatened him with hell and damnation. That amused him. No, that's too innocent. It inspired him."

Joe folded his arms and leaned back in his chair. "These phone records have calls going both ways, Father. Some of them go on for quite a while."

"Pearce would call to gloat. To update me on his progress and conquests. I shouldn't have listened, I suppose. But I told myself that I might get something from the contact that I could use. Know thy enemy and so forth. I didn't help. I'm afraid I was just mesmerized by the hiss of the snake."

"And the last call?"

"The boy I mentioned. There was a rumor that he had died. I'd been quite upset. But then Pearce called to say he was alive and claimed to know the address of some crack house in the city where the boy might be living. He told me to come over and that he would tell me where it was."

"Well, well..."

"I knew he was lying. He sounded stoned. But how could I say no? It's like the old joke about second marriages—'the triumph of hope over experience.' In any event, Pearce was gone by the time I got there."

Joe returned his chair legs to the floor and retrieved a sheet of scribbled notes from his folder. "Mrs. Flynn says she found a bunch of wet clothes in the rectory laundry the morning Billy's body was fished out of the lake. You want to explain that?"

Gauss smiled. "It wouldn't have been a good idea to be seen driving up to Pearce's hovel in the church station wagon, Sheriff. I rowed there in my skiff."

"Did you fall out?"

"Very nearly. Some maniac in a speed boat practically cut me in two as I came into Wilson Cove."

Joe watched Gauss light another cigarette—his fourth in ten minutes. "Too bad Billy was gone when you got there. You might have saved him."

"He was beyond redemption, Sheriff."

"Did he leave a note, or anything to explain why he wasn't there or when he might be back?"

"Not that I noticed."

"Did you notice anything at all? Anything unusual?"

"Just that he was supposed to be there and wasn't. Though in itself, that wasn't unusual—Billy Pearce telling an untruth."

Joe removed a sheaf of photographs from a manila envelope and handed one to the priest. "Does anything in this picture look familiar to you?"

Gauss examined the photo and moved his head from side to side. "No."

"Do you notice anything unusual in it?"

"It looks like the rumpus room of a frat house after an all-night party, if that's what you mean."

"But you don't recognize the room or anything of its contents?"

"Should I?"

He put the photo back in the envelope. "Okay, Father. You can quit fan dancing now. You just screwed up."

Gauss inhaled a lung full of smoke and ignored the invitation to respond.

"That photo was taken in Billy Pearce's boathouse loft a few hours after his body was pulled from the lake. If you were there when you say you were, that picture is what his room looked like."

Gauss opened his mouth to speak.

Joe cut him off. "Don't say a word. Just listen."

Gauss drew a lung full of smoke and waited.

"You never made it to the boathouse. The boat you say almost swamped you was hauling Billy Pearce, trussed up in a sleeping bag. Only it wasn't going fast enough to cut anything in two. It was just put-putting slowly through Wilson Cove, like any other boat going through that rock garden in the dark. Then along came the Coldwater Patrol Boat—me—and the boat with Billy turned off its engine and lights. If you were there in your rowboat, it may even have floated right up to you. You would have heard voices and seen Billy's sister shove his head over the side to keep him quiet."

Joe eyeballed his quarry. "When I turned on the patrol boat spotlight, you would have seen Billy clearly, hanging over the side. And he would have seen you in your little rowboat, if that's where you were. Maybe that's why he started to struggle and make noise.

"When I pulled the patrol boat alongside the Pearce's Chris Craft, I heard a thud and then a few seconds later a splash. If the splash was Billy going into the water, then the thud was him hitting something first. It was a long couple of seconds between the thud and the splash, Father."

Gauss opened his mouth. Joe held up his hand.

"The way I piece it together, Billy Pearce fell right out of that boat and into your lap."

Gauss stubbed out his cigarette, started to light another and then seeing it was the last in the pack, put it back. "Then what?" he asked, sarcastically. "Am I supposed to have muttered a brief prayer before helping my adversary on to his final resting place?"

Joe gestured at the portrait of Pius XII. "You said that Pope missed his chance when he had it. That he froze in the face of evil. I figure that's another way of saying that you think you'd act differently, if you had the chance. I think you did. I think you had that chance and you acted."

Gauss folded his hands as if in prayer and propped his chin on tee-peed fingers. "And what is our Sheriff going to do with his own crisis of conscience—if he believes this clever theory?"

"Don't bait me, Padre."

"Would that be unwise?"

"Not even Billy was that reckless."

"So what are you going to do?"

"Nothing."

"I see."

"No you don't. So let me spell it out." Joe put his hands on the conference table and locked eyes with the priest. "What I care about is keeping Coldwater safe. I do that by locking up the dangerous and letting God, or whoever, take care of the guilty. You're an arrogant son of a bitch; but you're not dangerous. So I could give a rat's ass what you did, or didn't do, out there on the lake that night. I also know that you don't corrupt little boys."

"His Eminence would be happy to hear you say that."

"Maybe I'll tell him. But I want something from you first."

Gauss shook the last cigarette from the pack, lit it and inhaled deeply. "What?"

"I want you to use that priestly influence of yours to get my brother off that phony financial merry-go-round he's got himself on. Susan Pearce isn't around to get in your way anymore. Finish what you started."

"Anything else?"

"Your silence. You don't tell Tommy any of this. Not ever. You let slip one crumb and he'll figure out the rest in a nanosecond."

"That's it?"

"That's it."

Gauss smiled. "You're walking away from quite a coup, Sheriff, if your theories are correct. You must love your brother very much."

"I'm not here for love of the church."

"Are you afraid that one more fallen hero might be too much...?"

"That's right, Father. You and our old man put a clamp on my brother's head so tight the poor bastard can't feel without thinking first. Lay this on him and he'll never throw it off."

"You don't know your brother as well as you think."

Joe took another envelope from his jacket pocket and dropped it on the table just outside the priest's reach. "Maybe. But I'm pretty sure I've got you figured out."

Gauss looked across the table at the envelope. "More phony letters?"

"A lab report. Comparing fibers from the bag Billy was found in with some I took from the front of your rowboat. Want to guess what it says?" Gauss looked at Joe and took a long last drag on his cigarette. "Or do we have a deal, Padre?"

CHAPTER 32

Moe Silverstein called first. He'd gotten through to the New York State Attorney General. No charges would be brought against Tom or his firm in connection with the Eurocon matter. The AG's office would officially drop the case in a few days. "They're waiting for the right spot in the news cycle so it doesn't get too much attention," he explained.

"Thanks, for getting through to the right people so fast."

"No problem, Tom. Every level of state government is looking good right now. They're anxious for it to stay that way through the November election. But it's a shame that you and your brother aren't going to get a medal or something. That was a hell of a thing you did, and no one is ever going to hear about it."

"We got what we wanted, Moe."

Tanner called next to say that the London office was Tom's if he wanted it. Moe Silverstein had been circumspect about what had happened. But he made it clear that it was Tom's doing and that the firm would be nuts if it let a Houdini like Tom Morgan get away. "We're all proud as hell of you," said Tanner. "Whenever you're ready to come back, you've got your pick of assignments. Any office, any continent. There's a mega-project in Russia that's got your name written all over it."

Tom knew he should feel flattered as well as relieved to know that he was no longer headed to jail or to the poor house. But he felt nothing. Susan was dead, and his capacity for feeling seemed to have died with her. Physically he was healing, but mentally and emotionally he was numb. Dr. Sayed said he could leave the hospital soon. But to do what? He no longer cared.

A voice at the door interrupted his gloomy musings. "Sorry about not returning your messages," said Gauss. "Bishop's orders."

Tom sat up in bed and smiled at the priest. "I assumed as much. The Church's defense fund must be scraping bottom these days. If you got stuck to the Billy Pearce murder, they'd be passing the plate for decades."

"That's more or less the way the Bishop put it."

Tom waved a splinted finger at a plastic chair. "Pull that thing over. I have some questions."

The priest moved the chair beside the bed and sat.

"You're not so unkind as to pass along an eight hundred page tome on a whim. You had a message. I missed it."

"You were busy."

"I'm not now. And it's bothering me."

The priest placed his hand on Tom's forearm. "I'm sorry about Miss Pearce. That was a tragedy. She was misled by her heart, I imagine."

Tom shook his head. "By her genes, she would have said. I doubt that so-called terrorist told her what he had in mind."

"No, that doesn't seem likely. In any event, the last time we spoke you were intrigued by her work on emotions and brain chemistry. I sent you that book because its author made the connection between emotion and feeling three hundred years before Miss Pearce stumbled onto it. I thought you might be interested."

Tom smiled through cracked lips. "I am. But I doubt precedence was your point."

"No. I wanted to remind you that the quest for knowledge has been led by philosophy, not science: Heraclitus dreaming up the atom, Plato the modern fascist state. I thought the reminder might help you get back on track, that's all."

"What track is that?"

"Don't be obtuse, Tommy. You're floundering again. Not as badly as when I first met you. But you took a wrong turn after I let you out of my sight. You know it and anybody who knows you can see it. It's time you put that first class mind of yours to work on something more worthy than mergers and acquisitions."

Tom fidgeted as best he could, pressing his shoulders into the pillows. "My career is finished, Father. The firm is dangling goodies to get me back, but there's no gas in the tank. I wouldn't last a month in that scrum. As for what I'll do once I get out of here…"

"Have you tried reflection?"

Ouch. "I haven't been to church in a decade, Father."

Gauss's response was patient, but pointed. "I'm not talking about the Church, Tommy. Organized religion is one of many paths. It happens to be mine. But I'm not surprised, and certainly not offended, that it hasn't turned out to be yours."

Tom felt the telltale twitches of surprise and caution wrestle for control of his face.

"Catechism and ritual help some people lead better lives than they otherwise might. Others seem compelled by nature to seek their own answers. Like anything we're designed by nature to do, if we don't do it, we're not healthy or happy. And no celibacy jokes, please. Depending on what it is we're not doing, we can be wasting our lives."

"Is that what you think I'm doing?"

"I do. And what's more, you know it." The priest paused to let the sting raise a welt. "Do you remember your Socrates? The Apologia?"

"An unexamined life is not worth living?"

"That's right. If Frankie Heller or that terrorist had succeeded in ending yours… what would your own judgment be on the last ten years of it—excluding what you did here recently?"

"He wasn't exactly a terrorist. But why exclude that?"

"Don't be stubborn. When I saw you last, you'd already sensed the need to begin looking for a new path. Should I ask what you've done about it? And I don't mean lying here brooding."

Tom didn't respond. He didn't know how.

"You already know the answer's not on Wall Street." The priest's gaze pinned his former altar boy to the pillows. "But if you have the *courage* and *stubbornness* to keep looking, you could do worse than to start right here in Coldwater."

Tom's eyes found the window and the speck of Pocket Island in the distance. Courage and stubbornness. *Fortis et Obstinatus.* It might as well be the Morgan coat of arms.

"Something tells me you have something specific in mind," Tom said.

"I do."

"Go on. I can't get away." *Might as well be in that rowboat of yours.*

"I'm thinking of building a school out on Pocket Island," said Gauss. "Something along the lines of the old Greek academies…"

Tom lay back, closed his eyes and listened to Gauss expound his vision. At first, he couldn't help thinking: *do you have any idea of how much something like that would cost? The federal and state bureaucracies that would live in your pockets? The sheer regulatory and financial complexity of getting something like that off the ground?* But as Gauss expounded, Tom felt his heart warmed by the beauty of the idea, even as he mentally tallied the enormous hurdles. He opened his eyes to see the priest watching.

"I see two roles that need filling right away," Gauss concluded.

Tom laughed. "I'll bite. What?"

"Prayer and Finance. Pick whichever one you think you're better at."

Before Tom could answer, another voice interrupted from the doorway. "Sorry," said Joe. "He wouldn't wait."

Luke ran to the bed and climbed in next to Tom.

"We were out with your newspaper pal, Jack Thompson, trying to catch Moby Dick."

Tom smiled. "Season's over, Sheriff."

"Yeah, well, I had to get gabby here out of the house. He's been a bear since his fishing buddy's been out of action. Driving his mom and grandma *n*-adic-*uts*."

"Jack Thompson endorses my idea, by the way," Gauss added. "He says

269

that if I can get you involved in one project, he knows a dozen more waiting for someone like you to take them on."

"What project?" asked Joe.

Tom sighed. "Something about building a school on Pocket Island."

Joe looked sharply at Gauss, who smiled blandly in return. "It would be great to have you stay, Tommy."

Tom turned to Luke and poked him with a bandaged elbow. "So what do you think, buddy? If Uncle Tom helps Father Gauss build a school on Pocket Island, would you go?"

"There'd be no girls," Gauss apologized. "Just boys, boats and fish, I'm afraid."

Wide eyes above a gap-toothed grin moved up and to the right. "*Y*-adic-*es!*"

Excerpt from COLDWATER CONFESSION

(Book 2 of the Coldwater Mystery Series, due out April 2022)

"There was a little girl, who had a little curl, right in the middle of her forehead.

When she was good, she was very, very good. But when she was bad, she was horrid."

Children's nursery rhyme.

Lightning blasted the top of a tall royal palm and dropped it through the windshield of the parked rental car. Cacophonies of thunder and colliding debris overwhelmed all other sound and thought. Andrew Ryan watched the swirling carnage from the window of the vacation cottage, heard his wife scream and did nothing.

"Aaaann—Drew!"

Peevish bleats, pitched to dramatize minor annoyance, no longer penetrated the young man's consciousness, but the timbre of genuine terror is self-authenticating and his wife's cries eventually broke through. The swollen bathroom door yielded to his shoulder. A screaming woman careened through the opening. Behind her, a pale reptilian tail slithered through a gap where the bathtub and wall did not quite meet. Waves of adrenaline surged through Andrew's already overloaded system.

"I'm out of here," his wife shouted. But when she spotted the severed tree rising through their car's windshield, she froze. "ANN - DREW!"

"It's okay," he whispered.

"There's a *HURRICANE* out there! We have to get out."

"We're not going anywhere until this is over."

"But there's a *SNAKE* in here! I saw it."

"And stuff flying through the air out there at a hundred miles an hour."

"I CA....CAN'T STA... AY HERE!"

Andrew pressed the phone to his ear, tilted his head and then tossed the mute piece of plastic to the chair. "It's dead," he said. His wife wilted to the floor, wrapped her arms around her knees and began to rock back and forth, moaning softly. The sound that seeped out of her then was more ominous to Andrew than anything howling outside or coiled in a corner of the bathroom. It started as a low-pitched wail, like a Muslim call to prayer. Only it wasn't spiritual.

"Eye-eeeee. MMmmmmm."

"Karen?" he demanded. "Did you take your medicine?"

"Eye-eeeee. MMmmmmm."

"Karen? Did you take your Thorazine?"

"Eye-eeeee."

Andrew lifted his moaning wife and laid her on the couch and then began to search her suitcase. "Where did you put your pills, Karen?"

"Eye-eeeee. MMmmmmm."

"Karen, don't do this."

"Eye-eeeee."

"Did you pack them?" His wife's eyes were unblinking...scared and defiant at the same time.

"I don't like the way they make me feel," she whispered.

272

Her husband's oath was a weary amalgam of despair, resignation and foreboding. "Then knock yourself out before this gets ugly. There're some sleeping pills in my bag."

"Will you stay with me?"

"Of course."

***

Andrew Ryan lay in bed, listening to the sounds of lethal nature and mulling an ordinary marriage turned by slow degree to tragedy. Or maybe it wasn't so slow, but he was just slow to notice. A file of overlooked clues lay open against the back of his eyelids:

Late for their first date, the tanned coed in a white halter-top boasted of getting caught in a speeding trap on her way there, peeling-out and losing the startled cop in a chase through the residential hills. Aroused by the exotic combination of recklessness and sexuality, Andrew Ryan assumed that she was making it up. She wasn't.

Later came the serial drama of post-graduation employment disasters, masked for a time by the carnal pleasures of twenty-something life in the big city. Months between jobs lengthened into seasons. The fade from lioness to recluse accelerated.

The year the popular magazines were touting biological clocks on their final countdown ticking, Karen announced that it was time for her to have children. She could do it all, she promised. Andrew was tempted to note that she had yet to do anything, but he stalled at the possibility that this might be the missing piece, the thing that could fix whatever it was that had gone badly wrong.

But he was mistaken about that too. The daily responsibilities of motherhood made no claim on Karen. Day-long trances behind her drawing table matured into night time hallucinations. The doctors said it was a hormone imbalance, easily remedied by medication. But Karen resisted being "balanced," and she "forgot" to take her medication. The cops and the EMT drivers became frequent visitors at the Ryan house. They had their own professional diagnosis. Psycho and stoned have a lot in common, they told Andrew. Some of their charges simply liked how it made them feel.

Karen stirred under the blanket and reached a hand to stroke her brooding husband. "Come here," she whispered, her voice soft and come hither though the sounds of the storm had, if anything, gotten louder. Andrew slipped beneath the covers and snuggled close. Strange, he mused, that while everything else had fallen apart, this one thing still worked. No deception. No false promises. They came together like ice dancers to a music they heard instinctively. Or was he kidding himself about that, too?

"You lost weight in there," he said. "You look good."

"They should call it the Club Med for the Head diet," she answered. "Institutional food and major drugs."

"How do you feel now?"

"Scared shitless of that snake in there, thank you. I was hallucinating them so much in the bin that they had to strap me down. Most of the time it's kind of interesting, you know? But I really thought I was going to lose my mind this time."

Andrew looked away.

"You don't like to hear this, do you?"

"I don't like to hear you call it '*interesting*,'" he said wearily.

"I'm an artist, Andrew. How could I not?"

"Because your doctors have warned you a zillion times, **not** to find it interesting. Quote: 'Down that path lies madness.' Quote: 'One time too many and you don't come back.'"

"I can come back any time I want," she snapped. Then, "You want to hear why they had to strap me down?" Andrew stared at her, but said nothing. "There was this long, pale slimy thing under my bed that kept trying to poke through the bottom of the mattress. It scared the living shit out of me. But you know what my doctor said it was? She said it was you, nagging at me to 'get out of the wagon and start pulling.' I suppose she got that charming phrase from one of her chats with you. She says that you should quit acting so disappointed all the time. That you're supposed to forgive me."

"I do," said her husband automatically.

Karen shook her head. "You don't even know what you're supposed to forgive me for." Andrew closed his eyes and mentally perused a fat catalogue of forgivable misdeeds:

Wandering the neighborhood at 3:00 a.m. in your Victoria's Secret nightgown, ringing doorbells at the homes of neighbors with teenage boys. Maxing-out on a half dozen credit cards I didn't know you had. Getting shit-faced at a dinner party with my boss and passing out on your plate. Leaving our two-year old daughter alone in the house all day while you're out driving the interstate lost in the buzz of your latest medication—or refusal to take it. The jumble of images collaged a multi-year sabbatical from the responsibilities of adult life, but they did not explain it.

"Of course I forgive you," Andrew said.

"Bullshit."

Karen tossed the covers aside and strode unclothed and unselfconscious toward the mini-bar. Andrew stared after her, reminded of the line from Aristotle about a pretty face being the best ambassador. Despite the abuse she had put it through, his wife had somehow managed to preserve the body of a twenty-year-old. In rare moments of frank self-examination, Andrew wondered if he would have put up with half of her crap if she hadn't. Watching her fondle a handful of mini booze bottles, he suppressed a familiar surge of frustration. "Don't," he said. "You'll just make it worse."

"I'm just having one."

"Is that likely?"

Karen looked at him straight and wrung the cap from the bottle with a closed fist. "We have to talk."

Here we go, he thought. You've had Group and Dr. Feelgood twice a week for a year, and now you've just had six weeks of it straight, twice a day. The psychobabble gets more polished with every rehearsal. But your behavior keeps getting worse. And now there's a child.

"I'm listening," he said.

Karen smirked and then opened her throat for an exaggerated gulp. "No, you're not. Nothing I say or do gets through to you anymore. You're numb. You don't feel anything, you don't see anything, and you certainly don't listen—unless it's about Maggie." Andrew's chin floated warily toward the horizon. "See?" said his wife. "Now you're listening." Andrew opened his mouth to protest and she stuffed it with, "You don't love me anymore. You know it, and so do I."

Andrew expelled a hiss of pent-up breath and asked, as if to a child who has done her sums wrong yet again, "Then what am I doing here? How many guys do you think would stick with someone through all this?"

"Oh, you're a rock, all right," she said. "Pride yourself on that. But somewhere along the way, you switched girls. You're here for her now. Not me."

Not somewhere, he thought, and his mind unprompted screened a tape whose every sad and scary frame he knew by heart:

Arriving home from work, he found Maggie tearing through the house in a filthy diaper, screaming for a mommy who wasn't there. He tried to calm the hysterical toddler while he phoned the familiar round of police, hospitals and doctors. Father and daughter kept vigil at the front window into the evening. The child fell asleep in his lap hours past bedtime, waking finally to the sound of a car scything through the mailbox at the bottom of the driveway and her mother stumbling through the front door. The child ran to her mother and held onto her leg until almost the top of the stairs before losing her grip. Andrew stared frozen as the frenzied toddler hurled her tiny body again and again against the locked bedroom door, screaming for a mommy who either didn't hear or didn't care. Through the door, he could hear his wife on the phone with her latest doctor calmly asserting that she was not really sick at all and that she was not going to take any more goddamn medicine!

That was six weeks ago.

"Karen," he said, his voice almost without expression. "It's not a contest between you and Maggie. Kids her age are helpless. You've got to feed them, change them, play with them—keep them away from hot stoves. None of that is optional."

"Mr. Mom!" His wife emptied another miniature bottle of booze into her glass. "You think you're a better parent than me?"

"Frankly, I'm the only parent, Karen."

"Not for long."

Goosebumps erupted on the surface of Andrew's arms and across the top of his scalp, heedless of the moist, tropical air. *I guess we won't be going snorkeling tomorrow*, he heard himself think.

"I met someone," Karen explained.

"In the bin!" The surge of incredulous anger took Andrew by surprise, but it made no visible impact on his wife. "Some crack-head biker?"

"A cop," she said proudly. "And he's only mildly depressed."Andrew looked at his wife over the top of his glasses, wishing at that moment that she were wearing something more than just flaming nail polish. "You know the irony of it all is I did it for you."

"What?"

"Motherhood. I did it for you…to keep you…"

"Right."

"You don't get it, do you?" his wife hissed. "You never have. I LOVED YOU!" she shrieked. Then she grabbed her crotch like a ballplayer, "But all *you* ever loved was this!"

That's all you've left me to love, thought Andrew while the rest of his mind split and tumbled down a dozen different paths at once. *'Can I afford to quit work and stay home? Can Karen get medical insurance on her own? Is my mother too old to come and help take care of Maggie until things settle down?'*

Karen watched the play of emotions ripple her husband's face. "Let me guess," she said. "You're thinking about me. About how you're going to fight for me and win me back, no matter what." HHHhhhh

Her husband sighed. "I don't know what to think," he admitted.

"I'm so surprised."

A rumble of receding thunder filled the silence before he could respond. "What are your plans?" he asked, noting wearily the puzzled expression that was his wife's only response. "You haven't had a full-time job in over five years and your knight in shining armor is a patient in a psychiatric facility," he explained. "What are your plans, Karen?"

His wife opened another mini-bottle and took a defiant pull. "We're leaving as soon as Tom gets out."

"We?"

"Maggie and I."

Andrew Ryan's throat clamped shut over lungs that fought to surge their way up and out.

"She needs her mother."

"You're joking," he stuttered. "You're not fit."

"My doctor says I am."

"When you lie to her! *'Yes, doctor, I am taking my medication. No doctor, I haven't had any hallucinations in quite some time'.* And what happens when you crash and burn?"

"You'll come to the rescue. That's your role. Remember? 'The Rock.'"

"I'm worn out with it, Karen."

"Then you'll come for her."

Andrew sat hard on the rattan couch and waved a hand at his naked wife. "Put some clothes on, will you?"

"Oh." Karen looked around as if there might be a suitable change of costume nearby. "I guess I thought we might be making a fresh start on our romantic weekend," she said. "I thought I owed you one last chance, at least. You blew it, Mr. Perfect."

The long-time lovers stared at each other, the one numb, the other uncertain but vaguely triumphant. Then the telephone trilled back to life. Andrew picked it up, and his face, which a moment ago had been flush with blood, drained abruptly and then slowly engorged again. *"Jesus Christ!"* The receiver pressed the side of his head and his free hand cupped the ear on the opposite side. *"Get her to the Emergency Room!"* Andrew whirled on his naked wife and, in a calm more menacing than fury, explained, "It's the babysitter, Karen. Maggie found your 'candies' and ate them. What the hell was an open bottle of anti-psychotics doing in the nursery—on the nightstand—next to her bed?"

Karen Ryan did not respond, but the look on her face was chillingly familiar. Neither guilt nor fear, Andrew remembered it clearly from the very first time they met. "Oh, my god," he whispered. "You left it there on purpose."

***

Karen stared through the cottage window at the tow truck that was hauling away the wrecked rental car and at the men who had driven over the replacement vehicle and who were exchanging papers with her husband. Waves of nausea oozed through her pores in emulsions of heat and sweat.

"Radio says there's another one coming right behind this," she heard one of them say. "You got maybe twenty minutes. Waiver says it's your nickel for any damage if you get caught in it." The brew inside Karen's gut heaved suddenly and her legs propelled an unwilling head toward the bathroom. With her face half-buried in the toilet, she heard thunder begin to roll again. Then Andrew was standing in the doorway, the keys to the rental car squeezed through the side of his clenched fist.

"Do you have any idea how terrified Maggie must be?" he asked, in a voice that was no longer the patient instrument of reasoned persuasion she had come to resent. "Lying on a gurney, surrounded by strangers. One of them shoving a tube down her throat to pump her guts out, and no mommy or daddy anywhere near?" Karen gave him the deer-in-the-headlight mask, but nothing else. "You don't, do you?"

"Kids are tough," she blurted.

Andrew shook his head—not in disbelief and not in resignation, but finally and irrevocably, in dismissal. He hesitated for only a moment before pulling the door shut between them.

"Aaaan-Drew!"

The voice on the other side of the door was artic. "All those times you left her alone, Karen—scared, hungry, reeking in her own filth—how long is a day, when you're two years old and Mommy has suddenly disappeared? Again."

"AAAAA-Drew! There's a *SNAKE* in here!"

"I can't let you take Maggie, Karen."

"AAAA-Drew! Don't do this!"

"Can you feel now how Maggie must have felt? Can you imagine how she must be feeling right this second?"

"A-A-ANDREW!" Karen tried to stand, but the panic that inflated her lungs had also jellied her limbs. "I'LL GO MAD!"

Her husband's voice was a frozen whisper. "But you can come back. Remember? 'Any time you want.'"

A staccato rip of lightning plunged the cottage into darkness. In the silence between screams, the sound of spinning tires on crushed shell driveway

279

masked the hiss of something close, but unseen.

"AAAAAANDREW!"

Get your copy of Coldwater Confession here:

JamesRossAuthor.com/Coldwater-Confession

A Note From the Author

I have two sons, close in age. When they were about to enter high school, their mother remarked, "My worst nightmare is that they're going to fall for the same girl." Voila! The idea for COLDWATER REVENGE was born.

Of course, COLDWATER REVENGE is not simply the story of sibling rivalry run amok, with a dead body thrown in for color. It's a roman a clef of the place and people I grew up with. I wrote it, not to settle old scores (though there may be one or two zingers in there) but to capture in words a particular place and time, while there's still time.

I hope you enjoy the Morgan brothers and the place and culture that made them. Because they're coming back. COLDWATER CONFESSION, book two of the Coldwater series, is due out in April 2022. Watch out.

About the Author

James A. Ross has at various times been a Peace Corps Volunteer, a CBS News Producer in the Congo, a Congressional Staffer and a Wall Street Lawyer. His short fiction has appeared in numerous literary publications and his short story, "Aux Secours," was recently nominated for a Pushcart Prize. He has appeared on the MOTH Mainstage, and is a frequent participant and several times winner of the live story telling competition, Cabin Fever Story Slam. His historical novel, HUNTING TEDDY ROOSEVELT, was published by Regal House Publishing in 2020 and is available wherever books are sold.

You can connect with me on:
🌐 https://www.jamesrossauthor.com

Subscribe to my newsletter:
✉ https://www.jamesrossauthor.com

CPSIA information can be obtained
at www.ICGtesting.com
Printed in the USA
BVHW071837201121
621898BV00001B/19